PRAISE FOR
SUNNY SONG WILL NEVER BE FAMOUS

"Sunny Song is one of the most hilarious, heart-warming, relatable teen characters I've had the pleasure of encountering. Readers will fall head over heels in love with her as she goes all the way from shining LA influencer to unwitting farmhand! A must-have for any YA shelf."

—**Sandhya Menon**, New York Times bestselling author

PRAISE FOR
THE PERFECT ESCAPE

"Pure fun! A hilarious rom-com that head-fakes you into tumbling headlong into a techno-zombie-survival thriller propelled by banter and plenty of heart."

—**David Yoon**, *New York Times* bestselling author of *Frankly in Love*

"Suzanne Park's *The Perfect Escape* is just that—perfect. Filled with humor and heart, it won't let you go until you're smiling."

—**Danielle Paige**, *New York Times* bestselling author of the Dorothy Must Die series and *Stealing Snow*

"An adorable, laugh-out-loud YA rom-com with a lovable hero and an action-packed, zombie-themed escape room—what more could you want?"

—**Jenn Bennett**, author of *Alex, Approximately*

"Quirky and hilarious, *The Perfect Escape* has everything you've ever wanted in a rom-com. Suzanne Park has created the perfect mix of humor and heart against the backdrop of zombie adventures guaranteed to keep you laughing. Nate and Kate are absolutely adorable, and you'll be rooting for them until the very end. A must-have addition to any bookshelf!"

—**Sabina Khan**, author of *The Love and Lies of Rukhsana Ali*

"Suzanne Park's debut was a thrilling ride with lovable characters and plenty of belly laughs."

—**Gloria Chao**, author of
American Panda and *Our Wayward Fate*

"*The Perfect Escape* is the hilarious tale of two snarky teens who will win your hearts (and maybe each other's). It is indeed the perfect escape from, well, pretty much everything."

—**Sarah Henning**, author of
Throw Like a Girl and the Sea Witch duology

"The funniest love stories can start in the most unexpected of places. *The Perfect Escape* is a whip-smart, hilarious rom-com that boldly explores classism, family expectations, and how to outrun zombies."

—**Nina Moreno**, author of *Don't Date Rosa Santos*

SUNNY SONG WILL NEVER BE FAMOUS

ALSO BY
SUZANNE PARK

The Perfect Escape

Loathe at First Sight

SUNNY SONG
WILL NEVER BE
FAMOUS

SUZANNE PARK

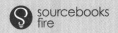

sourcebooks
fire

Published by Sourcebooks Fire, an imprint of Sourcebooks
P.O. Box 4410, Naperville, Illinois 60567-4410
(630) 961-3900
sourcebooks.com

Library of Congress Cataloging-in-Publication Data

Names: Park, Suzanne, author.
Title: Sunny Song will never be famous / Suzanne Park.
Description: Naperville, Illinois : Sourcebooks Fire, [2021] | Audience:
    Ages 14. | Audience: Grades 10-12. | Summary: "A social media influencer
    is shipped off to a digital detox summer camp in this funny
    coming-of-age story"-- Provided by publisher.
Identifiers: LCCN 2021001002 (print) | LCCN 2021001003 (ebook)
Subjects: CYAC: Social media--Fiction. | Camps--Fiction | Korean
    Americans--Fiction. | Coming of age--Fiction.
Classification: LCC PZ7.1.P3615 Su 2021 (print) | LCC PZ7.1.P3615 (ebook)
    | DDC [Fic]--dc23
LC record available at https://lccn.loc.gov/2021001002
LC ebook record available at https://lccn.loc.gov/2021001003

Printed and bound in the United States of America.
VP 10 9 8 7 6 5 4 3 2 1

To Trevor and CJ

ONE

"THANK YOU FOR COMING ON SUCH SHORT NOTICE, Mr. and Mrs. Song."

Mr. Lyons straightened the slightly askew HEADMASTER plaque on his desk before continuing. "I know the end of the school year can be hectic, especially for busy professionals like yourself." Headmaster Lyons looked at my mom, then my dad, then over to me with his signature poker face, washed over with indifference, an absence of humanity in his eyes.

He always looked this way. His lips pursed to thin lines during pep rallies and state championship basketball games when all the other school staff members let down their guard to cheer and scream our Westminster Prep school song. He never dressed up for spirit week. And once last year, the governor paid our school a visit and was all smiles for the newspapers and news cameras. But not ol' Mr. Lyons, with his pressed lips, straight like a flatlined heart monitor, with no sign of life.

On the brighter side of things, in the long term, he probably wouldn't get any laugh lines or forehead wrinkles when he got really old. Not like my parents, who already had worry lines so deep, you could hide things inside them.

This was the first time he had called my parents to his office, on the last day of my junior year no less, to discuss "a rather serious matter." He didn't give any more details. But no one ever used words like "rather serious matter" and had it turn out to be a rather serious great thing.

I studied him as he straightened other things on his desk. First the stapler. Then the cup that held pens. Next the pens inside the cup. His houndstooth blazer was a size too small, or maybe he was a size too big. I couldn't see his pants, but his khakis were usually so tight that the pleats along the front panel stretched flat, like a fully opened accordion.

My mom placed her hand on my knee, which I hadn't realized was jiggling from restless leg syndrome, or worry, or boredom. Or maybe all three. A single, firm squeeze to the left patella. *Stop it, Sun-Hee. This is a rather serious matter.*

Why were we here? My grades were fine. Not great, but fine enough. I wanted to take some easier classes my senior year to help boost my GPA a little, like seniors who weren't on the aggressive AP track were known to do. I hadn't gotten in any trouble at school. Not lately. So why single me out the last day of junior year?

C'mon, c'mon, tell us why we're here so we can go home.

Mr. Lyons folded his hands on his mahogany desk. He nodded once at his perfectly straightened desk and cleared his throat. *All right, here we go.*

"Thank you for finding time at the end of the school day so my husband and I could both be here," Mom said in a pinched, formal tone. She placed her free hand on my dad's arm and patted lightly. Her other hand still firmly squeezed my kneecap. "We always appreciate spending time with administration—outside of the fundraisers, school carnival, and book fair, that is." Mom was always dropping credentials. I was surprised she didn't throw in that she was PTA cochair, Head of WAA!—Westminster Alumni Association, plus exclamation point!—a donating alumna, former National Honor Society President, and salutatorian. She was the sole reason I was accepted into her alma mater. Mom had paved my way.

Her academic legacy remained in the hallowed halls of Westminster. And at Princeton. And at Yale Law School. Dad had gone to public schools his whole life (LA Unified, whoop whoop!), and he was as clueless about private school decorum as I'd been before I started here. So he sat there silently and let Mom do all the talking. And boy, did she like to talk. More frequently, she liked to argue. That was why she was such a good litigator.

I let out a big yawn, the kind that formed tears and messed up eye makeup. I'd been editing a video until three in the morning, and the stuffy, sleepy office didn't help with my exhaustion. I wiped my eyes with my sleeve and then, out of habit, instinctively reached for my phone to check on my notifications and video stats. Mom saw my movements out of the corner of her eye and gave me a second squeeze with all her unbridled strength, one that could extract juice from unripened lemons. I jerked my hand back like it had come near a hot stove, and Mom's one-handed choke hold on my knee relaxed.

Headmaster Lyons swiveled his computer screen toward us. "Let's first discuss the good news. Sunny is in the top twenty percent of the class." He showed my last report card. Three As, one A-minus, and one B. "She's is doing fine academically."

See, Mom and Dad? I'm doing fine academically.

My parents let out sighs of relief in unison while I waited for the other shoe to drop. There was a reason they were asked to come here, and apparently it wasn't for my fine academic performance.

"But unfortunately, I have some not-so-good news." *Down, down, down fell the shoe.* "There's a petition actively circulating around the school. Have you seen it?"

All three of us shook our heads no. What would a petition have to do with me?

He cleared his throat. "It's about Sunny's long-standing and prominent social media presence. Because Sunny is posting updates so frequently throughout the school day, even during AP exam season, some of our parents are worried it makes the school appear...how should we say it...*lax* in our academic standards—"

I blurted, "But I don't post at school! I schedule my posts. They go up during the day, but I've already written or filmed them ahead of time."

"Understood. But perception-wise, how do you think the school looks if you are posting snack food preparation videos while you're supposed to be taking exams? Or dry shampoo hair care tricks when you're in trig? To the outside world, it looks like you're posting during school hours because you have ample free time during the day."

He inhaled through his nose, puffed up his cheeks, then blew the air out through his mouth. "I've also heard parents are looking at Sunny's public account to see what's going on behind the scenes at school, since teenagers aren't forthcoming about personal and school matters. So while they're thrilled Sunny is so transparent and using her as a means to understand their own children, they're also worried about Sunny tarnishing Westminster's reputation for having a rigorous academic curriculum. It's frustrating to hear this, I'm sure."

Exasperated, I puffed up my cheeks and blew out a noisy breath too. "Okay. I'll stop autoposting during the school day. Can we please go now? I have a livestream in an hour. Which is after school hours, so it's *permissible*." I tried to sound calm and professional, but the last part came out with a sting.

Mr. Lyons pulled open his file cabinet drawer and pointed inside. "You know what's in here, Sunny? Over twenty cell phones and tablets, all collected today from students who have problems controlling their media consumption at school. Don't be a statistic. I know you've built a nice little social media empire outside school, but inside our walls, we need your undivided attention. Your education comes first."

My parents nodded in unison. They liked Mr. Lyons because he was old-school, but he was so clueless with technology. Everyone knew companies were paying people with big platforms to collaborate, and people like me were figuring out how to make a little bit of money by monetizing channels. Even colleges were catching on by admitting social-media-savvy students to be social media ambassadors for their schools. This would help them advertise to prospective new students, raise the school's profile, and educate their current students about school programs with just a few posts and photos. If I wanted to go to college, and that was a big *if*, this was my one ticket in. Not being first chair violin in orchestra. Not having the top GPA. And certainly not by listening to this old dude lecturing me about...honestly, I couldn't even remember.

By the worst luck imaginable, my best friend, Maya, called right then. My ringtone for her was set to Cardi B's classic "I Like It" at medium-high volume.

"Sorry about that," I yelped, silencing my phone just as Cardi B bragged about her banging body, too scared to look at Mom and Dad. Especially my mom.

This whole discussion was horrible, but for the record, I blamed my mom for all this trouble I'd gotten myself into. *She* introduced me to social media when she started her all-work-no-life mommy blog while on maternity leave seventeen years ago, with roly-poly baby me as her muse. When I was a wee elementary schooler, she uploaded a video of her "Little Turnip" to YouTube singing "Oppa Gangnam Style"—dance moves included—while wearing swim goggles and a unicorn bathrobe. That video spread like wildfire, and I became known overnight as Goggle Girl.

LA Weekly did an exclusive on me—cue cheesy movie trailer voiceover: *Can Goggle Girl handle the Goggle Girl-splosion? An inside look into instafame.* People *still* called me Goggle Girl to this day, for God's sake, so many years later.

At least from that point on, I was no longer referred to as Little Turnip. RIP Li'l Turnip.

I didn't understand what was going on back then, what being sort of famous meant. My mom handled all the media relations, and it was good conversation fodder at her boring law firm holiday parties and school alumni events. *You're the mom of Goggle Girl? OMG!* If I hadn't been thrust into internet fame, how would she feel about me?

Sometimes I wondered if things between us would be better. Or maybe they'd be worse.

"Unfortunately, there's more. Parents have also expressed concern with Sunny talking about other students in her videos without consent."

Leaning forward in my chair, I protested, "But...I never use people's names!" I looked at my parents. "I swear."

"True, but you do provide enough context so people can deduce who you're speaking ill of." He looked at a Post-it Note on his monitor. "For example, last week, you said, and I quote, 'Some annoying turdface dinged my car multiple times with his douchey, monstrous, red Land Rover door in the school parking lot.' And then you said, 'His vanity plate should read *ASSHOLE* instead of *ON FIYAH*.' Is that accurate?" He handed me the sticky note with those transcribed words.

It was true. All of it. I mean, ON FIYAH? How could I let that go?

"The problem here is this: there's only one student at school who has a Land Rover with that vanity plate. People can figure out it was Dylan."

Dylan Hightower. Driving his stupid douche tank that I wished I could set *on fiyah*.

Before I could explain that Dylan shouldn't have dented my car in the first place, and he'd committed a crime worth investigating because it was a clear hit-and-run incident—I had eyewitnesses!—Mom jumped in.

"Technically, this is within her rights to discuss online. As you know, freedom of speech is of course protected by the Constitution. And trust me, I'm well versed in the law." *Yes, we know. Yale Law School.* She gave a gritted smile and shrugged her shoulders. "But as you also know, I strongly believe in preserving the harmony at this school, my alma mater. To appease the other parents here, Sunny will absolutely refrain from this behavior in the future." Her words were pointy little daggers stabbing my heart.

"But—" I tried.

"But nothing. We're done here," she hissed under her breath, through her clenched smile.

"Yes, we are thankfully done here." Mr. Lyons smiled. "I appreciate you being so understanding of the severity of the situation. Just as you would feel free to come to me with any concerns, other parents also have taken advantage of my open-door policy. Some of them are named donors for the school. As you are."

My dad sprung to his feet first, hands jammed in his pockets, heels bouncing, ready to flee. He hated conflict. It was why he left law to sell real estate. It was why he caved to what Mom wanted or said, even if he was right.

He'd even put his dream of owning a consulting business on the back burner because Mom said it was too risky. I actually saw my dad's dreams crushed before my very eyes. We were at Olive

Garden for my fourteenth birthday celebration. The OG was my favorite restaurant at the time. The unlimited soft breadsticks were oh, so heavenly.

"What if you don't get customers or clients? How will we pay for Sunny's or Chloe's college if we're swimming in debt?" Mom barked at Dad while we were eating our garden salads.

It was an exclamation, not a question. The dining room went silent. Someone dropped a fork. A baby cried. My sister stress-ate three breadsticks in a row. I pulled my hoodie strings to hide my scorching-hot face so tight, you could only see my nose and an inch perimeter of pimply skin. Worst. Birthday. Ever.

My mom never apologized. And that night, my dad dropped the whole thing. He went on to climb up the ladder at the Koreatown real estate company he'd been at for ten years.

Mr. Lyons stood and extended his hand. "Thank you, Mr. and Mrs. Song, for being considerate of our tight-knit, well-meaning community." After a round of handshakes among the adults, we headed out the door. "Sunny, I'll see you back in the fall. No petition-worthy antics over the summer, okay?"

I took my phone off Do Not Disturb mode while we exited his office, and now it bleeped with a schedule reminder and a flood of notifications.

"Yeah, sure," I murmured while reading some of the comments. "No antics," I promised as Mr. Lyons pushed the heavy wooden door closed.

TWO

FAKE-SMILING FOR OVER FIFTEEN MINUTES IS HARDER than you'd think. How did news anchors do this on live TV? My cheeks twinged, and my watery eyes twitched, begging me for a brief time-out. But I had this livestream to do, and it was the first one I'd set up with donations. It was also the first time I'd streamed a cooking video. They were always popular, but I managed to forget that I'm a terrible cook before I went live.

With one wrong flick of the hand mixer, brownie batter splattered on the counter along with some of my mom's cookbook covers. Thick, brown droplets hit the ceiling.

I said in the direction of the tripod, "Whoops! Well, as my kindergarten teacher always said to my parents, 'A messy child is a happy one!'" Looking down at my clothing, it was clear that *messy* was an understatement. Brown batter and oil splashes speckled my entire front, turning it into a chocolaty Jackson Pollock.

Using a silicone spatula, I scraped the contents of the mixing bowl into a baking pan and set the timer. According to the livestream monitor, some contributions were starting to roll in. "Thank you, Janelle B! Christy Flores! Thanks for the Super Stickers, Chanelle M! It's my first time cooking live. I'll post the final video on all my channels! Thank you for all of your support, everyone." I grinned at the camera. "So there you have it. Thirty-minute brownies, including cooking time! Thanks so much for watching!" Waving at the camera, I tapped on the screen to turn the stream off and, with a sigh of relief, stripped off my soiled top and tossed it in the hamper.

Note to self: no more live cooking shows without prep and practice. That was a disaster. And how in the hell did I end up with a sink full of dirty dishes from making so-called One-Pot Brownies? Rachael Ray, you need more transparency. Maybe rename the recipe *One-Sink Brownies*.

I placed a mixing spoon onto the wobbly stack of measuring cups and utensils. The whole tower fell in a wince-inducing crash.

Adding to the noise, a message bleeped on my phone. I pulled it out from my pocket.

Maya

You're still streaming. I am watching you knock over dishes in your bra, like a seminaked human godzilla

Oh shhhhh—! This was what I got for doing the cooking show live. I thought I'd calculated the risks: live meant it was in the moment, and screw-ups would be hard to hide, but live also meant more interaction with my superfans. This was one of those days I should have opted for an apron, but who the hell wore aprons anymore? I looked down at my tattered exercise bra and high-waisted over-the-belly-button yoga pants and wondered if the camera really added ten pounds. Was my attire considered G-rated? I had on the bra equivalent of granny panties— there was nothing scandalous about my ComfortFlex off-white, low-impact-intensity brassiere. Zero sexiness here.

I glanced over to the tripod. The iPad app was still recording, the bright-red circle flashing, mocking my every move.

Blink.

Okay.

Blink.

Quick.

Blink.

Think.

A notification popped up that Rafael Kim—a.k.a. @Rafa007, a.k.a. my eternal crush since forever—had joined and sent me a direct message. My brain shut down. Or more accurately, my brain autofilled with millions of questions, like, "OMG, did he see any of my other livestreams?" and, "Does he want to hang out this summer?" My numb brain didn't have room for more critical thoughts like, "Shouldn't I turn off the camera?" or just as important, "Should you figure out if that's smoke you smell?" or, "Where'd the extra stick of softened butter go?"

Don't panic. Go over to the camera, say "hi-thanks-bye," and turn it off. Easy peasy.

But of course, it wasn't that simple. Walking straight to the camera would mean a full-frontal, grotesque cleavage assault on my viewers as I leaned into the tripod to shut off the video. There had to be a way out of this mess that didn't involve smothering my viewers' screens with my not-quite-size-B chest.

But what could I say that wouldn't make me look like a moron who forgot to turn off the camera?

I glanced over at my kitchen counter. Next to my cookbooks was a stack of unopened *Self*, *Women's Health*, and *Fitness* magazines with glistening cover models wearing string bikinis. It gave me an idea. My only idea.

"Th-Thanks for hanging in there...um...this is like one of those movie post-credits scenes. Surprise! I'm still here! While we wait for the brownies to bake, let's do some exercises! Everybody on their feet!"

Ugh. Exercise. Just the thought of flipping pages in those workout magazines made me tired. Stretching my right arm across my chest, I tried to think of what to do next. I repeated the stretch on the left arm and considered my options.

I lifted my arms above my head and mimicked climbing a

ladder. Running in place was next. Then jumping jacks. These were all exercises I remembered from elementary school PE.

God help me.

I looked at my YouTube stats while side-stretching. I'd jumped from 300 viewers at the show's start to 1,200, getting more views and likes than ever before, aside from my pre- and post-tonsillectomy hospital videos.

2,000.

2,300. Surpassed my tonsillectomy video views.

2,400.

2,900.

3,000 viewers! New likes!

Comments poured in.

» **Daphne_OC:** Never expected brownie making to be this fun!

» **HarryUppp:** WTF is going on?

» **JustinN:** Nice rack, GoggleGirl

» **ShereaScott:** Cannot unseeeeeee

» **JaydenLovesChurros:** Seriously, WTF is going on?

I grabbed a pan of brownies I'd made earlier that morning and walked toward the camera. "After a few more minutes in the oven, you'll end up with something like this," I chirped, tilting the dessert toward the camera lens.

While still holding the pan, I took a butter knife to cut out a sizable square and lifted it from the giant brownie loaf. "Mmmm, one-pot brownies in just thirty minutes. What could be better than that?" I took a giant bite. It was immediately clear that I'd accidentally used ground sea salt instead of coarse sugar in my recipe. Leave it to me to take sea salt brownies to a whole new level. But I gratuitously chewed and smiled for my audience.

I gulped it down, eyes watery and twitchy from the sodium overdose. "See you tomorrow for day two of summer break!" I used the brownie pan as a breast shield and barreled toward the camera, flicking it off.

With the back of my hand, I swiped my sweaty forehead. I breathed out a sigh of relief as Maya text-bleeped again.

Maya

> OMG DYING! Where'd you learn all those Zumba moves??? That was your best episode this year! Maybe ever

For months, my YouTube channel views had stagnated, so I thought I'd change it up by varying the programming during the summer, when I would have more time. I usually posted every day, sharing everything from my first time trapezing to being deathly vomity with the stomach flu to one-pot cooking. *Seventeen* magazine named me "Teen Hustler of the Year," and I finally hit ninety thousand followers but then hit a plateau. So damn close to breaking the 100K milestone. YouTube gave people who surpassed one hundred thousand followers a fancy plaque, the coveted Silver Button Creator Award. No one in my friend circle had gotten one. But nothing I did lately helped me gain more subscribers, even though I spent several hours every single night and my entire weekends trying to add and edit more content.

Nothing until now.

With the one-pot brownie livestream, brand-new viewers and subscribers had liked, commented, and shared my video. Maybe I needed to make more of them. I mean, who wouldn't want to see a seventeen-year-old wearing geriatric undergarments doing Jazzercise on a cooking episode?

The back door opened, and in walked my dad with my younger sister, Chloe. They'd just come back from her piano recital at the Walt Disney Symphony Hall.

Chloe crossed her arms and gave my attire a once-over glance. "I thought you were busy with summer camp preassignments. So instead of coming to my performance, you filmed a porno?"

Mom walked in behind them. "You filmed...*what*?"

THREE

MOM'S EYES GREW WIDE AS SHE SURVEYED THE MESS. "What are you doing? What is all this? You need to clean it up. Now!" She took a salt-laden brownie and bit into it. "Wow, this is terrible!" She placed the brown square back in the pan, then spit the chewed-up brownie bits into the sink. Mom paused and looked down. "Did I step on a melted stick of butter?"

My dad's mouth fell open as he took in the immediate setting: his seventeen-year-old daughter standing in the kitchen, filming herself in her never-meant-to-be-seen exercise bra when her parents were away. I had to admit, it didn't look good.

"It's complicated" is all I managed to squeak out.

Low-pitched and barely audible, Dad growled, "Go upstairs." His voice, acrid and tinged with fury, sent a shiver down my spine. Dad never got this mad. Not even on that fateful night at Olive Garden.

Even so, I wasn't done in the kitchen. "Hold on. I need to do one thing." Rafa's message. What did it say? In the half-naked frenzy, I'd misplaced my phone.

Dad bellowed, "No 'one more thing'! No more YouTubing." He grabbed my phone from the countertop. "This has become a real problem, Sunny. First the principal's office, and now...this? Aeeeesh!" He nodded toward the dirty dishes and the oil-splattered counter, then waved his hand from my neck down to my toes. "Look at you!" He shook his head slowly, his anger seething. "Does this look normal to you? You're grounded! All summer!"

In Korean parent-speak, *grounded* meant we were done talking and there was no opportunity for rebuttal. Even if I hadn't done anything wrong. It didn't matter. In this case, the conversation was over because they thought I made an R-rated cooking video while they were at a piano recital. End of conversation.

The oven timer beeped.

The brownies.

Before being banished to my room, I pulled out the pan with my slightly charred Williams Sonoma oven mitts. "I made a new batch," I said with one last attempt to reopen the dialogue. Met with cold stares from all members of the household, I trudged up the stairs, calling out, "Someone throw out the old ones!"

The first thing I did in my room was put on a fresh T-shirt. Then, flopping backward on my bed, I closed my eyes and replayed the recent events in my head. The livecast had gone pretty well, given the circumstances. I had crept up another thousand followers give or take, inching closer to one hundred thousand. That was when I could unlock new monetization opportunities, and companies would really get interested in working with me.

Improvisation was typically out of my comfort zone, but if doing something different was what it took to keep me from plateauing, or worse, falling, there was no question. I'd do it.

But first, I needed to get ungrounded. And get my phone back.

Dad's earlier words echoed in my head during my few hours of quiet time. My mom yelled at me a lot—okay, pretty much all the time—but never Dad. Mom always said he and I were cut from the same cloth—we were easygoing, introverted geeks. Mom and Chloe were similar to each other: stubborn and argumentative, partial to schedules and routines over spontaneity.

Dad's disappointed, woeful eyes haunted me. I'd really messed up this time.

Even though my phone had been confiscated, my messages could be accessed through my computer.

I could see what Rafa wrote.

Rafa

Hi.

That was it. I'd freaked out about a stupid two-letter word.

Meanwhile, Maya had sent me at least a dozen messages, and scrolling through them was hard because she wouldn't. Stop. Texting.

Maya

That video was hilarious

So many new subscribers, wow

You need a new wardrobe tho

LOL

Seriously, you do

Rafael just messaged me OMG

He said he tuned in for the first time today 😮

He was impressed 😊

He told me to tell you to message him back

why are you not writing back

Your video's getting shared with the hashtags #BROWNIEPORN #BROWNIEGATE

Um, you're trending?!

WHY U NO WRITE MEEEE?!?! 📸

Oh no

Rafa said that Dylan's mom sent the video to Mr. Lyons

My unintentionally racy one-pot brownie summer video had exploded in the worst way possible. This was #GoggleGirl level viral all over again, but a million times worse, because now it was not cute. #BrowniePorn. Why did the dumbest things always get picked up by everyone? And I didn't have a single clue about how to undo any of this damage.

Think, think, think.

Damn, damn, damn.

I did the only thing that came to mind. I logged into my YouTube channel, clicked on the video that had gotten me thousands of new followers, and made the video private. Only I could see it, but I didn't delete it. Maybe, just maybe, Mr. Lyons wouldn't be able to view the link in time.

Chloe messaged too, from her bedroom down the hall.

Chloe

OOOOH YOU'RE GONNA BE IN TROUBLEEEEEEE 😁

When my mom's phone rang with the ringtone I'd programmed two days earlier as a joke ("ALERT! ALERT! MELTDOWN IMMINENT!"), my heart thudded hard against my rib cage. I opened my door to eavesdrop.

"Hello? Mr. Lyons! Good evening. I didn't expect a call from you after our meeting. How can I help you?" She'd switched to her corporate lawyer professional voice. The really obviously fake one.

Pause.

"What do you mean *hashtag brownie porn?*"

Oh no.

"Hold on. I'll go check my email now."

Oh...nooooo.

A long, uncomfortable pause.

"Yes, we understand. I have no words to describe my disappointment. And if this is your recommendation, my husband and I are fully on board. We want to keep Sunny in school."

WHAT? I tiptoed to the staircase so I could hear better.

"Thank you. The second we get off the phone, I'm giving them a call. I'll mention you referred me. My sincerest apologies, and thank you again for giving Sunny another chance."

Pause.

"Much appreciated. Take care."

The murmurs of my dad's voice clipped the tail end of my mom's conversation with Mr. Lyons. He sounded calm.

Mom snapped, "Ed! Not now! I need to call this person right away, or Sunny can't go back to Westminster next year. SHE. WILL. BE. EXPELLED. They're waiting for my call!"

"Who is it? Who is *they*? Who are you calling?" He barked back, so loud that I shivered. Dad rarely raised his voice, and if he did, never twice in the same day. That was more of a Mom thing.

"Shhhh!" she hissed, then switched modes to instantly chipper robo-mom. "Oh, hi! Is this Sunshine Heritage Farms... Camp? Am I calling too late? Oh...okay...good! The headmaster at Westminster Prep referred me to you. He said you might have an opening for one of the digital detox sessions? Oh...oh, thank God. We need an intervention."

"I can't believe I'm spending a whole month in Iowa."

Maya flopped onto her back on my bed, her black curls splayed on my pillow. "Whyyyy did this have to happen before our senior year? This was supposed to be *our* summer. Both of us. Hanging out."

Maya was the only friend my parents allowed to come over during my grounding. They said she was a good influence on me, with her straight As and admissions-worthy hobbies like debate and community volunteering. A self-starter, she'd founded the Black Student Association *and* the Westminster Coastal Cleanup Club. She was also a social media logistics whiz who helped run my account. I'd offered to pay her, but she said I could be her first business reference when she applied for jobs. Leave it to Maya to already be thinking about stuff like that.

She continued moaning. "Now I'll be all alone, nerding it up in summer immersion at UCLA without you."

"You won't be by yourself. You'll be with Rafa," I said, joining her on my bed, staring at the ceiling.

She snorted. "He's more your friend, or should I say your forever crush, not mine."

"Hey, it hasn't been forever. I've had boyfriends!"

"Two. Two guys you dated a few times. And that doesn't mean you weren't still hung up on Rafa. It just meant you were... distracted for a while. Maybe going away to Iowa will help you get over him." Her body jerked, and she shot up to seated position. "Oh! I forgot. I did some research on your digital detox camp! I printed some things."

Because I had limited access to the internet now, Maya googled Sunshine Heritage Farms for me. Scrambling off the bed, she pulled a thick stack of paper from her messenger bag and handed it to me.

I sat up. "Thank you!"

Wow, the camp website was antiquated, and not in a kitschy, nouveau-rustic farm sense. The copyright at the bottom of the page was five years old, and the events page listed activities from when I was in junior high. From the home page description,

Sunshine Farms was a year-round organic farm but had educational tours where they dressed up like people from the olden days to teach kids how they used to churn butter, milk cows, and salt meat. Like *Little House on the Prairie*, but creepier because it was with real people. During the summers, Sunshine Farms had opened their residential facilities to become a long-standing Christian camp. Now that it was almost July, it made me wonder what the deal was with this place. Would it still be a church camp in tandem with the digital detox camp? Would us detox kids mix and mingle with the Christians? Maybe things would get ugly and territorial and we'd all rumble in the cornfield after dark.

I muttered, "Oh God, one whole month in farm hell."

"With a name like *Sunshine* though, how bad can it be?" Maya pressed her lips together and stifled a laugh.

At the bottom of the stack was a printout that wasn't camp-related. "What's this?"

"I didn't know whether I should share it or not." She peered over my shoulder. "Sorry the ink faded. My toner is low. There's a search going on for the next 'it' influencer." She showed me the same article on her phone. "Starhouse, a collective of content creators, is looking for their last member."

I grabbed her phone to look it up. "*Starhouse* sounds a lot better than *Sunshine Farms*."

"One of the members dropped out. There are rumors, but I think she was charged with possession of a controlled substance, although it's still unclear if it was prescription or not. Anyway, the door just opened for you, my friend. They're looking for an up-and-comer. Someone who has a lot of followers but has room to grow. Don't be mad, but I already submitted you yesterday. The only requirement was to submit the most popular video on your Goggle Girl channel."

I sighed. That Goggle Girl video was both a blessing and curse. Posted nearly ten years ago, it had over twenty-six million views and still received comments from people discovering it for the first time. I hadn't made my brownie video public again, but other creators had copied the video and tagged me. I was secretly hoping it would overtake the popularity of the Goggle Girl one. I'd rather be known for #BrownieGate or even #BrowniePorn, which spoke volumes about my feelings toward my old content.

"They're looking for someone who posts high quality content often. But honestly, if they look at your account and see the brownie video memes you're tagged in gaining traction, you'll be a shoo-in. It shows you can go viral more than once."

I smiled. "There's one other problem though. I'll be heading to farm camp this weekend. And that means no more posting."

"Well, that's where your brilliant friend comes to the rescue," Maya said with a smirk. "Let's work on some content ideas this week before you leave, and I can be admin while you're away. People won't even know you're gone for a whole month."

This was a great opportunity. Influencer houses were

cropping up all over the place, and being part of one was a surefire way to score high-profile collaborations and brand deals. And if I had some money saved up by the end of my senior year, I could make the decisions about what I wanted my future to look like. Not just do what my mom and dad wanted for me.

And why wouldn't Starhouse want me? I was like one of those child actors in Hollywood who made a comeback later in life but cooler. My brownie livestream had been liked, shared, and memed. Winning this contest was a long shot, maybe even one a mile long, but it was still a shot. I clapped my hands together. "Will you be my business manager when I get super famous?"

"Yes, and you need to buy me a fancy dinner if you actually get selected. And I'll need you to promote all my future businesses someday." She threw a pillow at me.

I caught it before it hit my face. "Deal."

FOUR

IOWA.

Honest to God, I didn't know where Iowa was on a map anymore. We had to memorize states and capitals in the sixth grade, and I purged all that out of my memory when I finished the school year.

Dad tossed me my phone, loaded my luggage, and slammed the trunk door. "Iowa, the Hawkeye State. Your mom also looked into these scary digital detox boot camps in China and Korea, so in comparison, Iowa's the least-terrible option, trust me. Plus, your headmaster was very keen on you going. We need to go to the airport though. Hurry up, and say bye to Chloe and Mom."

Iowa. Why couldn't it be Hawaii? I was supposed to take precollege classes with Maya and try coding, but instead they were shipping me off to some camp at some farm in the middle of Nowhere, USA? That was BS. A crap-ton of BS. And there would probably be actual bona fide bovine crap everywhere on this farm too. I'd rather go to SAT test prep classes full-time all summer long with no phone breaks than do this.

My phone buzzed with a message from Maya.

Maya

Did you leave for the airport yet

No, I'm packing up the car

Oh good timing! Look at the street

A fleet of bicyclists rounded the corner in tight, neon spandex. All the lime-green helmets had Westminster Prep Cycle Club insignias, making the group look fancier than they actually were. They'd formed the club at the beginning of the school year, an intramural organization that biked together on the weekends for fun. Rafa was the lead cyclist in the pack. When he whizzed by, he managed to flash a smile and wave with one hand. I couldn't see his eyes: he was wearing a pair of those narrow, wrapped sports sunglasses with rainbow lenses. He nearly blinded me with his ensemble of neon-blue biking gear. Looking directly at him probably had adverse health effects, possibly causing worse damage to corneas and retinas than looking directly at the sun or opening your eyes in a tanning bed.

Maya was the last to roll down the street. She only got into biking because of bad knees and a torn tendon. The torn tendon was a result of a ten-second video dance routine gone wrong, and now Maya couldn't do any sports involving jumping, running, or twisting, which was basically any sport. The physical therapist gave her two options: biking or swimming. She double-thumbs-downed swimming because she hated the smell of chlorine and said swim caps looked like condoms, so biking it was.

If you forced *me* to choose between the two—swimming or biking—I'd go with biking, but a stationary one. Ideally one with a place to put my iPad so I could watch Netflix. A poor man's Peloton.

"Were you pedaling and texting at the same time? That's a road hazard!" I shouted, trotting down the driveway to meet her at my mailbox.

She removed her helmet and shook out her hair. A wayward curl fell forward and stuck to her sweaty forehead. "I pulled over to the side of the road to text you, thank you very much, but people honked anyway. I can't catch a break around here, so many angry drivers everywhere. Anyway, I wanted to see you in person before you headed out." She leaned in close. Worry lines formed on her perspiring forehead. "Write me often, okay?"

"Of course I will. There might be SOS postcards. Just warning you."

She laughed. "I can't wait. And I'll make sure your autoposted content works, and we'll do a big online celebration when you're back. Memorize my number, too, in case there's any opportunity to call or message me. And I'll let you know if I hear anything from Starhouse." She checked her watch. "I need to head home. Did you know they gave us another round of preassignments at the UCLA enrichment camp? I need to ask Rafa if he's finished his yet. He's always done early."

My cheeks flushed when she said his name. "He's probably already got everything lined up for the summer: his assignments, his extracurriculars, a girlfriend. Maybe even two of them."

She fastened her helmet. "I'll report back on Rafa in my mail updates. Maybe he'll come to his senses and realize he should have been dating you all along. But try to have fun. Find a hot summer fling, a hunky Midwestern boy. And while you're there, maybe you'll come up with new content ideas to keep your social media empire growing. Think more brownie and less porny." Maya wobbled out of the driveway on her bike and coasted down my street.

"Bye!" Maya held her thumb and index finger together, slightly offset, over her head. A goodbye heart.

Chloe emerged from the garage sporting head-to-toe, size zero tennis gear, with an oversize Nike visor and perfect swinging ponytail. She was signed up for tennis and music camps all summer. "Leaving already? Have fun at farm camp!" She smirked. "Take some pics of you tipping cows! Oh, wait, they won't let you have devices there. You can draw me a picture and mail it." She smiled way bigger than she should have and pulled out her phone from her pouch. "My dear older sister, the wannabe Korean Kardashian, going to device detox camp. That's just perfect!"

Click.

I lunged for her phone but she was too quick. She wagged her index finger. "Uh-uh." Stuffing it back into her tiny purse, she said, "Don't worry. I'm not going to post it. I'm keeping this photo as a cherished summer memory or maybe future black-mail." She leaned in and gave me a light hug. "Don't get kicked out. And don't mess up my makeup. Bring me a souvenir if they allow you to buy things with prison dollars."

Chloe could be a real piece of work sometimes. When we were younger, we got along better. At just two years apart, we were joined at the hip, waving our chopstick wands and building elaborate castles with trapdoors in *Minecraft*. My parents wanted us to stay close as we got older, but it never happened. Maybe it was because she turned super high-fashion in eighth grade, and I was more of an Old Navy clearance girl. Or she became a Sephora girl, and I stayed my tinted ChapStick self. Or she had her first kiss in seventh grade at a party, and I hadn't managed to date at all this entire school year.

She was Mom's favorite, of course. Maybe we didn't get along anymore because Chloe could connect with Mom in a way

I couldn't. Mom and Dad pulled her out of Westminster to go to Webb Academy for Girls because she was hanging out with the wrong "boy-crazy" crowd, but Mom never laid into her about it like she would have with me. Chloe moved schools, they argued a little, and that was it. In contrast, Mom and I fought practically every day.

Now I'd be leaving home for four weeks, creating even more distance between Chloe and me. Literally and figuratively.

Mom came out the front door in her fancy Lululemon yoga clothes, far different from her weekday corporate America fancy law firm uniform: Chloé blouse, Ted Baker skirt, Valentino pumps. I went in for a goodbye hug as she took a huge step back.

Both palms up and arms outstretched, she protested, "Oh, no, I just did a fifty-minute Pilates workout. I'm so sweaty." She patted my upper back once, which was more like a light scoot-push to the car. "Remember, you're doing this because we want you to get a fresh start and be back at Westminster in the fall." Her face fell, and her forehead creases deepened. "You need to take this seriously, Sunny. No kidding around. You need help, and we want to make sure you get it. Nae mal jal deul-eo. Araso?"

"Okay." I shrugged. *I'll behave. I'll listen.*

"In Korean, please," my mom said, crossing her arms.

I lowered my head. "Ne."

Mom nodded at Dad, signaling it was time to leave.

I yanked the door handle, but Dad hadn't unlocked it yet.

Yank.

I hate speaking Korean.

Yank.

Hate it.

Beep-beep!

Yank.

Finally.

I plopped down into the passenger seat. Shoulders hunched, I fastened my seat belt. Both of my parents grew up speaking Korean at home, but Chloe and I didn't. Mom and Dad were born in Korea and had come to the United States at an early age. We always defaulted to English when Mom and Dad spoke to us, even when our parents bribed us with candy, ice cream, even Disneyland. I stopped going to Korean school so many years ago that I barely remembered anything. My childhood memories were plagued with not-so-fond recollections of writing pages and pages of Korean characters and memorizing useless, antiquated Hangul vocabulary words for weekly quizzes and drills.

After years of fighting constantly about this, my parents gave up. I won! Or so I thought. The more Hangul I forgot, the more self-conscious I got about it. It had gotten to a point where my parents' Korean friends and our family in Korea would rather revert to broken English than see me struggle to communicate in Hangul on even a basic level. By the time I turned sixteen, I pretty much forgot most of what I'd learned.

Dad punched the directions to the airport into his phone. "You should practice Korean more. It'll get more comfortable if you do," he ironically said in English.

Some of the other Korean kids I knew were in the same boat: they'd given up, like me. Others quit but ramped up learning Hangul later in high school by hiring private tutors and binging K-dramas with no subtitles. At the time, it seemed like a waste of effort and time, but sticking with it paid off for them. Now, my inability to speak the language would become the biggest barrier to ever really feeling "Korean." Any time a situation required me to speak it, I prickled with embarrassment and anger as toddler-level Korean words stumbled out of my mouth.

My eyes teared up, and I gulped hard, as if trying to swallow my sadness. I wished they'd just give up on me trying to speak it. Every time Korean words clumsily formed on the tip of my tongue, it was a painful reminder of how much time had passed since taking Hangul classes and how many words and phrases I'd forgotten.

Dad turned on the ignition and turned down the volume to his audiobook, *Getting to Yes*. Dad loved those self-help books that teach you how to be a better businessperson, leader, and negotiator. He said it was pleasure reading so he could be more effective at work, but my suspicion was he was building up an arsenal of knowledge to be able to go toe-to-toe with Mom one day, when it really counted. Too bad shipping me off to detox camp wasn't that time.

"Are you nervous about flying by yourself?" Dad asked at a stoplight, fiddling with the air conditioner. "We wanted to come with you, but Mom's working on a big case for a few months and needs to be in town for her client tomorrow, and I have some big client showings lined up next week."

I shrugged my reply. I hadn't talked to him much since the #BbrowniePorn incident. After that night, my parents had been fighting constantly about my future. Half the time, they spoke in Korean. Though they tried to talk quietly in the bedroom, I still had my trusty spy kit from a fifth-grade Scholastic order and could eavesdrop by putting the stethoscope thingy to the drywall. Dad wasn't on board with shipping me off to Iowa at all. It was too hasty, he said, preferring to limit my phone use and confiscate it at night and on weekends, weaning me off electronics slowly. Mom preferred the cold-turkey, drastic approach. Mom won, unsurprisingly.

None of it mattered now anyway. Mom and Dad had put down a full nonrefundable camp deposit, so I was going, end of story. But I at least wanted Dad to know the truth. He was the only one who might believe me.

I cleared my throat. "You know I didn't mean to record that livestream in my, uh, bra, right? I want to set the record straight before I get shipped away. This wasn't anything I did on purpose." Dad kept his eyes on the road and remained expressionless. "Seriously, if I'd planned it, I would have invested in a new bra."

His face turned red, and I got a chuckle out of him. But then he let out a disappointed sigh from his nose. "Sunny, you're not getting *shipped away* like an Amazon free return. And this isn't only about the brownie video. You understand that, right? You're on your phone every minute, every second of your free time. You don't have any interests outside social media. You hole up in your room for hours and only see us for meals, if we're lucky. You go into zombie mode as soon as you turn on your phone, iPad, or laptop, and you zone out to what's around you. We can't even have a normal conversation because you're always getting messages and notifications. Grunting out one- or two-word answers to important questions is your norm. Sometimes you stay in your room and forget to eat and drink water. As a parent, this is frustrating and, more importantly, really scary, because soon you'll be in college and won't have us to look after you." He glanced at me, taking his eyes off the road, but I didn't dare call him out. "You used to be such a happy, curious, silly girl. You never smile anymore."

I let out a snort. "I do, sometimes. You just never say anything funny."

He shook his head but smirked. "You never listen to me anymore, so how do you know? I'm the most hilarious dad around here, especially compared to my fellow stiff, unfunny dad comrades at Westminster."

That got a big grin out of both of us.

I studied his face as he changed lanes. His hair had gone grayer in the last few months. He officially had salt-and-pepper coloring, and the new wrinkles on the outsides of his eyes gave him a friendly look. I hadn't noticed either of these things before.

He made a ticktock sound by clucking his tongue, imitating his blinker as he made a left turn.

My phone buzzed, and I looked down to see several goodbye messages from my friends. Maya mostly, but even Rafael had sent me a tear-eyed emoji. I studied the breadth of emoji options before replying to him with the same one. For years, Rafael and I had a one-notch-above-platonic thing between us, but it never developed into a full-blown relationship. I'd hoped this was the summer it would happen.

Dad sighed. "See, there you go again. I asked you a question about needing money for camp, and you didn't even hear me because you're texting."

"I'm sorry." I wanted to put my phone away, but what if Rafa wrote back? I compromised by flipping the phone over on my thigh.

Shaking his head, he muttered, "When you're fully unplugged, we hope you process everything leading up to this moment. Maybe, when you're there, you'll learn how to become the person you want to be. Or even *used* to be—that would be good too. Someone present in the moment. Someone who lives life without her eyes glued to a device."

He wasn't wrong. The amount of time I spent online was higher than anyone I knew, but a big chunk of time every day was spent on my YouTube channel. I was building trust, relationships, and engagement through my platform, not just doing mindless social media scrolling, although that did happen sometimes. I pressed the side of my head against the cool window and marveled at the bright-blue sky and tall palm trees lining Sepulveda Boulevard.

Goodbye, LA.

Goodbye, beach I never went to anyway.

Goodbye, civilization.

Dad turned down a street that wasn't on the direct path to LAX. He was taking the long, scenic route to the airport...which meant one thing.

I jerked upright. "Wait! Are we going to In-N-Out?"

"Maaaaybe." He pulled into the drive-through and rolled down his window. "This is to repay your hilarious dad for sacrificing his weekend midmorning coffee to take you to the airport. But I also know you'll miss your Double-Doubles when you're in Iowa, so I thought it would be a nice thing to do for your last meal."

"Thanks." I let out a small whimper. "Last meal...that sounds like the end of a death sentence."

"With Mom, sometimes it kind of feels like it," Dad said with a faint, knowing smile. It was hard to get back into Mom's good graces once you were in the doghouse. She was the queen of holding grudges. Five years later, she was still furious at her own mother for sending Chloe and me some boys' sports stuff for Christmas. I thought the Korean soccer team shirts were cool and wore mine as a sleep shirt, but Mom took it personally, saying Grandma was passive-aggressively pointing out she wished she had a grandson. Honestly, knowing Grandma, it was probably just on sale.

And when Mom made a decision, boy did she stick with it. I was going to camp. Period. The more I protested, the more she scolded me. She had no problem with punishment either: all my attempts to reason with her failed, and challenging her authority made it worse. I already lost driving privileges and nonessential phone access after the brownie incident. She was clever for keeping my bedroom door open at all times as a form of penalty too. There was no greater punishment to a teenager than loss of privacy.

Next on the chopping block was her shutting down my YouTube channel permanently. That was when I stopped fighting back. This online life I'd created was a huge part of who I was. Years of hard work. Fame was within my reach, and I couldn't give up now.

Bzzz.

BZZZ.

Maya. There was no way my dad would be okay with me talking to her in my last minutes in the car with him. I texted a quick one-character reply, which was our shorthand signal for *too busy*—a code we'd developed in junior high. The other person knew not to reply back under these circumstances.

Well, except Maya broke the rule this time. She sent a picture, which I tried to sneak a look at while Dad ordered our lunch through the drive-through speaker.

"Two combo number ones, with grilled onion, ketchup instead of sauce. Extra pickles. One Coke and one Diet Coke." Dad pulled his head back into the car. "Anything else?"

"Can I get a chocolate milkshake?" If this was my last good meal for a while, I wanted to make it count.

I glanced at Maya's text. It was a photo of her wearing overalls, her hair pulled to the top of her head in a bun. She wore a shirt she'd designed herself that Westminster Prep's Black Student Association sold for fundraising during Black History Month. With outstretched arms and a pouty face, she'd added the caption, I'll miss you thisssss much.

I smiled as I put my phone away. *I'll miss you too, Maya.*

"And one chocolate shake. Actually, make that two shakes. That'll do it."

The speaker repeated back the order. "Nineteen fifty. Please drive around."

As we pulled up to the second window, my mouth watered from the smell of grilled burgers and fresh fries. In an odd contrast, my stomach went sour with a sense of dread. I'd be on a plane in less than two hours, with wheels on the ground in Iowa in roughly six.

The window guy handed over our food and drinks, and my dad passed the bags and boxes to me. With In-N-Out in my lap, my appetite returned quickly. I took my first bite of fresh-cut fries and savored the flavor, but I knew this fix was temporary. By the time the day was over, I'd be at a weirdo camp with device-addicted strangers on a farm in the middle of nowhere.

"Is this an evil way of teaching me a lesson?" I asked suspiciously. "Like to make me miss LA food like In-N-Out so much that I get homesick from the start?" Seemed like something Mom would come up with. Subtle mind trickery to get me to rethink my ways. She knew how I loved to eat, and I'd miss Korean food especially. When Mom or Dad didn't have time to make dinner or pick up premade food at H Mart, we had a nearby restaurant that delivered the best soon tofu chigae, kimchi fried rice, and kalbi on the Westside. Even with a delicious burger in hand, my mouth watered at the memories of sizzling meat and spicy stews. It hadn't even crossed my mind until now that I'd be deprived of Korean food for four long weeks.

Suddenly, the In-N-Out wasn't satisfying anymore.

Dad hit a pothole, and everything in my lap toppled, including my shake. Luckily, the bag of fries was full of napkins, so the chocolate leakage onto the upholstery was minimal. I couldn't say the same for my pants.

He looked down at the mess and frowned. "Well, you need to throw those pants out anyway. Too many holes."

"What? These jeans came this way and cost a lot of money. I actually added more fraying yesterday," I protested. Chloe had the eye for fashion in the family, but Dad was in last place in the Song family ranking of fashion sensibilities—given some of his college photos, he'd worn his signature polo shirts and khaki shorts for, like, thirty years. He had perpetual midcalf sock tan lines. Why bother explaining anything to him?

He shook his head. "You look like you've been attacked by a weed eater. Twice." If he didn't like my distressed pants, he would really hate the shredded-sleeve cardigan I had in my carry-on. His half smile turned to a half frown. "Wait, where did you get money to pay for those ragged jeans?"

I'd been monetizing my site for a few years now, which Mom and Dad kinda-sorta knew about when they approved it a few years ago, but the income was minimal. At best, it was barely above tooth-fairy money and allowance levels, meaning occasionally going to R-rated movies with friends or buying some romance audiobooks every few months. I didn't have to bother my parents about small discretionary purchases like that. After #BrowniePorn, my earnings shot up overnight as new viewers watched my new and older content. Enough to buy a couple of pairs of torn jeans and a ripped sweater. I wanted to keep that quiet for now, otherwise Mom and Dad would know how much the cooking incident had blown up.

It was also just enough to purchase a burner phone to sneak into farm camp for when my real one got confiscated. Mom was the smartest one in the family, but I was definitely the craftiest.

"I got the clothes at a consignment store. The stores on the Westside have high-end, designer shiiii—um...I mean...inventory." When Dad dropped the fashion discussion, I took a messy bite out of my Double-Double. Big mistake—one medium chomp pushed all the burger innards out of the bun. This, in turn, resulted in needing a crapload of napkins for the dribbling burger juice and lettuce leakage seeping through and overflowing from the not-very-effective paper wrapper.

Before I knew it, we pulled up to Terminal Seven. I swiped the last bit of ketchup off my chin with a napkin as thin as low-quality toilet paper.

Des Moines, wheels up in eighty-seven minutes.

FIVE

THE LAX POLICE PATROL WAS ANTI-"PULLING OVER TO THE curb for lengthy goodbyes." As soon as my dad lifted my almost-Sunny-size purple roller bag from the trunk, one of the nearby men in blue yelled, "Move along, sir!" and blew a metal whistle at us. My ears rang from the shrill shriek.

Dad wasn't the sappy, huggy sort, so he patted my shoulder instead. *There, there, Sunny.* "Be good, okay? Jal ga. Call us or write us when you can. Oh, and take your gummy vitamins."

Leave it to my dad to mention gummy vitamins as his final parting words.

"I will." We weren't a family who said *I love you* a lot, or really... ever, but as those words formed on the tip of my tongue, the glaring police guy blew the shrill whistle again. A short staccato then a long blow at an eardrum-bursting decibel, as if to say HEY YOOOUUUU.

"Get moving!" In case we didn't know he was talking to us, he flapped his hands in our direction, shooing us like he was fanning away smoke.

"Can you guys send me Korean snacks in case I opt out of eating carrots and lettuce and whatever else they serve at farm camp? Mom and Chloe know which ones are my favorites." They knew because Mom always yelled at me for putting too many in the cart when we went to H Mart. Chloe knew because she always ate more than her fair share and played innocent when I confronted her with the empty wrappers. Maybe *she* was the craftiest one in the family, not me.

Dad took his hand off my shoulder and nodded at me. We both knew the policeman was going to escalate if we stayed any longer, so Dad gave me a little wave before getting back into the car. I offered a quick finger-roll goodbye and wheeled my bag through the automatic doors at the airport.

Luckily, the bag check-in line was short. The desk attendant scanned my boarding pass from my phone and weighed my overstuffed suitcase.

"It's over the weight limit. We need to charge you extra, or you'll need to remove some items." A quick look at the scale revealed it was over by only two pounds. Something she could have probably let go, dismissing it as a scale calibration problem, but didn't. She watched as I unzipped the main compartment. My holey cardigan was easily accessible because I'd thrown it in last minute. That was maybe one pound. Everything else was jam-packed in, practically vacuum sealed together as one solid mass, except for one thing: a ziplock bag full of tampons, pads, and liners. I had taken them out of individual boxes and consolidated my sanitary supplies into this gallon-sized, fully transparent freezer bag. Glancing over my shoulder, I could see that no one was watching, but a long line had formed behind me.

I grabbed the cardigan and my trusty bag o' menstrual supplies then rezipped the suitcase. She lugged it over to the conveyor belt behind her and handed me a baggage claim ticket. "Thank you for flying with Pioneer Airlines!"

My backpack needed reorganization before anything else would fit in it. At a nearby bench, I put my cardigan and ziplock on an open seat and hastily removed anything bulky. Magazines, books, hand sanitizer, snacks, notebook, laptop, a face mask, papers, and pens—all to be unpacked and repacked. Large tour groups streamed in through the automatic doors, making it imperative to get to the security line before they did.

With only a backpack in my possession, I headed toward the GATES 60 TO 80 sign.

Someone behind me bellowed, "Excuse me! You forgot this!" An older woman with stark-white hair in a short ponytail flapped her arms to signal she wanted my attention. She held my bag of Sour Patch Kids in one hand and the large, clear bag of menstrual supplies in the other.

Wincing hard, I sped over to her just as an airport security officer moseyed her way too.

"Ma'am, how long have these been unattended?"

The woman looked at me. "They're hers. She was coming back for them."

I reached for my candy and ziplock but he held out his hand. "Not yet. I still have a few questions. Ma'am, please put the candy and the baggie on the seat."

My pulse quickened, and my breathing turned to light panting. My flight was boarding soon. I needed to grab and *go*.

He examined the candy quickly then took his time with the ziplock.

I blurted, "It's menstrual supplies. I prefer you not open it because of sanitary reasons." His mouth pinched so tightly, his lips disappeared. I backpedaled. "But I'm cool if you need to. I don't want you to think I brought in any explosive tampons."

The woman shot me a look, one I'd seen many times from my parents. *Please shut up. You're making everything worse.*

He rubbed his chin and dropped his arms to his sides. "You can both go. Just try not to leave things lying around unattended. This airport has strict rules, and you could have gotten into trouble."

"Thanks, Officer. And thank you, ma'am." I swiped everything off the seat and shoved them into the large front pocket of my backpack, breathing out a huge sigh of relief.

A cluster of travelers crowded the bottom of the escalator as the TSA agent cleared PreCheck passengers and allowed passage. Going up to the next floor, I could get a good view of what I'd be leaving for a month. Loudness. Crowds. Frenzy. Things I loved about LA but also found overwhelming. LAX airport, and most parts of sprawling LA, were always in a constant state of loud, disruptive construction too. I wouldn't miss that one bit.

To pass the time in the security line, I responded to most of the never-ending texts from Maya and to the ones from school friends (who claimed their summers wouldn't be the same without me). Rafa was in a **Goodbye Sunny!** group text thread, but he hadn't said anything, which honestly kind of pissed me off, since everyone else had responded with a farewell message.

I took a quick video of me in front of a TSA officer and waved goodbye, pretending I was off to a fun vacation destination. Then I uploaded it as my final post before Maya would take over my social media accounts. Before I tucked the phone away, I took snapshots of all my accounts to see how many followers and subscribers I had so I could compare when I got back.

By the time I made it through security, the plane was already boarding. They'd already called group six, so I entered the plane, observing all the first-class people drinking their glasses of wine, reading their *Wall Street Journal*s on their iPads, watching the plebeian parade go by. I offered a princess wave. *Nothing to see here, folks. Just a run-of-the-mill teenager getting shipped off to* *digital detox camp, wearing purposefully tattered clothing reminiscent of swiss cheese.* I took a quick photo of one guy wearing a silk robe with matching black silk eye mask and face mask and a bunch of tiny bottles of alcohol near his armrest. I captioned it **#FirstClassCabinGoals** and uploaded it to all my feeds. Once I got to my seat, I adjusted the vent so it wasn't shooting air in a jet stream strong enough to part my hair and leaned my head against the cabin wall.

Thanks to the engine's white noise and my severe lack of REM sleep, I conked out the second we taxied to the runway and woke up to the worst turbulence just before landing, so bad, I almost needed that free barf bag in the seat pocket. As we bounced into the airport, I hoped this horrible arrival to the great state of Iowa wasn't foreshadowing ominous things to come. Looking at all the teenagers around me as we exited the plane, I tried to figure out if they were also headed to Sunshine with me. Did any of them look like they needed digital detoxing?

I took my sweet time making my way to baggage claim. I had weeks of prairie living ahead of me, and there was no rush on my end to get there. Walking down the drab, beige-carpeted corridor, I stopped at the restroom, bought a soda, and scrolled through my notifications. There were a whole lot of messages in a group chat about parties and summer meetups. Life was moving on without me, it seemed, and not a single person asked about me or said they wished I was there.

Maya let me know she'd gotten access to my account. No messages from Rafa. One from my mom—Let us know when you land. I clenched my teeth as annoyance overcame me. She was the reason I was here in the first place. Why couldn't she find out my status with an airline app?

I texted her one word. Landed.

She replied immediately. Good! Hope it goes well.

At least she didn't say "have a blast" or "enjoy your time away from home!" We both knew this wasn't one of those trips.

But an "I miss you" would have been nice.

I messaged, letting her know I would go dark and my phone would be confiscated soon.

My lone purple suitcase rode 'round and 'round the baggage claim carousel. Maybe this was a metaphor of my life this summer: Alone. Aimless. Abandoned. I used every ounce of strength in all my arm muscles and core to lift and hurl the bag off the conveyor belt, then I wheeled it to some benches, where I unzipped the side pocket to check for one thing—my burner phone. It was there and had no cracks or breaks that would cause transmission issues. Now I had a device for making fun camp content to use when I got home. Something with a "city girl, country girl" theme seemed unique and interesting. Taking a few deep breaths, I tucked away my phone and headed to the exit where the shuttle was scheduled to meet me. There were three freestanding signs: ground transportation, shuttles, and passenger pickup.

Stepping out of the airport was like walking straight into a dripping wet blanket, and I was outside for only maybe one minute before breaking into a fountain of sweat. I'd never dealt with stifling, humid weather before, and it made me miss LA so much more.

The Sunshine Farms logo was on one of the shuttles in the loading zone. The gray-haired van driver, wearing a bright-orange Sunshine polo shirt, waved at me, and I walked toward him. He wiped his brown mustache with a napkin and shoved the wad of paper in his pants pocket. "Sunny? Sunshine?"

You'd think saying words like *Sunny* and *Sunshine* in quick succession would be a happy-ish thing, but this man was the literal opposite of smiley. He was a giant, walking angry-face emoji. His way of offering to put my suitcase in the back of the vehicle was yanking it out of my hand and heaving it with the other luggage. After he slid open the passenger door and I found a seat, he barked, "Sorry, I need to confiscate any electronics you have. And please open the pockets of your backpack so we can do a quick electronics check. This includes Apple Watches or any other wearables, iPads, iPods, laptops, handheld gaming devices, and of course, your mobile." He pronounced it *mo-by-uhl.* Three syllables. "Hopefully you didn't bring a desktop PC." I think he was joking about that last part, but it wasn't really very funny, given he was taking away my freedom. If he turned out to be a serial killer, I wouldn't even be able to call anyone for help...

well, except for my burner phone that I hadn't tested out yet. He placed my real phone in a bag with my name on a preprinted label and put it in a lockbox in the front passenger seat.

I knew this was his job, and he was paid to follow orders but... what a monster.

We started to drive, and it took me a while to notice there was a welcome packet under my right butt cheek. According to the enclosed map with directions, Sunshine Heritage Farms was seventy minutes away. That was an excruciatingly long time, and I had no idea how to fill it without music, games, and photos to thumb through. I heard a grunt and, to my surprise, discovered other people behind me. The shuttle looked empty, but apparently there was a guy who had been sleeping in the very back row and another girl in front of him who lifted her head from lying on the van seat and gave me the longest death stare when I made eye contact.

The girl pulled her bag off the floor and put it in the seat next to hers, as if I would actually get up to sit next to her in the middle of the drive, with all the open rows available. She braided her hair in one of those wispy, bohemian side braids and narrowed her eyes at me. *Nice to meet you too.* She looked vaguely familiar, but I couldn't put my finger on it. Maybe she was someone I followed online? Whoever she was, it was pretty clear we weren't going to be camp BFFs. No need to continue this tense stare-off. *Mental note: if applicable, unfollow Side Braid when you get home.*

According to packet materials, we were headed to a town called Promise City, Iowa. Promise City was known for only one thing: corn mazes. A cough-like bark escaped my mouth. LA-born Korean Sunny Song was going to the Promise City. Of freaking Iowa. Home of world-famous corn mazes. *Could I get a hallelujah? Could I get an AMEN?*

A seven-question questionnaire was the first page in the camp materials. Based on the instructions, our answers would determine our placement in an appropriate peer group.

On a scale of 1 (strongly disagree) to 5 (strongly agree), please rate the following, and provide additional commentary as needed:

I find myself preoccupied or obsessed with any aspect of the internet.

5. (*Didn't everyone?*)

I experience withdrawal symptoms when I'm not able to access the internet.

Maybe 3. (*What were these withdrawal symptoms?*)

I have experienced a buildup of tolerance (needing more time) in order to get the "desired feeling."

(*Left blank. WTF was a desired feeling? Like...sexy times?*)

I have tried to stop or curb my internet use.

1. (*Nope*)

I have lost interest in other life activities.

1. (*Nope. Okay, maybe 2 or 3*)

I have put at risk or lost an opportunity or a relationship because of my internet use.

5. (*My mom and dad wanted to straight-up murder me after #BrownieGate. Yup.*)

I have an addiction to the internet, phones, gadgets, devices.

1 or 2? (*Maybe?*)

I stuffed the survey back into the envelope and pulled out a crumpled printout from my backpack. It listed where my Westminster classmates would be this summer and how I could contact them. Maya had asked classmates to include their information on a shared spreadsheet document so I would have everyone's addresses in case I wanted to write anyone. Sunshine restricted access to email and phone calls, so Maya had given me a stationery kit plus a roll of Forever Stamps to write her. We'd agreed that the phrase "The food's not bad here" was code for "Help! This is a cult! Drop what you're doing and call the police ASAP!"

The summer activities listings were sorted by geography, and it looked like my peers were staying local and either doing something sports-themed or—like Maya—participating in an advanced program with precollege coursework. Like her, I was supposed to be at UCLA. A few of my wealthier classmates were traveling to Europe or Asia with their families. You know, to go to their second or third homes. A few kids had summer retail jobs, but not many. Rafael Kim was starting the summer at UCLA but had gotten a few offers for late-summer internships and hadn't made a final decision. His backup plan was to go to Aspen for their esteemed summer music program because he was also a piano virtuoso, in addition to being a soccer star and an academic god. Rafa with his tall, lean frame, broad shoulders, and full lips. My Korean friends and I joked that he had good Asian hair. It was thick but not stick-straight like mine—it had an enviable wave to it. Maybe I would write him. Or maybe he'd write me.

Great. With all this free time, I was daydreaming about and drooling over Rafael Kim, more than I did before. Surely, this couldn't be healthier than being on my phone.

I was listed on the spreadsheet too.

Name: Sunny Song
Place: Sunshine Farms
City: Somewhere in Iowa?

For the description, someone had included *Certified Organic Farm. Church camp, home to Evangelicals, Traditionalists, and Nondenominationals.* This same someone had lifted this church camp description verbatim from the website as well as listed the facility phone number and general email address. But was the real description—*digital detox camp held at an old-fashioned, historical farm*—any better? Probably not.

Folding the paper in half, I stared out the window. What would my summer have been like? How had my life taken such a drastic downturn? Things were going so well until, all of a sudden, they weren't. My parents—Mom especially—were freaking out about nothing. I wasn't any more addicted to my phone and social media than any of the other schoolkids, who were all living their best life the summer before senior year. And here I was, stuck in a van, being escorted to delinquency boot camp for losers. Something they'd show on *Dr. Phil* as a life lesson to teens: Don't be a statistic like these kids!

I gazed outside and took in what the Midwest had to offer. Bright-blue skies, multiple Culver's restaurants, and sparse side-street traffic. And so many Arby's. The Arby's per capita ratio alone was impressive—we'd driven by three so far. I also couldn't get over the hazy, Iowan humidity. The air conditioner in the van blasted away, cutting the hanging moisture to a somewhat reasonable level, but the second we stepped out of the van, I'd probably suffocate from the thick, damp air. I'd never experienced anything like this in my life.

Oh God, I hoped the cabins had air-conditioning.

A voice boomed from the front, startling me. "Where y'all from?" The van driver looked at me through the rearview mirror, his angry eyebrows and tired eyes framed in the reflection. Well, this made the ride all the more awkward.

"LA," I said flatly. While I wasn't thrilled with my new conversation companion, having some level of human interaction seemed marginally better than silence. My tendency with older adults was to chat about safe topics: that was what Mom and Dad always instructed me to do. Things like favorite school subjects. Books I'd read. The weather. Oh God, this weather.

When my other van companions didn't reply, I turned around. The guy in the last row was lying down on his back with his knees up. But the girl with the side braid wasn't asleep. She was busy glaring at me. My face grew hot, and I whipped my head back around. I could still feel her eye laser beams penetrating the back of my skull.

The driver snorted. "Not a talkative bunch, eh? Aren't you all social, uh, instigators? Isn't being *social* supposed to be something you do well? I've been shuttling you folks all day today, and I'm tired. And I'll be honest, I'd rather hear those church kids who used to come here singing their Jesus songs than endure all this quiet. If you have any questions, give me a holler. Otherwise, I'll put on the radio."

I did have one question. "Will there be any church kids at the camp too?"

He shook his head. "Not this summer, and it's a shame really. Helicopter parents aren't paying for camps like ours anymore; plus, with churches being low on funding, they've been doing more activities on-site, like lock-ins and picnics. Luckily for us, we got all the licenses now to run this digital detox camp, and there are about a hundred of you campers here. We're hoping it's sustainable long-term. The camp owner's son really has a good mind for all this business stuff. Real smart guy." He tapped his head with his right index finger near his temple.

A band my dad liked came on over the speakers, and the driver turned up the volume. The Smushed Pumpkins or something? They were okay.

With my eyes closed, I leaned my head back on the torn vinyl seat. Between the dread of going to camp, the oppressive heat and humidity, and the mild car sickness, this was the worst I'd ever felt in my whole life.

In just over an hour, I'd be in Promise City.

Insert double-praise-hands emoji.

Nah. Scratch that.

Double-X-eyes emoji all the way.

SIX

WHEN WE TURNED IN TO THE CAMP PROPERTY, THE RIDE got a lot bumpier, as if this were extended turbulence from what I'd experienced earlier. The long, dirt road was dusty, and it wasn't easy to see out the windows. I sat up straight and clutched my backpack to my chest.

Along the potholed pathway were mounds of what appeared to be horse crap, all over the place. If this crap were snow, you could make a *lot* of snowmen. The driver pressed the recirculated air button on the front panel, but not in time. Even though the shuttle windows were closed, the sour smell of horse manure permeated through the car and nearly made me gag.

The van driver made eye contact through his mirror. "Sorry about the smell. You probably don't have to deal with this over in the City of Angels."

"Oh, we have other unpleasant smells, especially in

downtown LA in the summer after a long stretch of no rain." Was it worse than horse crap though? Tough call.

Up ahead, the worst sight imaginable came into view: dozens of camp workers riding on whinnying horses. Horses, horses, everywhere. Was this their main mode of transportation? The horses' giant marble eyes on the sides of their heads made them look like four-legged mutant goldfish. The bar was already low for this camp experience, but it was now at subterranean levels.

Our vehicle slowed to a leisurely walking-horse pace, but that didn't make navigating the potholes on the road any easier. And unlike LA's bike lanes, there was no separate horse path. They were oblivious to us creeping along behind them. Horse tracks, and presumably wagon tracks, wore deep into the dirt road, making it sound like the underside of the shuttle would drop out with each rise and fall.

Lift...thud!

Ba-boom! Ba-boom!

I sneezed. Then again. And again. A few bless-yous came from the driver, but after the fourth and fifth one, I was so annoying, I wanted to punch my own face.

"I forgot to take my allergy meds," I said to no one. I tried to breathe from my mouth alone, but it wasn't easy. This dusty, airborne horse manure was way worse than the smog back home. I wanted to breathe air free of dung.

While the unhurried horses hogged the path, I took in the sights. Cows and goats grazed near a large, red barn, the kind you saw in postcards of rural America. A man riding on a lawnmower waved as we drove past. I couldn't help but notice how tan and weathered he looked from the Iowa summer sun. He had a cowboy hat, but that clearly didn't help much.

Chicks and chickens wandered the field. It didn't seem like they were fenced in, but it was hard to tell with all the dirt clouds around us. Off in the distance, there were rows of crops, presumably corn. I had this idea of what Iowa was like in my head, and corn fit that image. I didn't see any scarecrows though. Maybe it wasn't corn. Or maybe scarecrows were only in movies and fiction. Or maybe crows had evolved and outsmarted humans. That was the most likely.

As we bumped along, we passed a pond, a small baseball field, and a volleyball court. Finally, we pulled into a large lot near a cluster of four wood cabins and two beige cinder-block buildings. The driver parked the van and scrambled off his seat.

The passenger door slid open. "Welcome to Sunshine Heritage Farms, established 1913. Registration is straight ahead. I'll bring your bags inside once we've unloaded everything." The driver stepped aside, and I hopped out.

He didn't outright say he would be snooping in our bags to make sure we didn't smuggle anything in, but that was likely part of his job, in addition to shuttle driving, luggage handling, and making idle conversation. It didn't matter though; my burner phone wasn't with my luggage anyway. Not anymore at least.

Slinging my backpack over my shoulder, I headed straight for the main building, eyes wincing from the bright sun and the oppressive humidity. *It'll be fine, Sunny. You can do this. You survived #BrownieGate. This is nothing.*

An oil slick formed on my face and spread down my body vertically, like I'd gone for that dewy look you see in magazines but went overboard. There was one piddly air-conditioning unit in one of the windows. From the racket it made, it was undoubtedly on full blast but still barely making a difference.

There had to be more than fifty people in the room in a few different registration lines, and none of us had phones or devices to pass the time. Most of us probably skipped lunch, and boy, were some people hangry. So much sighing. So much eye rolling. And that was just me. Others were in the same boat but handling it a little better.

The scrawny, freckled kid with the high fade in line ahead of me proclaimed he was teen prodigy Daniel Goldberg, a.k.a. DJ Goldrush to his fans on the Jersey Shore. He wore a basketball jersey with his own name stitched on the back. Gross. "What do you mean there's no VIP cabin?" he roared.

I took a sip of water from my stainless steel bottle and

swallowed an extra-strength Tylenol. After DJ Goldrush yelled, "I hate this place!" and stormed off, leaving his empty potato chip bag and Red Bull on the table, I stepped up to the registration desk. The pungent smell of horses still lingered in my nose, and it mixed with the sweet Red Bull aroma, making me dry heave a little. The registration person grabbed DJ Grossness's trash and took it to the nearest bin.

"I have a jug of ibuprofen if you need it."

I looked to my right. A fidgety, wiry kid in an Orioles baseball cap over in the next line shook a plastic jug-like container of all kinds of medication mixed with gummy bears.

His eyes darted left and right before he focused on my face. "Bear gummy vitamins. I hate swallowing regular ones. And the chewable crunchy kinds are so nasty. I have Dramamine too. And CBD gummies, but they're not bear-shaped. I took some a few minutes ago because no one warned me how twisty the roads would be once we got on the campgrounds. Shouldn't all the roads in Middle America be straight and flat? We're out in the middle of nowhere. Oh, I have some weed too. Legally bought. Somewhere."

Wow, he had a lot of thoughts about medication. And thoughts about everything. Overall though, he was much friendlier than DJ Grossface, and I was happy to have some company, even if I didn't get a word in edgewise.

"Thanks!" I said. "Ibuprofen upsets my stomach, unfortunately, but I'll take a gummy. The vitamin one."

He opened the container and shook it. By some weird jug magic, only one bear rolled out.

"I'm Sunny," I mumbled, mouth full of gummy bear bits. "Thank you." I drank the remaining water from my bottle.

"I'm Patrick. *League of Legends* is what I'm known for."

I didn't know anything about the gaming influencer world. And I sure as hell wasn't about to say what *I* was known for: wearing swim goggles in a viral video ten years ago and practically getting kicked out of school for a PG-13 baking incident.

"Next!" The registration person had come back from trash cleanup. I handed her my driver's license and she checked my name off the roster, handing back my identification. She leaned over to her other registration helper and whispered, "These kids are way different from the Christian campers, right? None of them want to be here. The ones I checked in earlier had a pretty bad attitude."

Did she mean DJ What's-His-Name? He was rude. But was she talking about me too? Was I eye rolling unconsciously now?

The other registration helper whispered, "Did you see the famous ones who came in earlier? Clementine the esports gamer was here. She has, like, three million followers. And the disrespectful one, the guy who's internationally famous for a video where he ordered from McDonald's in forty-five different countries in different languages. As soon as he arrived, he asked a staffer if we'd be allowing some free time throughout his stay so he could go get himself Quarter Pounders. Then he asked if he could borrow a phone to film it. Apparently, if he doesn't post every week, he's in breach of his corporate contract with the restaurant? I bet he gets paid, like, hundreds of thousands of dollars."

That McDonald's guy was all over the internet. Damn, so many serious influencers here. Ones who had made it big because they had an "it" factor and were good at something, or at the very least good at making content. Maybe I could learn something from them these next four weeks.

My registration person looked at me and smiled. "Sunny Song. Seventeen years old. Los Angeles, California?" I nodded and watched as she wrote 2 on the printout. According to the key next to the roster, that was *tier-2 social media addiction*.

She said, "Great, I'll check your name off. Do you have any other names you go by? We don't have any others listed."

"Oh, my mom filled out my forms, not me. I go by *Goggle Girl* on Insta and YouTube and *Sunny D* on everything else."

She laughed. "No, I meant, like, a family nickname or something. In case someone calls the office and is trying to contact you in case of an emergency?"

Heat flushed my cheeks, and my body flicked on the maximum-perspiration switch. "Oh, jeez! I'm so...oh my God. I go by Sunny, or Sun-Hee at home, usually when my parents are angry with me." I scrunched my head down into my shoulders like a turtle backing into its shell.

Out of the corner of my eye, I could see the guy with the vitamins and drugs give me a pitying look, like he wanted to stand up and give me an "aww, poor thing" pat on my back.

As she scribbled *Sun-Hee* on the registration paper, the back door burst open. A tall guy with a strong, chiseled face breezed in with boxes of granola bars, animal crackers, clementines, and bags of popcorn. The campers immediately flocked to him, anointing him with praises. The snack messiah had come to save us all from starvation!

Behind him, a younger, more regular-looking guy carried two cases of a much heavier water bottle load and pushed his way through the door. They looked a lot alike, but the water bottle guy was shorter, less muscular, and had a flushed, shiny face covered with beads of sweat—a lot like mine, but he had beard stubble.

The first snack guy was likely the taller, athletic, more charismatic older brother. The water guy was, well, that guy's shadow. Poor thing.

Water Boy tore the plastic off one of his crates and handed everyone in the back of the lines a room-temperature bottle. The camp attendees grabbed it from him without acknowledging his heroic duty of keeping us hydrated in the overbearing heat.

While he made his way up to me, the girl behind me stuck her hand out and made a *stop* gesture right in his face. "I don't know if you know this, but plastic bottles are destroying our environment." Her eyes rolled so far back that I wondered two things: if she wore contacts and if they ever got stuck back there.

He smiled politely. "My top concern is to make sure you all are hydrated. Your health and safety mean a lot to me right now."

A very diplomatic answer, but she wasn't satisfied. "Fewer than half the bottles in the world are recycled, and seven percent of those that are collected are turned into new bottles. Instead, most plastic bottles end up in a landfill or in the ocean. U.S. landfills are overflowing with more than two million tons of discarded water bottles!" Each new sentence was shriller and more panicked than the previous. Her stress made my own anxiety spike. My pulse thumped hard along my jawline as she badgered the water boy.

She snorted like a bull. "I don't know why I'm at this stupid place. I have two hundred thousand subscribers on my environmental YouTube channel, and we talk about ways people like you can stop being selfish by destroying Mother Nature with your consumerism. If I'm here, that's fewer people out there getting the message."

A hush fell on the remaining campers. She stopped talking. Finally. Her breathing was labored, probably from spouting all those facts, but had slowed a little by the time the guy spoke.

"You know, you're actually surrounded by a lot of nature here, Karynne. Yes, I know who you are because we reviewed your applications before you arrived. Honestly, I think you'll be more at home here than where you live now, in Manhattan's Upper West Side. As for the bottles, they were donated from a local county fair that had ordered too many, so drinking them is doing them a favor. Otherwise, they'd be tossing them into the trash."

She crossed her arms and huffed out her nose again. "Okay."

After all the hemming and hawing, that was all she said. *Okay.* She didn't even apologize!

He offered a polite smile. "There are water-filling stations by the outdoor bathrooms and also inside the commissary. It's a five-minute walk from here, and I'd be happy to pull you away from the line and walk you there myself, assuming you have a reusable water bottle."

I tried to not laugh. I really did. But a single cough burst out of me.

Water Boy switched his gaze from Landfill Girl to me, and I raised my reusable bottle in my hand, like I was cheers-ing him.

"I take this with me everywhere," I said. It wasn't true, but I wanted to help him out.

An amused look filled his eyes. "Would you want an extra water if she decides she doesn't?"

"I'd love an extra. I wouldn't want it to go to waste."

He held out the extra bottle so I could grab it, but she snatched it out of his hand at a lightning-fast speed.

"I don't want to lose my place in line," she grumbled. Or more accurately, venomously hissed.

The registration person handed me a yellow envelope packet and waved me on. "Next in line, please!"

I rubbed my nose with the back of my hand to stop a sneeze. Examining the map, I asked aloud, "Wait, where do I go?"

The water guy came over to me and grabbed the paper from my hand. *Um, rude!* "You're in Cabin D, which is straight out the door you came in and down the path to the left. The welcome assembly's in an hour."

He stepped even closer to show me the map key. His fresh-shower smell must've been heat-activated—the pine mixed with spring-rain scent enveloped me completely. Moderate suffoca-tion...in a good way. Was that even possible? I'd never experienced anything like this before. As he pointed his finger at a path on my map, I noticed his chest was so close to my head, I could headbutt it. What a stupid thought. This was why I never dated.

"I don't get this at all," I said, squinting at the legend. "It's nowhere to scale. Where's Cabin D?"

He grabbed a marker from his back pocket and made some edits to the key.

Cabin ~~Apostle~~ A

Cabin ~~Bethlehem~~ B

Cabin ~~Canaan~~ C

Cabin ~~Damascus~~ D

Cabin ~~Ecclesiastes~~ E

He circled my cabin and handed the paper back to me. "Sorry, this map is old and we didn't get a chance to update it. If you need anything else, my name is Theodore. The guys here call me Theo. You might hear Teddy too. Or even T. rex?" His face turned more crimson with each word he spouted. A strong contrast to his soft-green T-shirt, which matched his eyes.

I grinned. "I like the name Theodore a lot. Were you named after Theodore Roosevelt?"

He shook his head. "I wish. It's embarrassing. I was named after Theodore from...the Chipmunks."

My eyes widened. "You mean, like the *chipmunk* Chipmunks? The ones with those...chipmunk voices?" *Wow, Sunny, bravo. You really have a way with words today.*

"Yes, those Chipmunks. Alvin, Simon—"

"Theodore!" I shouted so loudly that everyone around us hushed to silence. "Sorry," I said in a whisper. "It's just so hilarious! But...I can't tell if you're joking or not."

"Well, I guess you'll need to get to know me better to find out." With a lopsided smirk, he handed the two waters he was holding to people behind me.

His brother came over and gripped both of Theo's shoulders from behind. "There's still more cases of water in the van. Hurry up."

Theo sighed. "Okay. Well, if you need anything—"

"Yeah. I'll come find you," I finished. I retrieved my bag

from the luggage area, and dragging my wheeled suitcase behind me, I walked toward the building exit with my map in my hand. I glanced around and caught Theodore looking at me over his shoulder as he walked in the other direction.

I didn't want him to leave me. He was the nicest person I'd met. "Hey! Theo!" My throat was dry, like it was lined with sandpaper.

As he jogged over, I realized I didn't need him for anything.

Think of something.

Think of something.

Hurry.

His face brightened as he drew near.

Then the unsexiest words possible spilled out of my mouth before I could stop them.

"Where can I go to the bathroom?"

SEVEN

THEODORE'S CONTORTED FACIAL EXPRESSION SAID everything: I'd committed a classic Sunny social faux pas.

Note to self, don't blurt out bathroom talk to a stranger. Especially someone you'll keep encountering over a four-week period. Just...don't. What was worse was I didn't even have to go pee or anything—I needed to take my contraband phone out of my sweaty sports bra. It wasn't waterproof, and it had been pressed against my drenched skin since I stuffed it in there at the airport, causing more discomfort than I'd expected. It had been a good idea at the time, but the bra cups didn't have much give, and at the wrong angle, my right boob had a lumpy, rectangular shape through my clingy shirt, one I couldn't adjust in public.

I had to get it out before someone noticed. I hoped Theo didn't. Not that he'd be looking at my boobs anyway.

If they sent me home for smuggling in the illegal phone,

my mom would straight-up murder me. RIP Sunny. My tombstone would read, *Herein lies Goggle Girl, known by many for #BrowniePorn.*

Theo laughed so hard, he had to wipe both eyes with his sleeves. "I get that bathroom question all the time. You're the first person today who hadn't asked me right away. I was beginning to wonder what was wrong with you. Um, not that there's anything wrong with you." He coughed, still laughing. "Nothing's wrong with you. You're great. I'll shut up now."

He grabbed my map and circled the closest restroom. There was his body heat and scent again.

"There are two on your way to your cabin. The closest one is nicer. It has a hand dryer. The other one is always out of paper towels, the doors don't shut right, and there's always toilet paper on the ground. It's like a pig sty." He laughed. "Sorry, I use farm references a lot."

I almost asked him to text me so we could stay in touch, but I stopped myself. Right. Digital detoxing. "Thanks, Theo. I'll see you around."

He headed back the way he came, and this time, he didn't turn his head. Maybe I scared him off? I had a way with guys, and not a good one. Rafael and I sort of had a flirty thing between us for *years*, but it never developed into a relationship. We were always good friends—a platonic default. He dated the kinds of girls who wouldn't start a conversation by asking where the bathroom was.

Speaking of bathrooms, the one closest to the registration building was bleach-cleaned, and it was so run-down that it had rust stains in the toilets and sinks (hopefully those were rust stains). There were no disposable seat covers, and the toilet paper was the scratchy, thin kind—the type you could use for papier-mâché. Polar opposite of the Charmin we got from Costco. Who knew the first thing I would miss from home was the TP?

After making sure no one was in the bathroom with me, I took the phone out of its hiding place and turned it on. No signal. None of my apps would load. Of course there wouldn't be any signal at a digital detox camp. What was I thinking? I let out a deep sigh and slipped the contraband in the side pocket of my roller bag. Once I got settled, I could explore. Maybe there was an area of the camp that got reception.

The side-braid girl from the shuttle entered the bathroom and brushed by me to the sink area, even though there was plenty of room near the mirror for both of us. I had to decide if I was going to be the person at camp who stepped aside for girls like her or pushed them right back.

We stood in silence as she put on pale-pink lipstick. After glancing at me quickly in the mirror, she narrowed her eyes. How could she apply lipstick so evenly with her lip all twisted into a sneer?

"Why are *you* here?" she asked in a tone so unfriendly, it was borderline murderous.

"Same reason anyone else is here," I quipped. I wasn't revealing my story first. This was like one of those prison situations on TV where the veteran inmates try to figure out if the new inmates are soft criminals or there for violent crimes like cold-blooded murder. For sure, she had sized me up as a softie.

"I hate this soap," she muttered with less of an acidic bite. While I washed my hands, she hit the nozzle a few times, and pink, pasty goo shot out in microspurts. Maybe she knew I was dodging her question and was doing something similar. Or maybe she passionately hated soap. The pearly liquid smelled faintly of roses and bubble gum. It was a pleasant smell that reminded me of my elementary school's restrooms first thing in the morning, before the kids dirtied up the toilets, floors, and sinks.

She struck her palm on the silver button that activated the air dryer. A deafening *whoosh* filled the room, which was good because I didn't feel like talking to her anymore. We stood in silence as she briefly wrung her hands under the hot air. She checked herself in the mirror once more before leaving the bathroom, and relief flooded over me when the door closed behind her.

I stared at my reflection in the warped mirror. Did I pass her weak-girl sniff detector? After wiping my forehead with a paper towel, I put on my backpack. On the way out, I scratched my hand pulling the suitcase on the rough, wooden door frame. Great, I hadn't even been at the camp for an hour, and I already injured myself. This place had a rustic vibe but not in a charming, farmhouse-chic *Architectural Digest* way. This was like someone hadn't bothered to repair anything in twenty years and had added thick layers of paint to cover it up. No splinters from the hand scrape though. And I didn't need a tetanus shot from exposed nails.

Maybe things were looking up.

Back into the baking hot sun I went. In the distance, horses near the registration area snorted and whinnied. I couldn't smell them from where I stood, thank God. Someone in tenth-grade biology class had told me you basically taste everything you smell, and it really messed me up. I didn't want to taste nasty horse.

Cabin D was a one-story building with a log cabin veneer and some light prison touches. The mesh door creaked as it opened. It was hard to see anything because the lights were off and the dark-brown interior walls, ceiling, and floors matched the exterior. A brilliant design for trapping in the Iowa heat.

"Hello?" My voice echoed in the brown chamber.

No reply. Only the hum of the ceiling fan.

In the entryway, a stack of welcome packets caught my eye. How many of these manila envelopes were we going to get? I spotted my name on a medium package resting on the same table: a reused Amazon box with their signature branded tape. The return address was from Maya.

Hastily, I ripped off the tape and opened the package. Inside, there were all kinds of snacks (including my favorite, Korean dried squid!), celeb gossip magazines, sudoku and crossword books (boring, but on the approved list), and a stationery kit with a sticky note on it:

Girl, you better write me ASAP. I want to know how messed up that place is. Love, Maya

She also included a photo of Rafael from the last day of school, one she had doctored so there were smoochy kiss emojis all over it. On his T-shirt, she'd written *Property of Sunny Song!* I blushed. Maya had been so sneaky to snap a close-up picture when he wasn't looking. His thick, wavy black hair and playful brown eyes charmed me, even though he wasn't staring in the camera's direction. For about half a second, I considered kissing it.

If he ever came across this photo, I'd die. Sunny Song, dead from mortification.

Did attractive people know the rest of us did this kind of thing in secret? That people had crushes on them and their friends doctored photos and shared them privately? It was one of the great mysteries in my teenage life.

I'd had a crush on Rafael Kim since seventh grade. He wasn't even cute back then—he was all gangly and awkward, and Rafa was the only kid I knew who had to get braces twice, once in junior high and then a year ago. We shared notes in our harder classes, and he even let me copy his homework sometimes, and we texted, but he never asked me to a dance or movie or anything. It was always some other girl for him. We were basically friends with no benefits. Well, other than our friendship, which was actually a pretty nice thing. I wished it was so much more. I wished *he* wished it was so much more.

"Get anything good?"

My stomach dropped as I spun around. Theo's brother stood in the doorway. What was his name? Did he ever mention it? Was it Alvin?

He took a step forward, knocking loudly on the doorframe and announcing his presence in a booming voice. "Henry's here for repairs!"

Henry talked about himself in third person.

Scooting past me, he headed straight for a curtain rod that rested above the main window on the other side of the room. After examining it, he went to the maintenance closet and pulled out a small ladder, then used it to reach the top of the window frame. Then he screwed in the askew curtain rod bracket.

"This thing falls every few months. It's a real pain, especially when it happens in the middle of the night. People think it's a black bear or a bobcat sometimes, but they rarely come in."

I blurted, "Bears? You have, like...bears?" Eloquence was thrown out the window when there was talk of large mammal infiltration.

He laughed as he put the ladder away. "I don't want to scare you. It's virtually impossible for these predators to get close to our residents' sleeping quarters, since we have safeguards in place. Rattlesnakes are a different matter though. I'd watch out for those."

"Rattlesnakes?" I whimpered.

He shot me a dazzling smile. "If you see one, don't try to pet it."

While Henry examined his handiwork, I put my bag and backpack next to the nearest empty cot. I must've looked queasy, because Henry shoved his hands into his pockets and shot me an apologetic look.

"I was just messing with you. You might get mice or raccoons in here, but no big animals. If you want an expert tip, there are more beds in the back in semiprivate rooms. Given that it's late afternoon, they might all be taken. But you should look anyway."

"Thanks! I'll go check it out." I left him to go deeper into the cabin.

There were two smaller back rooms, each with a few single cots, partitioned with five-foot-high dividers. Semiprivacy was better than no privacy. Most of the beds had been claimed: people were apparently saving their sleeping spots by putting welcome packets on top of pillows. I threw my stuff on the last available bed and unpacked some of my clothes into the top wall drawer.

The front door slammed. "Henry's leaving!"

A second slam reverberated seconds later. Female voices filled the front area with excited chatter. I could tell some of these girls already knew one another by the familiarity in the way they spoke, which didn't bode well for me, the outsider. But maybe being on the outside was okay for now. I could hopefully make connections later.

This place was full of internet celebrities—maybe I could get to know some of them after we got settled. In the meantime, I could semiprivately relax before the welcome session and didn't have to deal with chitchatting with strangers. After a long travel day, self-selected solitary confinement suited me.

The bedsprings squeaked from my weight when I sat down. The coils stretched so low, I was nearly touching the ground. This was nothing like my full-size, Tempur-Pedic platform bed at home. I pulled out my second welcome packet and looked over the schedule. Theodore was teaching archery at ten in the morning. I smiled. Archery wasn't exactly something LA kids like me had ever tried, and I wondered if it was possible I had an inner Katniss in me that I'd never tapped into before. Picturing Maya and me trying to fool around with a bow and arrow made me laugh, but then my thoughts immediately went negative.

I missed her. I missed LA. Who knew where we'd be next year? This summer was supposed to be filled with us doing all the things we loved for the last time as high schoolers—626 Night Market, Twilight on the Pier, and of course, finding LA's best

Korean fried chicken and brown sugar bubble tea. Instead, I'd gotten myself exiled to Iowa.

Shaking my head, I put the daily schedule back into the envelope. *Maybe you shouldn't bother making friends here, Sunny. You're here as punishment.*

To echo this sentiment, the universe delivered the worst thing imaginable. Side Braid waltzed into the back room, wearing high-waisted jean shorts and a white halter so cropped, it looked like a low-impact yoga bra, along with another girl who dressed like her twin. The Sneery Sisters of Sunshine Farms, with the matching ghostly pale midriffs.

"Oh, great, it's you." Her icy-cold tone cut through the hanging heat. "I already claimed this space." She swept her arm around, gesturing to the entire section.

I stood up. "Nice to see you again too. Look, I've got no beef with you. I just need a place to sleep. You don't even know me—" I looked down at her welcome packet label, but her name was illegible. "*Jersey City.*" I said it slowly and deliberately and hoped she took it as a somewhat sarcastic insult. I didn't know anyone from there, but my dad made fun of New Jersey a lot because my mom lived there, so I assumed it could be part of my verbal arsenal.

The boar-like snorts from her nose suggested she did in fact take it as an affront. Was this going to turn physical? We were no match. Our builds were the same, but she was all hard muscle, and I was like one giant stomach pooch.

I wanted to put up at least a verbal fight and stand my ground, but she seemed like a sketchy, petty girl who might destroy all my belongings when I wasn't around. I didn't want to start a bunk turf war, especially when it was two against one.

"Assembly time!" someone yelled from the front.

Thank God.

"Fine," I said, relenting. "It smells back here anyway." As I pulled my clothes from the drawers and dumped them back into my bag, I also tore open the pouch of Korean dried squid and pushed it back between the dressers. The fishy odor would probably hit peak pungent stink later that night. The two girls watched me leave, and I was tempted to flip them off but instead fought hard to keep my cool.

By the time I made it to the front room, all the cots had been claimed except the one under the speaker directly in front of the bathroom. Three other campers shoved their things away in the open closets, slamming drawers and doors, all refusing to talk or make eye contact with anyone.

Yeah, I didn't want to be here either.

A soft, calm voice next to me interrupted my underwear sorting. "Those girls in the back are the worst. I overheard some counselors saying they're spoiled rotten—like they have families with yachts and know the Vanderbilts and Kennedys through their family connections."

I looked up to see a Black girl smiling at me. It was nice to see someone beyond the sea of whiteness that had been at registration. My new conversation buddy had chin length, thick, jet-black hair and the best shimmery eye makeup application I'd ever seen.

She asked, "What are you here for?"

"According to my principal and parents? Social media addiction."

She raised her eyebrows. "Well, that's vague. What does it even mean?"

I nodded. "I know! It seems like BS, right?"

"No. I mean, yes, kind of. Is it deeper than that? Like are you here because you're addicted to something social media enables? Are you obsessed with likes? Subscribers? Views? Fame?"

I laughed. "Yes, yes, yes, and...YES." Those things mattered to me. They made me happy. And they were a big part of my life since the Goggle Girl video vaulted me into the limelight so many years ago. It was one of the few things that made me unique back home. But here? At this camp full of influencers? I was a small fish in a big pond full of snapping turtles.

"What about you?" I asked.

The girl bit her lip. "I'd rather not say. It's embarrassing."

I was about to let it go and had turned back to my clothes organizing, but she volunteered information. "Okay. I'll tell you, because it'll likely come out anyway. My parents are military, and I spent a lot of time moving, but we've been in Korea for five years." She took a deep breath. "I do mukbang livestreams."

"I know mukbang! You're very Korean." Mukbang videos always baffled me—who would pay to watch people eat a ton of food on camera? The food always looked so good though. When I got home, I'd definitely check out her channel.

"A Black girl doing mukbang. Weird, right? Made a ton of money too, from Koreans and international viewers, but my parents freaked out when they saw how much I was spending on food and clothes." She tilted her wrist so I could see a Swiss watch and a Cartier bracelet.

Making food videos seemed harmless to me, but I knew from #BrowniePorn that things could go wrong. And dropping cash on all those fancy accessories seemed like it could be a problem. A very expensive one. "So are you here for video addiction or spending addiction? Or even maybe attention addiction? I would totally pay to see you eat, by the way."

A sly smile spread across her face. "Aren't they all one and the same these days?" She looked at the clock on the wall. "I'm going to see if there are any snacks left at registration before the assembly starts. I'm Delina by the way. Annyeounghaseyo. Mannaseo bangawoyo!"

Her Korean pronunciation was perfect. As good as my parents' even.

My face flushed hot. "I'm Sunny." Heat rushed to my neck and ears. "My Korean's not that good. Um, so I'll see you around then."

With a cocked eyebrow, she nodded in slow motion, as if to say, *Okaaay, I'll still be your friend even if you don't help me practice my Korean.*

Knowing I'd let her down with my inability to speak even a few Korean words in a casual conversation, I regretted more than ever not having learned the language, especially with so much of American pop culture being influenced by Korea these days. This was something I'd never admit to my parents though. It would mean they were right all those years and I was dead wrong.

Delina opened the mesh door for us to leave, and a new stream of people came in, presumably the other bunkmates.

B-BAM! THUNK!

A crash of metal hitting concrete by the window made all of us flinch and scream. The curtain rod Henry had supposedly fixed was on the ground and had rolled toward us. Rather than try to fix it ourselves or move it (yay, teamwork), most of the campers simply stepped over it and trudged to the main hall for the camp's official welcome.

No one, including me, cared about this place.

EIGHT

"GOOD AFTERNOOOOOOON, CAMPERS!" THE CAMP director, a blond with a swishy ponytail, did a little cheerleading move with her arms and chirped into the mic, "I'm Cindy. Welcome to Camp Sunshine!"

The response was shy of lukewarm. A few whistles and a number of sarcastic slow claps. Someone in the back row booed, and I cough-laughed in response. Tough crowd all around.

Poor Cindy.

"We have nearly every state represented here, including Hawaii. Aloha!" We all looked around, searching for someone who looked Hawaiian. As I scanned the crowd, it dawned on me that I didn't exactly know what someone from Hawaii would look like, since I didn't know anyone from there. Other people had the same problem, because a few people fixed their stares on me, one of the only three Asians in the room.

"A-T-L!" someone in the back shouted. That started a frenzy of city, state, and territory callouts.

"Two-one-two!"

"Oakland! A's!"

"South-siiiide!"

A girl's voice directly behind me yelled, "DTLA!" If this meant Downtown LA, this person was my neighbor. Well, sort of. Los Angeles was so spread out, each neighborhood was basically like a different county.

With my neck not quite turned, I said, "Hey. I'm from LA too."

"You're not from where I live. I bet you're Bel Air."

I was Brentwood, actually, but she didn't seem like the type who wanted to discuss urban planning.

A guy next to me pulled his cap down over his eyes and slid down into his chair. He muttered, "Daaaamn, that was cold," and everyone around us laughed. Thanks to DTLA, I was shoved down to the bottom rung of the Sunshine Farms pecking order. *Daaaamn* was right.

A different girl directly behind me hissed, "Look, y'all don't need to get nasty. None of us want to be here. So stop making trouble."

Cindy walked away from the podium and took center stage. "Here, you'll be device-free, but you'll also be obligation-free, for the most part. We want you to live life. Live it hard. Love it hard."

With her palms up, she closed her eyes and joined her thumbs with her middle fingers on each hand, taking a deep breath in and out. In and out. Her nostrils flared with the exhales. She opened her eyes. "The only requirement for you each week is daily group sessions with your assigned camp counselor in the morning. Most afternoons, you are free to do as you please. Throughout your first week, we will want you to rotate through a few activity and task stations so you can assess your leisure preferences. Later, we'll need each and every one of you to pick a community contribution. This can be a farm task, barn cleanup, animal feeding, harrowing fields, or anything else that could help the greater good. If you don't choose one on your own, one will be assigned to you. This isn't required for your stay here, but we hope to get full participation."

Several of us looked around and made WTF eye contact. What use would these skills be? It's not like I could shuck corn as a side hustle when I got back to LA. What a waste of a summer.

Murmurs from the crowd swelled, and Cindy had to practically shout into the microphone to override our chatter. "We have expert staff on-site who know how to work the farm equipment and tend to our animals, and they will teach you what you need to know. Don't worry."

It was still hard to hear, so she used her thumb and pinkie to do one of those taxi whistles. That shut everyone up. A bunch of us tried to imitate her whistle, but it didn't work for me or anyone else. Maybe, by the end of camp, we'd be able to figure it out. It'd be the only useful thing to come out of this experience.

The room settled down. "We eat what we sow here, and most of our food comes from within the camp. So if our crops fail, we all fail. If we fail, we don't eat. Everyone needs to chip in for this to work. We need corn pickers, vegetable washers, and line cooks. We need milkers for our cows and honey harvesters for our bees. Your counselors and staff will assist with picking your activities and chores, but you're free to choose your own as well. We may also assign you a nonfarm project based on your abilities and our urgent needs, such as answering the phones, volunteering outside our Sunshine community by helping those less fortunate, or assisting with minor repairs."

She walked to the podium again and banged her palms on the wood like bongos.

"Annnnnd finally, at the end of the camp session, there will be a talent show held jointly with the nearby assisted living facility. We encourage everyone to participate in some way or to help one of their residents with their performance. We're still working out details, but participants who volunteer may get their electronics back a day early."

More groans. One of those was from me. I had quit most of my extracurriculars to focus solely on my grades and my social media platform. My Korean lessons, all sports, music, and hobbies had been tossed aside. I didn't have any talent to show. This was going to be a disaster. It's not like I could play "Yankee Doodle" with only my right hand on the piano with other people here my age being music virtuosos. Even that jerk DJ from registration probably had more talent than me. And it's not like I could reenact my only claims to fame, my #BrowniePorn or #GoggleGirl videos: they had brought me likes and subscribers, but they were both dumb luck and evidence I indeed had no natural talents. At least not in singing, dancing, or baking.

"Does anyone have any questions?"

The Downtown LA heckler behind me yelled, "I'm starving, and I don't want farm food! I want Burger King! I need my Whopper!"

The crowd roared with laughter, and even though I'd made a pact (with myself) to not enjoy a single second of this whole camp experience, I joined in. Here we were, a bunch of device-addicted teens in the middle of Nowhere, Iowa, on some kind of weirdo farm, with no fast food for miles, and someone was asking for BK.

I bent down to reach into my backpack pocket to get my phone and remembered it had been confiscated. Damn, all this would have made such a good livestream video. Did other people here have the problem of reaching for their phantom phones?

The camp director paced around onstage as the noise died down. Back and forth. Swish, swish, swish went the ponytail. "You should have loaded up on fast food before you came, because all you're getting here is homemade, delicious organic food. Any other questions?"

"You got fries, then?" someone cried out from the back of the auditorium.

Cindy's grin rivaled the Cheshire Cat's. "Those are actually on the menu. Potatoes that someone here will dig up fresh from the garden. Someone else will wash and cut them. We'll have other people helping in the kitchen to fry and salt them. I promise, they'll be delicious. Crispy, crunchy, savory goodness. Better than Burger King."

"Not better than McDonald's fries though!" a camper in the front row said.

"You can be the judge, but I think you'll be surprised," Cindy said with a wide, toothy smile.

Honest to God, her description of the potato-cooking process made my mouth water. Even though camp would suck, at least the fries would be good.

NINE

AFTER A TERRIBLE FIRST NIGHT'S SLEEP ON A CREAKY COT and wolfing down the world's most free-range, organic, GMO-free breakfast sandwich, I ran to the meeting location listed in my welcome packet, Trailer Number One. Did this mean there was more than one trailer? Or this was the best trailer on the farm?

All of us detox campers had been placed into morning small groups, each with an adult supervisor. This was one of the mandatory activities for camp: the afternoons we were free to do as we pleased.

"Y'all need to scoot in a little closer. I swear I don't bite!" Our counselor chuckled hard at his own joke while wiping his brow with a bandanna. The mere act of laughing made this guy sweat. He took the cloth and patted the top of his bald head.

The chair legs scraped the worn, vinyl floors of the classroom as we all drew closer to him. Like metal nails on a metal chalkboard. The flickering fluorescent light above him didn't seem to bother people, but it made my eyes twitch.

He wrote the words *Our Sunrise Mission* on the rolling whiteboard, following with four more words.

Courage.

Respect.

Accountability.

Passion.

Our mission's acronym was CRAP. Not something I could ever forget now.

"I want you all to know how brave each and every one of you are for being here. And I applaud you for getting the help you need."

He clapped, and someone in the group, surprisingly not me, cackled.

"Contrary to what you might think, I'm not a counselor per se. I'm here to facilitate discussion. I'm a retired PE teacher, but for the past few years, I've been working with youth both in person and online as a wellness and mindfulness coach. I'm here to root for you. To help you strive to be your best. To keep you focused. With that said, you can call me Coach Will."

I rolled my eyes and made eye contact with a cute guy across from me. He looked away and stared hard at the whiteboard.

"We've broken our campers into groups of six to eight, so hopefully you will feel comfortable sharing your thoughts and feelings in a more intimate environment of your peers. In our small group, we won't need to address one another by our names like in the outside world. When you walk through this door"—he gestured toward the trailer door entrance with both hands—"you will shed your identities. In here, in this space, we will simply call one another *friend*. Or if you're uncomfortable, you can address one another as *fellow human*."

What the hell kind of hippie BS was this? I snorted so loud that Coach looked directly at me.

Busted.

"Friend, would you like to say something?"

I shook my head no, as social cowards like me do. All snort and no action.

"Anyone else?" A few hands soared into the air. He pointed to a blond girl next to me. She looked familiar, in a "we're mutuals on Instagram" or a "perpetual suggested friend on Twitter" sort of way.

Her eyes teared up as she spoke. "Can I be honest? It's really hard for me to not be addressed by my real name. Or my usernames." She sniffed, and the cute guy who had ignored me jumped up to hand her a tissue box he snagged from a nearby desk. Screw him.

"I mean, I don't know if any of you recognize me, but I have more than four hundred and fifty thousand followers on Insta. My name is my brand. *I* am my brand. And if you take that away from me"—she blew her nose into the tissue—"I'll be nothing."

Heads nodded and murmurs filled the room. People were resonating with this—unbelievable. I needed a new peer group of the eye rolling and snorting variety. This girl had almost half a million followers. I'd die to be in her shoes—she was famous!

But maybe that was her problem. She was famous.

Coach clapped his hands together. "Now we're getting somewhere. Listen, everyone, no one wants to take away your identity. On the contrary, we want you to strengthen it. When you go back home in four weeks, you can get back to your old life, if you want it." He smiled at Blondie. "But here, at least for the time being, we want you to start off with a blank slate. Where no one makes assumptions of who you are because of any preconceived notions." He paused. "All of you are here because a parent or guardian wanted you to uncouple from your devices and believed you were addicted to them. And yes, we will discuss ways to be healthier about our daily choices and whether you need all that screen time. Our group will come together as a safe space to explore your true selves. And figure out what you want to do and want to be."

Two out of the six of us clapped after his soapbox speech. The rest of us, including famous Blondie, were still not buying into this #BestLife BS.

The door flew open. Side Braid waltzed into the room and collapsed into an open chair across from me. "I got kicked out of my group, so they put me in here." She pulled on her hair elastic and reweaved her braid. "What did I miss?"

I tried to imagine what she could have done in just twenty minutes to get banished from her previous group. Yet somehow, her getting ousted didn't surprise me either. She was a horrible person and basically the antithesis of what *community* stood for.

Coach tilted his chin up and nodded at her. "Welcome, friend," he said with a smile.

Hell no. Not my friend. She wasn't even human. She had no soul and no heart.

He continued, "We have twenty minutes left before lunch. In every session, we will have one assignment to complete, and the one I've chosen for you today will be to write a letter, postcard, or journal entry. You can write anything you want, and you'll be writing by hand because there are no keyboards here."

Groans all around.

"Get used to it because you're going to be writing a *lot* the next few weeks. But for now, send a note to your family or a close friend to let them know how you're doing. Write a diary entry about your feelings. I have scented glitter gel pens and stickers for anyone who wants one."

Stickers were always a special treat, no matter your age. I wanted first dibs on those. And these were scratch-and-sniff ones too. Mmmm...artificial bubble-gum fragrance.

Everyone else jumped up to grab a pen out of Coach's hand, and there were some heated arguments over who got what. Who knew glitter gel pens could cause major beefing among "friends"?

I drew one of the boring brown ones I thought no one wanted and got a sea of protests from other jealous campers.

Sitting alone at a table, I wrote a very insightful postcard to my family.

> Can you guys send me some squid snacks? Maya mailed me some, but they're all gone.
>
> Living the dream in Promise City,
> Sunny

I drew a glittery, brown squid and swirly border around my sparse words, then added some flowers and balloons in the corners. I hadn't drawn anything in years, not even on my tablet, and I was surprised by how easy it was to pick back up.

As I colored, my mind drifted to what I'd do first when I got back home. Maybe post an "I'm back!" video? Share all my weekly postcards to my parents? Ooooh, maybe upload summer farm photos from my contraband phone? Speaking of which, I needed to test it out. And what did Coach mean when he said we'd get our old lives back in a few weeks *if* we wanted them?

Of course we did. If anything, coming back from a long hiatus might make me appreciate what I had even more.

"Pssst." My gaze followed the sound of the hiss. It was Side Braid, holding up one of her postcards. I leaned in to read her scrawled print.

Found the squid you hid.

She aimed her index finger at me, her thumb sticking straight up.

Bang, bang.

You're dead.

TEN

THEO'S BOWSTRING WAS PULLED TAUT, THE ARROW ready to fire at the target pinned on the haystack. I wanted him to know I was there, but I also didn't want to startle him and get speared in the chest.

A deep breath in and out. *You'll be fine. He's nice, and he'll help you figure out where to go first, like he did at camp registration three days ago. Cool as a cucumber, Sunny.*

A voice behind me boomed, "Don't fuck up your shot, Bro." Theo's bow arm spasmed, and he released the arrow, missing the target completely. It soared past the haystacks and nearly hit one of the cows in the field. It looked up and asked in bovine speak, "Moooo?"

I whipped my head around to see Henry laughing so hard, his rock-hard abs joggled up and down, visible through his spandex shirt. He whistled and walked away—or should I say, swaggered away. Unbelievable. He'd only come there to mess with his little brother.

When I turned back to Theo, he said, "Henry's heading over to the woodworking station if you want to go see him." In the distance, a long line of girls formed around Henry's tent, like they were waiting for a celebrity autograph. "This afternoon, he'll be rotating other camp activities, like fishing and horseshoes, if you want to see him later."

My face flushed. He'd caught me studying his brother and had the wrong idea. "Uh, good to know, I guess? But I'm here to learn archery."

He cocked his head. "I didn't realize you were the bow-and-arrow type."

"You think I'm more the Smith and Wesson type?"

He chuckled hard. "Yeah. Exactly." With each easygoing laugh, my shoulders relaxed. And his cute, messy, dark-brown hair and dimples were easy on the eyes. His brother had the chiseled jaw/underwear model/ten out of ten in the looks department going for him thing, but it didn't make my senses spin like Theo's boy-next-door appeal did.

In contrast, I was definitely not his girl-next-door counterpart. Did he even know anyone who looked anything like me here in Iowa?

I said, "Honestly, I'm here because every other activity was overbooked or worse than this. No offense."

"None taken." He repositioned the next arrow in the bow. "So basically, archery was your least crappy option, if I'm hearing you right."

Whoosh!

Bull's-eye.

I smirked. "Yeah, something like that." I tried to pick a bow-like contraption, which was just as heavy as it looked, up off the ground and nearly toppled over. "Okay, maybe I can't do this. I need two hands to lift it. Maybe even three."

Theo laughed. "Okay, California girl, that's a crossbow. Put it down before you injure yourself. You need one of those." He pointed to the side of the nearby shed. I walked over to the bows leaning on the wall and picked out a midsize one. "It's one of our practice bows. It's not fancy, but it's more durable to heavy abuse. Um, not that you'd abuse it."

I watched how he positioned his own arrow on a bow and copied him. With a serious look, he nodded at me. "The nock part of the arrow has a notch in there to fit in the string, like this." Theo demonstrated his archer prowess by pulling back the arrow on the string.

PFFFFT!

His arrow soared and hit the target fifty feet away.

Another bull's-eye.

I stretched back my string and let go.

DOYYYYYNG.

The arrow soared in slow motion and hit the outer target perimeter with a timid thud. Then it fell to the ground. The aim was decent. But there was zero power.

"Are you sure you're new to this?" Theo joked. "That was so good. But I can help teach you a few things." He puffed his chest a little.

I inserted another arrow and hit the outer ring of the target. This time, the arrow stuck in the hay.

"Well damn," he muttered, his thrust-out chest sinking back in. "I take everything back. You're pretty good once you steady yourself!"

I knew I'd pay for all this arm action later because I was overdoing it to impress him. I had no upper body strength and couldn't do a pull-up to save my life. "My parents would never let me do this. Or woodworking. And if they knew I tried worm composting yesterday and almost forgot to add worms, they'd be so embarrassed." I smiled at him. "It's actually really nice doing this with you."

Blotches emerged on his cheeks and neck, resembling a personal pepperoni pizza. I loved pepperoni pizza. "Well, you look happier than a pig in mud." He gulped. "Um, I mean you're a natural, and if you come back, I can help you with your posture, and we can build up your strength through repetition. And you have the place all to yourself since no one comes here. Keep going and let me watch you." He handed me five more arrows.

My face flushed to a million degrees. The thought of him staring at my moves made me hot and sweaty, and not in a sexy way. I closed my eyes and took a long, deep breath. Opening them slowly, I shot all five in a row with surprising ease. Who knew I had all this instinctive hunting and weaponry potential? I was actually good at something! And that something was...archery. Not exactly talent show material.

"Let me go get those." He raised his arms. "Don't shoot me." Theo walked to the target and pulled the arrows from the haystack.

I put everything down by my feet. My left arm shook from all the effort. Lactic acid was building up, and thanks to the soreness, extra-strength Tylenol was in my near future.

I swiped my sweaty hair out of my eyes, but my perspiration was unrelenting. "It's so hot that I'm sweating like a pig!"

He looked right at me. "You know, pigs don't actually sweat. It's a misconception."

"Well, look at you and your porcine PhD," I taunted.

He bowed. "I'm the king of farm facts."

"Okay, here's an easy question. What other activities do you recommend here?"

The red splotches on his face and neck turned to a darker crimson. "There's nonfarm stuff, like thirty-five-millimeter photography, beginner music classes, and knitting and looming, but you have to get up early for those. And honestly, who wants to get up at six thirty for anything in the summer?"

I shook my head. "Definitely not me."

"My mom makes butter and cheese in the kitchen every Friday, and that's good because you get to sample everything with homemade bread. You know, the fresh kind with the crispy outside and the soft, warm middles."

My mouth watered. It was amazing how gluten and saturated fats were so intrinsically connected to my happiness. I would definitely have to check out those classes.

He added, "There's soapmaking and candlemaking tomorrow. Not with me, but those are popular."

"What else do you teach, besides arrow shooting?"

With a sheepish grin, he said, "My stuff isn't too exciting. And I usually fill in, like a substitute teacher. The horseback riding instructor's been out sick a while. I also sometimes set up nature walks, and those are late afternoon when things get a little cooler. Oh! And I do fish drying and meat curing with salt and spices. So horses, walks, fish drying, and meat curing."

Ew, no, nah, and nope. Those were nowhere nearly as appealing as gluten-y bread.

His eyes gleamed. "Did you know ancient societies of the high-altitude Andes were thought to be the ones who invented beef jerky?" He handed me five more arrows and kept five for himself.

"No?"

He beamed at me. "It was made by alternately drying the

meat in the hot sun and freezing it during the cold nights. I read all about it in my favorite science magazine."

I nodded, not knowing how else to contribute to a conversation about ancient beef jerky.

Theo's oddball knowledge of pigs and dried meats was surprisingly fascinating. Maybe he could help me figure out other information, like where someone with an illegal phone might pick up a signal on a farm. "Are staff allowed to carry phones? Or do you have to communicate with postcards like we do?"

He smirked. "We have to keep them in our lockers. The signal's not good here anyway. We have limited cell service on the entire lot. But when you do get spotty service, it's endless dropped calls and useless internet. We haven't had many camp emergencies, but when we do, we have to use the landline in the office. Although—" He pursed his lips. "Never mind."

"Although?" I cocked my head. Was he going to tell me how to get signal? *C'mon, Theo. We're friends here. TELL ME.*

"I was just going to say that there are rumors that one of the camp counselors got decent service near the barn." He smiled at me and shrugged. "But he's a big talker—who knows if that's true."

A potential key to a connection to the outside world. Thank you, Mr. Theo. If the rumors were true, I could hunt for that signal and check for Maya's Starhouse updates.

He lined up his body to the closest haystack and positioned his bow and arrow. His thin T-shirt pulled against lean arms and back. I couldn't help but stare at his hard-to-miss muscle definition.

He shot all his arrows while my eyes drifted from his arms to his shoulders and back, then down to his—

"Want to grab your target and help me clean up?" he asked, startling me.

My face flushed. Oh God, did he see me staring at him?

On my way to the haystacks, he asked, "Soooo, on a scale of one to ten, how do you like it here so far?"

I bit my lip and hesitated. "When I came here, it was a negative ten. Then it jumped to a one or two when I saw there were chickens everywhere and air-conditioning in the buildings. It dropped back down to negative when this annoying girl was assigned to my cabin and ended up in my counseling group. But archery is okay. And you're pretty okay. So maybe a three?"

I laughed at my own convoluted math. I sounded like a real downer. Not a glass-half-full kind of girl.

A glass-cracked-and-half-empty kind of girl.

"Looks like we have company," he announced. Behind me, a group of girls were coming from the woodworking station and heading straight toward us. Side Braid was leading the pack of laughing girls. None of them had noticed me yet.

"Oh, shoot, that's her. And it looks like she's found her people." I handed him a bow. "My day dropped back to negative ten. I'll see you around."

I darted off before we could exchange goodbyes and walked down a smaller path toward the lake, away from Side Braid. And sadly, away from Theo.

I moved fast but could hear the loud group reach the archery station. I heard one of the girls say, "Goodbye and good riddance, Goggle Girl."

ELEVEN

CREAAAAK.

I flipped from my side to my back on the squeaky cot and observed the sunlight creeping in through the front window, leaving scattered shadows on the ceiling. Did I bother trying to go back to sleep? Showering now meant no waiting for the bathroom. And no naked, awkward run-ins in the shower area with my nemesis.

She was everywhere. Side Braid—a.k.a. Perma-Scowl, a.k.a. She-Demon—was literally everywhere. Haunting my nightmares. Every shadow and every rustle made me paranoid she was messing with me somehow. She knew I was Goggle Girl in the outside world, but how? I didn't know a single thing about her. I didn't even know her real name because we didn't disclose them in Coach's sessions, and she was so influential that she got all her friends here to call her *Queen*.

QUEEN.

I still had nearly three weeks at camp, and my only plan was to avoid her as much as possible until I could get a better handle on things. So far, I'd avoided her glares in Coach's sessions, switched mealtimes so I wouldn't have to hear her shriek-laughter dominating the acoustics in the mess hall, and ignored how she swept all the dirt, hair, and food crumbs under my bed during cabin cleanup. One fun week down, three more to go.

The worst part was that Side Braid was exponentially growing her posse of scowl-faced, *Queen*-worshipping fans. It was like she had ride-or-die followers, but in real life. She was a natural social influencer. Behind a computer, I was way more confident than I was at school and with my friends. Online Sunny was so much better than real-life Sunny. Online Sunny could edit and delete posts when she didn't like how they came out. Real-life Sunny hated actual conversations, because she could never think of something clever to say or blurted things out without thinking first.

This wasn't my first experience with bullying. I'd been made fun of and called names—mostly by neighborhood kids teasing about my flat nose or small eyes. When I was younger, neighborhood kids would complain that my house smelled weird because Dad loved making spam and kimchi fried rice, and I grew too embarrassed to have people over. But the meanness was never so hurtful and deliberate that I felt as lost and lonely as I did now. At home, I was lucky enough to have friends around who liked me for who I was, and I lived in LA, where there were at least a few Asians at my high school—I didn't stick out too much.

Often, my experiences with bullying were watching it happen to other people. There were times I regretfully stood by on the sidelines while some classmates made fun of others for bringing "weird lunches" to school or telling them to speak English at drop-off or pickup because this was AMERICA. I also didn't speak up when girls were teased for being flat-chested or ample-chested or for dressing differently.

It wasn't because I had my nose stuck in my phone and didn't know what was happening. It was a case of fight or flight, and I chose flight, scared of being a pariah and choosing to lie low so I wouldn't be picked on next. Paralyzed with fear, ignoring what was going on in plain sight right in front of me made me feel sick to my stomach. How could I be so powerless even though I had a platform?

And now, without friends here and with my social media platform taken away, I was not only powerless—I had a target on my back.

Would anyone help me if Side Braid's hatred went too far?

Was this the universe righting my wrongs?

Was this karma?

If it was, this was one hell of a punishment. Being banished to a detox camp was one thing, but being an outcast here among all these quasi-almost-famous people, well, that really was the ultimate lowest of lows.

Maybe things needed to change. Or I had to change.

Was this all just a mix of my insomnia and me overthinking everything, as usual? Wow. When I didn't have my phone as a distraction, I had a lot of time to think about these things. Maybe too much time.

I rolled back to my side.

CREAK.

My bedsprings groaned from the shift in body weight while the plastic mattress cover crackled with my movements.

Someone was snoring.

Restless and wide awake, I rolled back the other way.

CREAAAAAK.

The spring coils squawked as they stretched and retracted. The bed squeaked with every wiggle.

Every.

Single.

One.

I sat up and flung my legs over the edge of the bed. Yawning and stretching, I slid my feet into my rubber slides and trudged to my closet to get my towel and shower caddy. On the way to the bathroom, my brain defogged, and it hit me how badly I needed to get some protection ASAP, like I'd learned about from watching all those dystopian and prison movies on Netflix. I needed watch-my-back friends. People who would make sure I was safe so I didn't have to routinely sneak showers at five something in the morning. People whose backs I could watch too.

It was the only thing I could do to make it through this. I'd never been outgoing, and being around all these big personalities for the past week had been intimidating. It seemed easier to just skate through this process than get invested. But I had to find my people, because I currently had zero. Coach didn't count, and neither did Theo.

I hung my robe and towel on a hook near one of the shower stalls. Placing the shower caddy in the shower, I turned the lever as far left as it could go. In the morning, the showers took at least two minutes for the hot water to kick in, giving me plenty of time to use the toilet. As I took care of business, one of the commodes flushed at the end of the row. I lifted my feet, holding my breath.

The stall door creaked open and someone shuffled out slowly. My heart pounded as the *thump-thump* of the soap dispenser echoed in the room. The hissing of the sink water was next. More shuffling.

Then my shower water turned off.

Damn it.

"You shouldn't waste water."

Damn it.

After lifting my pants, I pulled the drawstring and tied a quick bow. "You're right," I said and flushed. "I was waiting till it warmed up. The first showers of the day are the coldest, based on my experience."

I opened my door and stepped out to face my accuser. It was Delina, the mukbang girl. We'd eaten together a few times. Well, sort of—a bunch of us from Cabin D who weren't in Queen Side Braid's dominion sat together in a big group. The closest I'd been to Delina was a few seats down at a long table, but still. She passed me the salt once. And the ketchup twice.

Delina wore a striped shower cap, a dark-blue robe, and a frown. She cranked on the shower in the stall next to mine and put her hand in the stream of water. With a quick yank back, she yelled, "Damn, it's so cold!"

"Sorry, I tried to tell you." I turned my shower back on and tested the water. It was warm now. Not steamy hot but acceptable by camp shower standards. "Why don't you take mine? It's ready, and I'm okay waiting."

"Are you sure?"

"Yeah. No problem." I puffed out my cheeks and exhaled when she pulled the curtain closed. If letting her have the shower was a baby step to becoming better friends, I was okay with that.

Seconds later, she called out, "Come get your shower caddy."

I grabbed my caddy from Delina's dripping, outstretched hand, then padded to an empty shower and turned on the water. After waiting a minute for it to heat, I undressed and hopped in the stall.

Lukewarm water shot out from the rusty metal shower-head. The stream pelted and cascaded down my back, warming the back half of my body. I closed my eyes to wash my face as she said, "You should hurry before those mean bitches get up." While I turned and put my face into the water and wiped stinging shampoo out of my eyes, Delina shut her water off.

"That was fast," I called out.

"I didn't wash my hair today. That's why. I don't have hair like yours." I didn't know if I offended her or not. If I did, I didn't mean it.

As I speed-scrubbed the rest of my body, I could see Delina's shadowy silhouette outside my shower stall.

"Seriously, you better hurry."

"I know, I know, before those mean bitches get up."

Through the curtain, I heard her cackle.

On the way back to my bed, I noticed a lone brown box on one of the empty cots. Was this here before? It was a new care package addressed to me, in my sister's handwriting! Someone had opened the box partway and probably abandoned it because the first thing visible was a bag of seaweed rice crackers with Korean writing on it.

Quietly removing the last portion of tape, I could see the box was filled with snacks—crunchy and chewy savory ones that were kochu spicy or soy-sauce flavored. A few bags of squid too. Individually wrapped mochi filled with red bean paste and black sesame made me giddy. There were some bags of candy and choco pies in there, but I wasn't a huge fan.

I hadn't even put things back in the box before Delina trotted over like she had a sixth sense for covert snack unboxings.

"Anything you can share? I'm getting a package today or tomorrow, and I'll pay you back in snacks. My grandma makes the best brownies."

I hadn't had brownies since my #BrowniePorn fiasco. I still wasn't in the mood for them. "Got anything else?"

She laughed. "Oh, so you're picky. Yeah, I should have homemade cookies and Takis."

Takis were a good trade. "Yep. Take a look."

While I towel-dried my hair, Delina meticulously examined each item and put them in little mysterious piles of some kind of rank order. I read the enclosed note from Chloe, which had been tucked in between two packages of Jollypong corn puffs.

Hey.

Umma and Appa are being jerks. Big ones. When you left, I honestly thought things would be about the same or better (sorry), like you were on a monthlong minivacation taking a break from us and us from you (sorry again), but that's not what happened. Now Mom and Dad are bickering with each other about him starting his own business, about how to handle internet access when you're back, and they're on my case about EVERYTHING. I've already been grounded for the entire summer for coming home past curfew a few times. Can I call you, or is that against the rules? Anyway, this is a box of snacks, which you prob figured out already. I threw in extra stuff from the pantry.

I snuck (sneaked?) some CBD pills in here to help you sleep in case you need it. Consider it payment for your future parent shielding.

Love (HALP),
Chloe

Mom's favorite kid finally got to see a glimpse of what it was like to be me. She'd never been grounded before in my knowledge and definitely never voluntarily asked to communicate with me, for anything. My God, it must be bad there. Poor Chloe. I kind of missed her.

Delina gave the jar of CBD capsules a little shake and handed them to me. She murmured, "You better hide those."

I put the container in my box of tampons, and Delina shook

her head. "You better hide those too," she muttered. "Tampons seem to be like currency here. The camp market only has those overnight pads with wings. And they're thick."

There weren't many hiding places in the cabin. I dragged out my bag of laundry and put the tampon box in there and cinched the top by drawing the string.

She nodded at me. Delina's stamp of approval.

"You also need to hide that phone of yours."

My stomach rolled. "M-my what?"

She wasn't buying it. "You're lucky I'm the only one who sees you sneaking around because I wake up early too. I saw you pull it out from your bag and try to get signal, more than once. You'll get kicked out if someone snitches."

My mouth opened, but no words dared to come out. Hadn't I been discreet? I'd been checking it sporadically in our cabin because I still hadn't had a chance to try at the barn like Theo accidentally recommended. The only way I could go there without getting caught would be to go in the middle of the night, and I was almost too chicken to do it, with all the snakes and God only knew what else. And speaking of chickens, the ones roaming this farm were not friendly. If they were near the barn, they'd chase me away, wings out, clucking up a storm. I never thought of myself as someone who had fowlphobia, but the chickens here were monsters. I'd need a plan B (and maybe C and D) for my barn expedition in case I was confronted by the irate rooster and hen mob. And now I apparently needed to be extra *extra* careful if people in my cabin were already on to me.

Delina lifted up a bag of shrimp crackers. "Can I have these? When I get my box, I'll let you have first pick, I swear." She stared at me. "Why did you get sent here again? To this camp?"

One of the campers stirred in bed. We both froze in our spots until she fell back into a peaceful slumber. I pushed my laundry bag back into the closet. "My parents made me come. The headmaster said I'd get kicked out of school if I didn't go. He thinks I'm addicted to social media."

"And you're not?" She studied the ingredients on the snack bag.

No? "Not any more than any other teenager. Oh, and my parents think I filmed a nudie video in my kitchen, but that was a big misunderstanding."

She glanced up, and her mouth fell open. "You?"

I grinned. "I told you it was a misunderstanding. And so what if I did?" Leaning forward, I jiggled my almost-B-cup chest at her.

She laughed. "Please don't ever do that again. Never. I mean it. It, like, permanently scarred my retinas."

I barked a laugh and clamped my mouth with my hand. Checking to make sure I didn't wake anyone up, I continued, "Okay, I promise. Now, your turn. Why are you here again? Like, what was the final straw for your parents? You mentioned the mukbang videos and spending too much money."

Her face twisted. "Well, I told you some of it but not all. I'll tell you...but you can't ask questions because I don't like thinking about it or talking about it. Deal?"

"Okay."

"When I did mukbang videos, I had so many people commenting on the posts. At first it was fun, but then there were lots of asses who made comments about my being Black and not Asian and how girls shouldn't eat so much, and it was just horrible. It was ugly. And the videos with the nasty troll comments went viral. My parents didn't even know until then that I was making mukbang videos. I couldn't sleep or eat because I was obsessed with reading the responses. It messed me up pretty badly. I was getting paid well, but all of it really screwed up my self-esteem. My parents worried that the bigger I got, the more harm it would do me." With both hands, she lifted a pile of gummies, Pepero chocolate sticks, and corn chips. "Can I get these too?"

"Uh, yeah. Just be sure to pay me back." Showing gratitude was important, but I couldn't be a pushover. Another thing those Netflix prison shows taught me.

With her bounty stuffed in her robe pockets, Delina said with a yawn, "Thanks for breakfast. I'm going back to sleep."

She walked to her bed and hid her snacks under it, then crawled back under the covers.

Outside, the bugle blared at seven. Bodies stirred from sleep, cabinmates' pillows pulled onto faces to block out the early morning sun. It was time for everyone else to start the day. My day had already begun. With a new ally.

It was amazing.

TWELVE

COACH ASKED US TO ALL HOLD HANDS AND FORM A CIRCLE.

"Nope. No way in hell," the guy with a man bun on my right said. Was it a man bun if the guy was only, like, maybe fifteen or sixteen?

"Thank you for telling me the thoughts weighing heavy on your mind, friend. I don't want to start today's session with negativity, so let's just stay where you are then. No hand-holding. No circle." Coach scanned the room and made eye contact with each of us. "We've talked about connecting, recon-necting, and disconnecting with communities in our last few meetings. Today's theme is identity." He stood from his chair and handed out name tags and pens. "Without writing your name or usernames or handles or gamer IDs, whatever, write down in only a few words why you're here. It doesn't mean you have to agree with the reason you were brought to Sunshine."

A few new disgruntled people had joined Coach's sessions over the last few days. Had they been kicked out of their own groups like Side Braid had been? Why couldn't someone like Delina join my group?

The girl next to me raised her hand. "Isn't this a violation of privacy? I ain't disclosin' *jack*."

One of the guys said, "They already know this information about us."

Huffing hard, she blurted out, "Yeah, the *administration* does. But the campers don't." She crossed her arms and scowled.

He shrugged. "Whatever. We're all on social media, or at least we used to be. Oversharing is in our DNA. The most we'd do is look each other up when we got home. Wouldn't be hard since everyone posts photos of themselves."

A conspiracy theorist blogger in our group muttered, "And who knows what the Russians are doing with your facial recognition."

Coach clapped to grab our attention. "This is fantastic discourse! And I can see both of your sides." He nodded at the conspiracy guy. "And yours too." Coach took a deep breath in and out. "So if it makes you uncomfortable to disclose anything about yourself, you can write *no comment*...okay? When you're done, go ahead and stick on your name tags."

This was easy. I wrote, Parents think I'm addicted to social media in lopsided print. Scratching that out, I wrote, Supposedly obsessed and addicted to social media (likes, follows, etc). I put the name tag on my shirt pocket, crumpled the backing, and took a shot at the trash can halfway across the room.

It landed perfectly.

The guy next to me leaned over. He was so tall, he cast a shadow on me while seated. His unkempt, reddish-orange, explosively curly hair made his silhouette look like a tall stem of broccoli or a high nuclear explosion. "I'm captain of my varsity basketball team, all-state three years, and I couldn't have made that shot."

I smiled. "I've thrown away a lot of trash in my lifetime, and I'm too lazy to walk to the basket. Those two things combined lead to high wastebasket toss accuracy." My ability to shoot trash can goals didn't make any sense given none of the people in my family were into basketball. Our school was notorious for having the worst basketball teams in the district, so I never went to those games either.

He stretched out his long, muscular legs to reveal he indeed was a basketball guy. This dude had to be at least six-six. "Well, maybe if we can find a court here, you can teach me your techniques. I can only do layups with that kind of accuracy. Oh, my name is Colin."

I grinned. "Nice to meet you. I'm Sunny."

Coach looked right at us and cleared his throat. "I'm thrilled you two are able to have a conversation IRL, as they say, and we want to encourage this interaction in regular circumstances, but

I need you to focus." He took his handkerchief out of his back pocket and blotted the perspiration on his forehead, temples, and upper lip. "It looks like everyone's wearing their stickers, great! Next, I want you to walk around the room and see if you can find someone else who is here for the same reason as you. Or find as close a match as possible."

Colin got up before me and held out his hand to hoist me up. I looked at his sticker. All it said was *fantasy basketball*. Maybe he'd find another super tall fantasy basketball fanatic here.

As he pulled me to standing position, he said, "I'm terrible with names. You're Sandy? Can I call you Trash Shot?"

I laughed. "It's Sunny. And I suck at names too. Trash Shot's good, or you can call me the female Jeremy Lin. But then I get to call you the white Yao Ming." He had a squarish face like Yao Ming, so it wasn't a terrible comparison.

He laughed. "Deal!"

I'd made another camp friend. And I'd already forgotten his name.

All of us milled around the room, including Coach. Most people had illegible writing, so it was hard to decipher words. But the ones I could read shocked me.

Online gambling with borrowed credit card
Took a selfie at a great-aunt's funeral (sorry, I wasn't think-
    ing) and it went viral

Addicted to esports/gaming

Addicted to reading and posting Reddit and subreddits

And Side Braid's reason:

Screw you

"Amazing. Did you notice one thing you all have in common is you're all here for different reasons?" It took me a second to register what he was saying. Coach was sometimes sneakily deep.

Honestly, I'd assumed everyone was here for being on their devices too much, but it turned out there was a wide range. Some were here for reasons much more serious or heinous than mine.

"Now, friends, I want you to take a piece of paper and a pencil then jot down, for your eyes only, your name or usernames or handles or gamer IDs. Whatever name you are most identified with outside Sunshine Farms."

I hesitated, scribbling down **Sunny Song** at first, then scratched it out and wrote down **Goggle Girl** instead. Peeking over to my left, I saw the guy who refused to hold my hand in the circle earlier write *DannyBoyGamer1215* in surprisingly nice penmanship.

"I have a question for you all to answer that you can journal about now, or you can think about it and answer it later. Do you think this username or handle encompasses you? The whole you? Is it a reflection of who you are today? Who you are right now?"

DannyBoyGamer1215 let out a loud "HA!" He shook his head. "Nope."

"Care to elaborate?" Coach's chair creaked as he leaned back.

He said, in as mansplainy a tone as a teen boy could, "Everyone knew me as Danny in elementary and middle school. I go by Daniel now, but I kept my old gamer handle. When I got to be a big-time esports guy, that made it worse. And now I'm stuck. I'll be an old man like you, and people will still know me as Danny Boy."

Coach smiled. "I see this a lot. Sometimes you get stuck with an identity that is associated with your past. Also, in some cases, you get stuck because you don't know what else you want in life, and you find yourself in a rut. Sometimes, change is good. For me, switching careers from teaching to facilitating was hard, but it has been positive and rewarding. Maybe now you have time to explore your identity. Maybe not, if that's not your cup of tea. But it's your choice."

I felt this deep in my core. Goggle Girl was a name given to me by the public when I was younger. I didn't even choose it. But over time, I didn't shy away from it. As a middle schooler, all I wanted was to be popular and famous, and that viral video catapulted me into the spotlight. And after the initial popularity died down, I had thousands of followers, and all I wanted was to hold on to fame longer. But that's the thing about social media: it's fickle and fleeting. You can be "seen" one minute and disappear into oblivion the next. My video rank plateaued and then plummeted, my notifications went quiet, and I was stuck with the Goggle Girl identity. It was like those *Star Trek* actors who go to comic conventions to stay relevant. I was the Wesley Crusher of YouTubing fame.

Who's that, you ask? Yeah, exactly.

Coach let us spend the last few minutes of the session writing about the identity crises he unearthed for us. As we all scribbled, doodled, or penned a journal entry, he cleared his throat. "I want to remind everyone that while I have a master's degree in postsecondary education and social work, I'm by no means a psychologist, psychiatrist, or therapist. I'm here to facilitate discussion and, as any educator should do, to maximize your potential. I don't have all the answers, or maybe even zero answers, but I want to help you. Anyway, carry on."

After pouring out my feelings on two pages of a college-ruled spiral notebook, I pulled out a postcard and chewed on my pen top, trying to think of what to send to my family. My sister had sent me that care package and filled it with all my favorites. Maybe a thank-you note was in order.

"Oh, one more thing. This week's chores and tasks will be posted on the community board just before lunch. As you know, these assignments will help the collective group of campers, will have you be a part of the greater community, and will help things run more smoothly here at Camp Sunshine. Before you leave, here are some ideas for things you can write to your loved ones if you're stuck." On the whiteboard, Coach listed a few writing prompts to try out with his squeaky dry-erase marker. I tried out a few, but none of them were natural. So I improvised.

Hi, Umma, Appa, Chloe,

~~I realized something about myself today.~~
   ~~There's something I want to share with you.~~
   ~~I did something courageous I've never done before.~~
   I liked the snacks.

I stopped writing when Coach peered over my shoulder to check my progress.

He pulled his reading glasses from his shirt pocket and perched them on his nose.

"Another postcard about snacks?" he asked.

I shrugged. "It appears that way." It sounded snarky, but I honestly had no idea what to write. I never opened up to my family about anything.

"Might I suggest digging a little deeper, then? Think about why their snacks are so important to you?" He coughed a few times and shuffled over to the next person.

A few things popped into my mind. The snacks were from the Korean supermarket thirty minutes away. Mom and Dad hated going to the post office and waiting in line. The average post office rating on Yelp for all the stations near our house was one star. And yet the box they had sent was custom-packed, heavy, and filled to maximum capacity.

On a fresh postcard, I wrote:

Hi, Umma, Appa, Chloe,

I liked the snacks you sent.
    I met a nice counselor here, and I've made a friend who liked the snacks too. And I impressed a basketball player with my trash throwing.
    The snacks remind me of home. Thank you.

Then I remembered I needed to let Chloe know I'd gotten her note.

And, Chloe, I hope you're having a fun summer. I miss you. You'd hate it here. I don't even think the word "rustic" can describe this place, but it's growing on me.
        XO, fam,
        Sunny

I attached my stamp and dropped it in the outgoing mail tray as Theo burst into the room wearing a large cross-body mailbag.

"I'm doing mail delivery and pickup today, Coach." He made eye contact with me and grinned, making my heart squeeze tight. I returned his smile but awkwardly held it too long, so I shifted my gaze to the floor. Why was I like this around cute guys? It was always the same thing with Rafa too.

Coach said, "Oh, that's great! We have some postcards to mail, and it looks like everyone has things to send. Do you have any mail for any of our friends here?"

"I do. Um, let's see, there's a letter here for—"

Coach interrupted. "In my sessions, we don't use any outside names in this safe space. In here, we go by *friend*."

Theo pursed his lips, suppressing a smile. "I see. Okay, well, this makes my job pretty hard. But let me try." As he sorted through a stack of mail and distributed letters to people in the group, I studied how he bit his lip before he handed every letter to a camper. I slid my gaze from his tousled hair down to his shoulders to his lean, muscular arms. Everything about him was easy on the eye: even his large, strong hands that held so many packages and letters made me swoon.

He flipped through letters and peered at me through his long eyelashes. Handing me a postcard picture side up, Theo said with a frown, "Um, one for you."

I'd expected a package from my parents, not a postcard. And not one that said, *Greetings from La La Land*. No one in my family would dare use the words "La La Land."

I flipped the card over to see it was from Rafael. Rafa Kim had sent me a note at camp!

WOW.

Clenching the mail with both hands, my eyes went blurry as I read and reread Rafa's words.

Hiya from LA, specifically UCLA, specifically the UCLA bookstore. It's Rafa. I never write anything by hand, so hoping you can read this. I don't know which is better, sitting in our dark classes learning genetics and Euro history with a virtual professor videocasting on our Chromebooks or being where you are, milking cows and husking corn all day with no obligations and no internet.

Anyway, there's something I wanted to ask you, but maybe I'll get the nerve to do it if you write me back ☺ So write me back, okay? Or call me if you have phone privileges!

—RAFA (Real As F*ck, A'ight)

P.S. That was embarrassing. Sorry.

P.S.S. (or is it P.P.S.?) Postcards are super weird. Why are they so OPEN. Anyway, it's my first one! EVER!

If I weren't in public, I would have smelled the postcard and clutched it to my chest in a modified bear hug. Rafael wrote me!

He included his address! And he had something he wanted to ask me. Rereading it a third time, my mind ran through possibilities.

Hang out more?

Go to a movie with his friends?

Go to a movie with him?

Maybe a hockey game? He loved hockey. Was that even in season? Probably not; it was summer. Also, I hated hockey. Scratch that.

He had written a smiley face, so what he needed to ask me had to be good, right? Smiley faces always preceded or followed happiness.

But this was Rafa. He always did this to me—sent me mixed messages. Or maybe I read into things that weren't there and they weren't actually mixed at all. RAFA. Raffish. Rakish.

But...the smiley face. And why would he go out of his way to buy a postcard and send it to me unless he had some kind of feelings for me?

Or maybe he was bored. Or felt bad for me.

Damn it, I was doing it again.

Stop it, Sunny. It's just a postcard with a Forever Stamp on it.

My gaze lifted from Rafa's words, and I locked eyes with Theo, who looked away in a hurry. He handed out the last of the letters and closed the flap on his messenger bag. Then Theo shoved both hands in his pockets as he walked out the door.

Sifting through the pile of blank prestamped postcards on Coach's desk, I picked one with a photo that screamed *WTF*

IOWA. An old-timey picture filled with bales of hay. The caption?
Haaaaaaay!

> Haaaaaaay, Rafa,
>
> I can't even tell you how happy I was to get your postcard.
> I'm bored out of my mind here, so getting mail is a huge treat.
> It's humid, there are lots of bugs (mosquitoes!), even in the
> cabins, so you can't sleep well, and most of the people here are
> on the left side of the bell curve of pleasantness. So much for
> Midwestern niceness. But the food is surprisingly pretty good, all
> homemade. Nothing else to report except I can't wait to get back
> home. How're things? And what do you need to ask me? ☺
>
> ♡ Sunny

With a great deal of care, I inserted my postcard in the front
zippered pocket of my backpack and made sure the corners
didn't bend. It was where I used to keep my phone during the
school year. Over the last few days, my urge to look for my phone
had dwindled to maybe only a couple of times an hour now. It
used to be hundreds of times a day.

Huh.

Maybe this place wasn't so pointless after all.

THIRTEEN

THANKS TO RAFA'S POSTCARD, AS SOON AS I STEPPED out of the trailer, all I could think about was getting cell signal. This camp detoxing seemed to be working, then it backfired. I thought I'd be able to wait until Rafa's next postcard to hear what his question was, but no, once I knew he had something to ask me, I couldn't get it out of my head. It was on an obsessive loop. After this many years of an unrequited crush, was he finally going to tell me he reciprocated my feelings? Did he realize, in the wise words of Taylor Swift, that the one he'd been looking for had been here the whole time? Within twenty-four hours, I'd finally snuck off to the barn. I had to talk to Rafa.

Once the barn was in sight, I slowed down and checked behind me to confirm no one was following me. When I felt safe, I pulled out the phone and turned it on.

Searching...

Searching...

Searchi—one bar!

I sent Maya a message.

> It's Sunny! I'm alive!

Rafa's number was one of the few others I knew by heart. I blotted my face with a tissue and smoothed my hair, then called him on the video app. On the second ring, he appeared, smiling sheepishly into the screen and running both sets of fingers through his jet-black hair.

"Oh, hey, Sunny! Are you still at the camp? Did you break out of jail?" Reception wasn't great. I could hear him speaking, but the screen froze while he was midwave, his hand fully filling the screen.

"I'm breaking the rules. You know me," I joked. "Thanks for sending me mail."

The video connection unfroze, and his adorable face filled the entire screen. "I'm glad you got my postcard! Thanks for calling me." He sucked in his cheeks a little. "So I mentioned I wanted to ask you something." He paused and leaned in toward the camera. I gulped and brought my phone closer too.

This was it, his big question. *Sunny, do you think we could be more than friends?* Or maybe, *Sunny, are you aware that I'm totally in love with you and have been this whole time?* Or, *Would you like to go to Cheesecake Factory with me?* Drumroll, please.

"I'll be quick in case the farm prison warden comes for you. I got this journalism internship I wasn't expecting." He moved his head, and I could see he was sitting at a desk in some kind of modern, sleek office. His face recentered in the camera. "They want me to write about unique summer experiences for seniors. Of course, you came to mind immediately. I'd love to interview you, because out of everyone we know, your summer is by far the most non-summery summer of all summers. And if you could send photos too, that would be great. Anyway, think about it and let me know."

My stomach sank. Stupid me.

A slender, manicured hand appeared on his shoulder. Long, shiny, brown hair came into view, then half of a gorgeous face appeared. No doubt, the other side I couldn't see was symmetrical. "Heyyyy, who you talkin' to?"

He stammered, "Just a friend." His tone was different with her. It was softer. Sweeter. Doting. He'd never directed that tone at me before.

A poor connection warning appeared as the video froze again. Rafa's face was tilted up, smiling at his companion, his hand holding hers.

Thank God he couldn't see my crestfallen face.

I dabbed my eyes with the tissue I'd used to blot my face just as the choppy connection resumed. His eyes sparkled, oblivious to my implosion.

Rafa spoke, charming as ever. "So maybe I could call you again? Is this your number while you're there? Anyway, think about it. Whatever's easiest for you. You better write Maya too; she's angry at you for not communicating. You might want to do that if you haven't already."

I nodded, smiling while a sob hung in the depths of my throat. "Gotta go," I croaked.

He nodded. "I hope you and me and Maya can hang out soon when you get back. Anyway, ahnyung! See ya, Triple-S." He flashed a gorgeous smile and waved again. The video ended, and the signal disappeared.

Bye, Rafael.

He was the only one who called me Triple-S, short for Sunny Sun-Hee Song, a nickname he'd given me in middle school. I thought for years it was special. It turned out it was simply a platonic, cute, and easy way to remember my name.

I wished Maya were here to talk me through this. It wasn't like he had ever misled me about wanting more than a friendship by making out with me then acting cold. Or told anyone he liked me and hoped a mutual friend would get the word out. Normally, I would have read into everything he'd said on this call—did he want me to call him again because he liked me? Was this an excuse to work together? But the girl changed everything. He didn't even feign any coy flirting this time, making me second-guess all those previous times. Had I imagined those too?

I put everything on the line for him. Sneaking to the barn to make a call, risking getting kicked out of camp and school, just to hear his voice.

I let out a sputtering sigh. What a letdown.

My phone vibrated in my hands just as I was trying to power down. A message from Maya.

Maya

> HOLY OMG you made the semifinals for STARHOUSE!!! I'm continuing to post your premade content, but please please please check in. I think we'll hear if you make the final rounds sometime this week. You've got this, Sunny Song!

Leave it to Maya to put a smile on my face when I was down in the dumps. What would I do without her?

> So sorry I've been MIA. It's impossible to get a signal at farm camp. I'm hiding behind a freaking barn right now. I'll try to find other places to connect. Thank you, love you, miss you x infinity!

It was a good reminder: there was only one reason to sneak around and break camp rules. Without Rafa distracting me, I could turn all my attention to the competition.

FOURTEEN

DURING OUR GROUP SESSION WITH COACH THE NEXT DAY, Theo came by to deliver mail again and told me I had a package in the office. I had to hand it to Chloe: she was really staying on top of these care package deliveries.

When I made it to the office to pick it up, Theo was organizing plant seed packets into little stacks.

"Do you have any cannabis seeds in there?" I asked from the doorway.

"It's against regulations. A few kids have tried to plant some anyway, but the soil and precipitation at this farm aren't ideal."

I took a seat by the desk. "I was kidding. Parents would get this place shut down in half a second if they thought you were growing pot at a rehab camp."

He laughed and ran his fingers through his hair. Then he

lifted the tray of seed packets and put them on a side table. "How can I help you?"

"I have mail to drop off and that package to pick up. I have to say, I've never been this excited about getting packages. Not even around the holidays when the Amazon Prime packages pile up on the porch."

"Summer camp mail is the best mail." He pointed to the hand truck and crate already placed on it. "It's unwieldy enough to need a dolly."

"That's weird. The last package I got was normal." I squatted on the ground next to the long, flat box and read the calligraphy-esque lettering. It was an overnight package from Maya! Why was it sent with one-day shipping? Why the urgent snack mail?

I lifted the box. "It's not actually that heavy. You all don't deliver these straight to the cabins anymore?" My other box from Chloe was sent directly to the cabin.

Theo sipped from his water bottle and choked. "You're looking at the entire Sunshine Farms mail system here. That includes farm equipment deliveries and supply shipments."

I was about to apologize, but then he added, "You must have our camp confused with some of your fancy LA spa and surf camps."

"Spa camps? We don't have that in LA." His anti-LA rhetoric was a little off-putting. "But okay, we actually do have surf and swim camps."

He gave me one huff and a sarcastic snort. "Figures."

I don't know why I was so compelled to defend surf and swim camps, but his judgy snorting really irritated me. "They mainly teach you about ocean water safety. It's not like they sit around yelling 'Duuuude' at each other and doing hang ten signs. And junior lifeguard certification is no joke. I had to take it twice." I didn't mention I didn't pass the second time either.

He shot me a skeptical look, raised eyebrow and all. No snorting or sarcastic one-word replies though.

"Well, if you ever need a water rescue, don't bother calling me." I tilted the hand truck back and was able to push the box with ease.

His forehead crinkled. "I can help you if you want."

Not feeling in the mood to be chaperoned by Mr. Anti-LA, I said, "I can take this to the cabin on my own...and I'll bring back the dolly later."

"Suit yourself," he said and sat down with a *thunk* into the desk chair. "Holler really loud if you need anything." Theo gave me a wry smirk that infuriated me, but I also noticed how weirdly cute he could be when he argued about something trivial. As I made my way through the door, Theo called out, "Duuuuude, let me know if you need any help with that!" Then he muttered, "Jeez, so stubborn. Stubborn as a mule."

I was a born-and-raised Angeleno, and his stereotypes offended me. It wasn't like I cracked farmer jokes all the time, even when he spouted his farm phrases and facts. I didn't ask where his overalls were or if the hay the farm kids dangled from their mouths was certifiably organic (okay, maybe that would be more of a California joke).

Plus, by no stretch of the imagination was I a surfer. In fact, I'd entirely forgotten about my junior lifeguard lessons until he was joking around about it. Did I even know how to swim anymore? I could dog-paddle still...maybe. I hardly went to the beach and sat by pools but rarely got in them. I'd dropped swim completely from my schedule once school, social media, and homework started to take up all my time.

It wasn't the only thing I'd dropped. There was Korean, and I also dropped my interest in improv and sketch comedy. *Yes, Theo, we had sketch and improv camps in LA too.* I enrolled when my parents sent me to full-day coding, animation, and video editing summer camp and I finished my daily programming assignments too quickly. The camp staff stuck me in the afternoon comedy class down the hall because they didn't have anything extra to assign me. To my incredible surprise, I enjoyed it. It was on my long list of things I loved but never got around to doing. But maybe that was part of the problem—I never had spare time anymore.

I'd given up all of it so I could invest and reinvest in Goggle Girl.

Wheeling my package down the path to the cabin, I passed

the community board by the commissary. Just as Coach had said, the individual assignments were posted, and the list was extensive. By each camper's name, one or two "community betterment chores/tasks" were listed, along with their locations and times. I skimmed to find my name and was overwhelmed by the breadth of farm offerings.

→ Salting/hanging/smoking meat and fish
→ Butter churning
→ Cheesemaking
→ Mulching
→ Collecting honey
→ Milking cows
→ Making candles and soap
→ Cooking supper and blowing the dinner horn

Then I spotted my name.

→ Sunny Song: Lady Pioneer @ Welcome Wagon

Lady pioneer? Welcome wagon? What the—

"Hey, are those new snacks for me?" Delina's jovial voice boomed across the courtyard. Relieved to see a friendly and familiar face, I smiled as she approached. I was so glad she'd become my camp buddy: over the past few days, we'd eaten most meals together and sometimes took walks and traded snacks. She had her eye on my box briefly but saw the assignment lists and stared at the posted pages. She pointed at my name on the board. "You're going to be a pioneer? Now *that's* as funny as *me* being a pioneer." Her smile quickly fell. "Oh no, they want me to shear sheep? What the—?" She dropped her voice. "You want to trade? Sheep freak me out."

Theo walked by us and did one of those whistles that sounded like a bomb dropping. "You sure you don't need help? It's taken you, like, half a year to walk fifty steps." He looked at Delina. With twinkling eyes, he said, "Ovinophobia."

She looked at me, like I would interpret his alien language. I shrugged as he laughed at us.

I asked, "Is that dark magic?"

"Ovinophobia is the fear of sheep!"

Delina narrowed her eyes. "And how would you even know that?"

His shoulders rose and fell. "Um, maybe because I've been around sheep for seventeen years?"

Delina punched him lightly in the shoulder. "Then you know what I mean, right? Those beady-eyed sheep are scary! Like, haunt-your-dreams and murder-you-in-your-sleep scary."

I chimed in. "They are. 'Mary Had a Little Lamb' is creepy. She had a stalker lamb. He went everywhere she did. Everywhere. Pretty messed up."

I had to wonder though...could shearing sheep be worse than dressing up and greeting farm guests as a pioneer? With shearing sheep, you could wear whatever, but as a pioneer, you'd have nonbreathable clothing and a hat, which would mean sweatiness and a lot of breakouts. Being at a farm camp, I expected farm chores, but it never even crossed my mind I might have to be part of the welcome personnel. They probably wanted me to smile the whole time too. Nope. Wasn't going to happen.

Unless Theo smiled at me. Which he did, making me blush and look at my feet. Delina continued ranting about how sheep regurgitated food, how she hated the smell of lamb, and how the taste of non-cow dairy products made her want to become a vegan. How the first sheep that was cloned way back before she was born died prematurely, and how there are shady clinics now that clone dogs for rich people.

I glanced up and grinned back at Theo. It was no wonder Delina was a social media magnate: she was so smart and funny and could talk about anything, even sheep, in an engaging way. For hours probably.

Pioneer or sheep shearer? A choice one could only make at a farm camp. I was definitely not in the mood to shear sheep now, especially with all that negative propaganda Delina was spewing. Cutting and bagging wool sounded so hot and uncomfortable. With temps already hitting the midnineties here, a woolly summer was NOT what I wanted out of my camp experience. It was pretty much the exact opposite of something I'd put on my bucket list.

"Oh, oh, oh! Look who else is pioneering with you!" Delina threw her head back with laughter.

Wendy H.? Who was that?

Delina scanned my face for recognition. "Seriously? She's that girl who has it in for you. She always has her hair in that raggedy, lopsided Elsa braid."

Side Braid from Jersey City? *Oh no.*

Delina smirked. "Sure you don't wanna trade now?"

Her name was Wendy? She didn't seem like a Wendy. Wendy was a normal-sounding name, and Side Braid was too mean to have that normal of a name.

Shearing sheep instantly moved up in my ranking, over standing next to seething Side Braid for hours each day, fake-smiling while she plotted my demise.

"Deal," I said.

"One more thing. If there are any good snacks in that big box of yours, I still get dibs, right?"

"I never knew you had dibs in the first place."

Theo added, "Wait, you have good snacks? I want snacks too."

These guys were like pigeons in the park. They saw me as a giant, walking loaf of bread. But if snacks helped me gain alliances, I was okay with it. "I honestly have no idea what's inside, but you're welcome to anything in here within reason."

Delina looked at Theo while she asked me, "Is it from a secret admirer?" His face turned bright red while my cheeks flushed with heat.

A secret admirer, ha! No secret admirers, nope. "Definitely not."

Immediately, I regretted my words. Would it have been better to act like I had any game in front of Theo? Should I have played it cool?

Still blotchy, Theo said, "I—um—if you need me to take your stuff to the cabin, I can help you. I was being kind of a jerk earlier. I'm sorry about that. My wood chopping shift is soon, but I have a little time beforehand."

I imagined Theo swinging an ax with his muscular arms, pulling his T-shirt tight against his back and shoulders, his shirt lifting a little so I could get a glance at what was underneath. My heart skipped faster, and Delina looked at me with her head cocked and her eyes slightly bulged. She placed her hands on her hips.

What?

"I'm good," I said with a little half wave and pushed the cart toward the cabin. To my surprise, Delina walked with me, quiet for the first time after what felt like hours of her antisheep TED Talk, and when Theo was out of earshot, she pulled my shirt-sleeve hard.

"You like him, right? And he seems into you. When a guy, or

anyone, offers to help lug heavy boxes to your cabin, next time, you say yes, okay? I thought LA girls knew stuff like this."

Well, obviously not *this* LA girl.

"What I saw back there was an embarrassment to all humans. You need to do better. He basically was like, 'Let's get out of here and ditch your friend. You can walk with me and touch all my muscles.'"

I barked a laugh. "Shut up, you liar."

"You know I'm right." She and I were buddies now, and she clearly was the "let me make fun of you till the cows come home, tough love" type of friend. Oh God, now I was thinking in farm phrases. *Damn it, Theo.*

Every night, while other clusters of campers in our cabin giggled and whispered after bedtime, Delina came over to my bed and we played Uno while talking about whatever was on our minds until we could barely keep our eyes open. She was the only person I'd "friended" at Sunshine. I hoped there was some truth to what she was saying, even through her teasing. Even after I saw Rafa with his new girlfriend on video chat, there was still a tiny part of me holding out hope for him—for us. But I was trying to move on. Delina was doing a good job distracting me. Theo too.

Theo was really cute. And if Delina could tell I liked him, oh God, did he know too?

But if he did, was that a bad thing?

She held the screen door open to our residence and gestured with her hand. "After you."

"Thanks!" I wheeled the dolly in and parked my box next to my bed.

Delina shrugged. "I'm not being magnanimous here. I wanna know what's inside that box." Her eyes shone. "This camp is boring, and this is the only thing worth my time." From her cross-body purse, she pulled out what I thought was a simple pocketknife. But then she pushed a button and swish! A blade flipped out.

She said, "Look, it has a ramen logo on it. It's hilarious what kinds of free stuff you get from Japanese companies that want you to promote their brand. It was already in my backpack from a camping trip, and I forgot to take it out. They confiscated our phones and devices but didn't really check for stuff like this." By *this*, I suppose she meant stabby, jabby, weapony stuff.

"May I?" Without waiting for an answer, she slid the blade on the taped box seam and tore back the flaps. Underneath a few sheets of Styrofoam were ice packs and two boxes of chocolates. *Thanks, Maya!*

Delina used the blade to open the truffle box packaging and then pulled off the top so I could see. The handmade truffles were from a chocolate store near Maya's house.

I asked, "You want one?" She pulled out one with gray sea salt and had already chewed and swallowed before I picked mine.

Delina licked her lips. "These are so good. They're a good blend of fudgy and chocolaty, and the salt helps balance the sweetness. There's a hint of nutmeg."

I laughed. "I had no idea you were such a chocolate nerd, Dee. Thank you for educating me. All chocolate tastes good to me. Even Hershey's."

"How dare you compare this to Hershey's." She raised an eyebrow. "My family calls me Dee. But yeah, you can too. I like that. I have to go to meet up with some people. Don't laugh. I met them when we were trying to milk cows yesterday. They're cool and invited me to hike. Err, I guess it's actually just a walk. Wanna come?"

"I'm a firm *maybe*; let me figure out what to do with this box and stuff first. What am I supposed to do with five thousand calories of chocolate in this heat? Can you take this other box to your friends? Maybe they'll wanna eat some. Where're you all gonna be?"

"My bovine buddies will be at the trail by the barn or at the one near the trout lake."

We looked at each other and burst into a fit of laughter. She gasped, "Did you ever think anyone would say something like that out loud?"

I shook my head and wiped both eyes with my palms. "You say those things, and they sound so normal now. Anyway, I'll catch you in a few minutes."

She left, and I took the ice packs out of the cardboard box. Lifting the bottom frozen packaging layer, my fingers bumped up against something hard.

Another cardboard box. When I lifted it, a folded paper fell out. I grabbed it midair.

Sunny!

I hope you're having a blast at farm camp. Things are going well here.

But enough chitchat. If you're seeing this note, it means you didn't get so distracted by the chocolate that you threw out the REAL reason I mailed you this package: I've enclosed a cell phone signal booster! It's pretty easy. You just put it somewhere high like a roof or a tree and flip the switch. According to Consumer Reports, this one is a "value buy" that gets a good rating and it's "ideal for truck drivers" lol. It's also the only one I could afford. Good luck! Can't wait to hear from you soon. And OMG STARHOUSE!

Maya

The signal-boosting equipment was enclosed in infuriating packaging that wasn't easy to open without a proper Delina-style switchblade. After tugging open the seals and rubbing my thumb and index fingertips raw to the point where I may have rubbed off my fingerprints, I finally opened the plastic encasing and shook out the contents: a booster, antenna, battery pack, and various mounting brackets. This was some 007-level craziness here, just to get a cell signal.

Clearly, this cell booster manufacturer had sophisticated truck driver clientele who were handy with screwdrivers and wrenches. My plan was simpler: to lob it onto the gutter of the barn. And if that didn't work, to tape it to a tree branch.

Maya had included one more thing inside the box. A roll of waterproof tape. She knew me well. *Thank you again, Maya!*

If I got caught with any of this, I'd be expelled from this camp and from school. It was risky, but the enticement of Starhouse instant fame made my pulse race. Maybe I wouldn't be a fleeting blip. With Starhouse, I could be remembered for something other than goggles and brownies.

Voices nearby scared me into swift action, and I dumped all the packaging back into the box and took the booster equipment and wrapped it in a T-shirt. My mind raced to think of a hiding place.

No...not inside your bra again.

No...under your bed is a stupid hiding place.

You already have a phone in your laundry bag.

I had no other options. Maybe I had to keep it in plain sight.

I shoved the booster and remaining candy inside my backpack, then zipped it closed. As campers noisily made their way through the cabin, I tossed the ice packs in the trash and flattened the box. It wasn't until I tidied up that I noticed the folded stack of clothes at the foot of my bed.

A petticoat.

An apron.

A white bonnet.

And an engraved name tag. SUNNY SONG, SUNSHINE HERITAGE FARMS TOUR GUIDE.

No.

I couldn't swap jobs with Delina.

I was stuck with Side Braid.

And I had to wear this god-awful *Anne with an E* poofy, unflattering dress in public. I unfolded the dress to inspect it. People would be taking videos and pictures of me in this, wearing a god-awful bonnet to match.

Oh no.

But wait.

The period dress had...pockets. I had no idea who designed this costume, but I thanked the fashion gods that they were thoughtful enough to include what every girl wants in a dress.

Deep pockets.

A place to smuggle a secret phone.

My day turned around in an instant. Who cared about Side Braid? Okay, admittedly there was risk—getting kicked out of camp and school if I got caught, which my parents would murder me for—but I potentially had a bright future ahead of me, thanks to the Starhouse talent search team. And if I had a shot at fame, I had options.

Popping a truffle into my mouth, I left the cabin with a spring in my step.

FIFTEEN

I NEEDED A SIGNAL. THE STORY OF MY LIFE.

I couldn't pick up service anywhere around the barn this time. Would putting the booster there even help?

I'd put on my heavy pilgrim attire *before* hunting for reception, in one hundred percent humidity. A terrible idea. A very sweaty, overheated, pore-clogging idea. For over an hour, I trudged around to all the places I'd seen the administrators and counselors go on their breaks, hoping that would offer a clue to where I could connect. When that didn't work, I gave up and made my way toward the welcome station. It was my first day as the pioneer tour guide, and Theo intercepted me on the path with a bottle of water and some sunscreen.

"Hey! Have you seen the mail hand truck? I thought you returned it but was wondering if you saw anyone with it and—are you okay, Sunny?" His brow furrowed to a deep V. "You look like you might have heatstroke."

He put the bottles on the ground and placed the back of one of his hands on my forehead, then on each cheek. If I wasn't already overheated from the sun and the heat, his hand touching my face was definitely enough to make me flush. I studied his long lashes, his kind eyes, and brow line as he said, "You're really warm."

Oh God, of course I was. Theo was touching me.

"Maybe you should go to the nurse's office."

Nooooo thank you. I flicked my wrist. "I'm a little overheated is all. It's nothing. I'm an LA girl, remember? I'm not used to humidity and all these clothes." With my right hand, I pulled the front part of my dress away from my damp skin. It made a slight suction sound.

Gross.

I asked, "Can you help me undo the lacing? It's tight." My previous feeble attempts to untie and loosen the corset-like top failed. Theo's presence made my hands tremble, and I couldn't think straight.

His face and neck flushed, and red speckles appeared. "Uh, sure." He brought his hands up to my chest and looked around. "Um, maybe I should get someone else, like a female counselor who can help you better? I—I've never done this before."

My breathing became more labored. Partly because he was

just inches from me, so close I could feel his body heat, his hands hovering over my breastbone. And partly because the costume had either shrunk somehow, or I'd maybe expanded from the heat, making everything cling tight like Saran wrap. Science suggested it was the latter.

"Please, I need help now," I panted.

Squatting to the ground, I scooped up the bottle of water and chugged. The coolness helped, but only a little. I'd nearly finished the whole bottle, and I'd sweated out maybe two bottles' worth over the course of the hour. This squeezing corset was going to be a real problem soon if I couldn't get relief.

I tried again with the laces, but the beads of sweat dripping into my eyes caused my field of vision to blur, making it even harder to see what I was doing.

Theo said, "Okay, let me," and took the laces from my hands. He was able to unknot the bow while I closed my eyes slowly and steadied my breath. The water was helping.

"You want me to loosen it too?"

I nodded. The oxygen deprivation plus Theo's proximity made my head fuzzy.

"Um, this is all new to me. Is it okay if I, you know, touch you up here?"

"Yes! Please touch me," I blurted. *Okay, that came out all kinds of wrong.* Surely he knew I needed to breathe though?

With his gentle and swift grip, Theo unknotted, yanked, and

loosened the ties, decompressing my chest so I could inhale and exhale freely. Huffing hard but inhaling and exhaling steadily, my brain shifted gears to notice Theo breathing harder than me. Through his lashes, he peered down at me with sincere concern, his hands tightly clenching to the strings attached to my body. My heart thudded hard and fast against my chest as my breaths became shallower and more frequent.

Just when I'd been given the ability to replenish my oxygen levels, he made it nearly impossible for me to breathe again.

More deliberately this time, his fingers worked down the front of my chest, tugging at my crisscrossed laces and giving them more slack. I'd never had any guy work his fingers down my front like this, and the more I thought about it, the warmer I became. He made his way down to my navel, then looked up triumphantly and met my gaze.

I glanced at his lips. Those soft, full lips. I wanted to tug him toward me and draw him close so I could see how kissable they were.

"Theo."

I put my hand on his, and a drop of my forehead sweat fell onto his fingers.

Without a beat, he pulled his hand free and let go of the laces like they were two helium balloons he was releasing into the air.

Mortifying. "Sorry," I mumbled. "My LA forehead isn't used to this humidity."

He bent over to pick up the sunscreen. "Today we're supposed to hit a hundred. You're also out here in the sun when you should be at the welcome station, which is actually in the shade, under a canopy." He cocked his head and crossed his arms. "So why are you over here anyway? The welcome station is close to your cabin."

I slid both hands into my dress pockets, a nervous habit of mine, and grazed the phone. I drew my hand out so fast, you'd think I'd had an electric shock.

With the back of my sweaty hand, I wiped my continuously perspiring brow. "I was giving myself a tour so I could answer any questions about the camp better." I flashed him a smile, or more accurately, a giveaway wince.

He curled his lips into a smirk, sending my heart racing. "Well, there's not much to see there. It's an old barn and a bunch of fallow land we'll use next year for corn. We like to have corn every year."

Pointing past the lake, he said, "Across there's where it's more interesting. It's funny, that land used to be abandoned for decades because some guy who inherited it from his great-granddad refused to sell. But he died a few years ago, and it's been developed by some rich dude. There are rumors flying all over town, saying it's a high-end farm hotel with a winery, equestrian lessons, and hunting, with PlayStations and jet tubs in all the rooms. But it's got private-property signs all over the place, so we can't snoop to confirm. We've lost some of our best handymen and groundskeepers to them." With a deep sigh, he added, "They obviously pay more."

His words made my heart tighten, but in the back of my mind, I couldn't help thinking that if an obscenely rich dude owned the place across the lake and other rich dudes stayed there, wouldn't they have good LTE service and maybe even guest Wi-Fi? Sneaking over there vaulted to the top of my to-do list. Maybe I could check it out later in the evening.

I peered around Theo to get a better view of the lake perimeter. Could I walk around the lake, or would I need to boat or swim across?

He shoved his thumbs into his pockets and shrugged. "I can take you canoeing if you want."

I wasn't expecting such a generous offer, especially one that gave me exactly what I wanted. "Really? I'd love that. But if you fall out, you know, I'd be conflicted because all of your surf and swim trash talk."

He smiled. "It was the surf camp part I was trashing. You up for a lake swim? One where we swim across and I beat you so badly, you eat your words?"

I looked down at my outfit. "Now? I'd get caught and probably condemned to farm bathroom duty for the rest of my time here."

"I can talk my mom out of giving you janitorial duty for that. It's the one advantage to being the director's son."

It took a couple of seconds to register his words. The director was his mom? "Well, she'd be pissed. Also, I'd need to change into something less cumbersome. Or...you could wear the same outfit so we'd be fairly matched. You'd look pretty good in a hoop skirt, I bet."

He laughed and motioned for me to follow him. "Not *now*. I meant sometime soon. Let's get you to the welcome station. If you're late, I promise you'll never hear the end of it from Mom."

Sure enough, when we arrived, she was there and said in a cheery voice with a hint of sarcasm, "Nice for you to join us. You too, Theo."

A large group of young children came down the dirt path, zooming like airplanes with their arms out, tagging and hitting one another, and running in circles as they made their way down to our welcome committee. *Promise City Preschool* was emblazoned on their bright-orange T-shirts. A smart idea. They were like walking highlighter markers and hard to miss. They all wore handwritten name tags, presumably in the kids' own writing because most of the letters were illegible.

Three harried teachers accompanied this group of miniature people. Each of them held the hand of one errant child who needed extra supervision. A blond, husky boy with a perfect bowl cut tugged hard at his teacher's arm. "I want apple caaaaaake!"

I looked at Theo, who pursed his lips, holding back a laugh. "We sometimes bake fresh apple crumb cake. Kids really like it."

My nemesis Side Braid was there, wearing a nearly identical outfit to mine. She glared at Theo and me and muttered under her breath, "Spoiled apple cake jackasses."

The blond boy nodded vigorously. "I want apple cake jackasses too!"

The children all chanted, "Me too!"

Tension ran high as boys and girls stamped their feet. Tears spilled down one girl's cheeks as she whimpered, "I'm allergic to apple peels, but I want it too! It's not fair!"

The preschool teachers tried to calm the riotous crowd, but it was no use. They had lost control of these little people, and this unruliness was getting worse by the second. Honestly, who would even want apple cake over something like chocolate cake or ice cream?

A loud, shrieking whistle ripped through the air, and dead silence followed. Everyone stopped what they were doing. I turned my head to see where it came from. Theo was in my peripheral view, his thumb and middle finger in both sides of his mouth. Was this something everyone who worked here knew how to do? He pulled his fingers away from his lips and grinned at me.

Argh, his lips. Never before had a shrieky whistle been so attractive.

Theo cleared his throat and spoke. All I could do was watch his mouth move. "If I could have your attention please. First of all, we don't have any cake today. I'm sorry."

The group of kids let out a collective *awwww*.

"Our baker is out sick, but you're in luck...we have a famous baker here in our midst!" He tipped his hand toward me. "I've heard rumors that Sunny here, our renaissance pioneer woman, has a reputation for making some killer brownies." His eyes sparkled with mischief. How did he know about my brownie disaster?

Of course he knew. All he had to do was a Google search.

But if he googled me, did that mean he wanted to know more about me?

Before I could get too excited, Side Braid sneered, "I told him everything." My fists balled and flexed in response. How come she knew all about my life and I still knew nothing about her? Who *was* this girl? If she was famous, I would recognize her, right?

All along, I'd had a feeling there was something menacing about her I couldn't place. And I still couldn't figure it out, not without an extensive internet search. Was she an online troll who had it out for me? Or someone who ranted about how much she hated my goofy content and tagged me so I would see it? I never understood why people would tag a creator and trash them in a review in the first place, but Side Braid totally seemed like one of those hateful people. Personally, I didn't bother to waste time on stuff I didn't enjoy, so this type of commentary was always so perplexing to me.

Another mystery of the universe.

And she was glaring at me. Hard.

Actually, everyone was staring at me. Every single one of those preschool kids and their teachers. Over forty eyes. On me.

Next to one of the teachers, a kid with a fauxhawk sighed loudly. "I asked why you were a pioneer. You don't look like a pioneer."

A girl to his right had her name embroidered on her shirt. She was the only one. Kalani. "I thought paneer was cheese."

I laughed. "It is cheese. Paneer, an Indian dish. Pioneers are different. They're people from...uh, long ago."

Kalani asked, "You mean like when my mama was born?"

"Before that, like two hundred years, maybe more."

She pointed to Coach walking by. "Older than him?"

I nodded and laughed. "Older than your grandparents' parents."

"Whoaaaaa!" The class marveled in unison.

Kalani wasn't done talking. "Yeah, you don't look like people in the pictures we see about people long ago." She pulled out a Sunshine Farms map from her jacket pocket and pointed to all the photos of people. All the images were older white men and women and indeed looked nothing like me. Historically accurate.

"So why did they pick her?" Kalani asked Fauxhawk. "She looks like Tinkerbell's friend, Silvermist." Silvermist was the gorgeous fairy in Tinkerbell's girl gang with dark hair and dark eyes. It was never called out that she was Asian, but I'd seen the

Silvermist character walking around Disneyland, and she was most definitely Asian. This Silvermist comparison was a compliment, as far as fictional characters went—it's not like she said I looked like SpongeBob's pink friend or Ursula the Sea Witch. I'd definitely be happier donning a fairy costume instead of this horrible prairie outfit. My dress was insanely tight in some places and super loose in others, in the most unflattering combination of the two. It was hard for any clothing to beat out the amorphousness of a Korean hanbok, but this one did, by a landslide.

One of the little boys stood on his tiptoes and shouted at me, "You don't look like someone who was a farmer. Or someone from the old times." He pointed at Side Braid. "She looks more like a farmer."

All the kids quieted down and nodded in agreement. Apparently, preschool field trip chaos can briefly subside if the kids need to collectively decide who looks like a farmer and who doesn't.

Theo shot me a sheepish grin. My heart melted like cultured butter on a warm cast-iron skillet. I returned his smile and dropped my gaze.

Brushing out the wrinkles on my skirt, I said, "I think what we are all noticing is I'm Korean American. Someone whose ancestors came from Asia and settled down in the United States, but far after what you see in history books as 'the pioneer days.' My parents both moved here from South Korea a few decades ago, but not what you describe as 'long ago.' They came here after the TV was invented."

Theo's mom emerged from behind the preschool class. "Perhaps to avoid future confusion, we should consider switching our camper volunteers around." She looked directly at me. "I'm sorry. When I saw the name Sunny, I assumed you were American."

Oh no. Casual racism. At a popular tourist site. In front of preschool kids.

Looking at all these impressionable little faces, I had no choice but to address it. "Well, I am American. I'm ethnically Korean, but I was born and raised in LA." I raised an eyebrow. This was not a discussion I planned to have while wearing a pioneer woman costume in front of four-year-olds. I preferred to have my "look, bish, I'm just as American as you" conversation in my regular street clothes versus a corset and an itchy bonnet. My face heated with anger, and the added degrees in temperature made the outfit even more unbearable to wear.

Theo placed his hand on my shoulder and whispered, "I'm so sorry. I'll talk to her. Sometimes she's completely clueless." His looked across the field. "Seeing as how we live and work on a historical farm, she's kind of stuck in the past."

His mom smiled at me the way a politician does when surrounded by cameras. "Of course, of course. I'm sorry if you thought there was a misunderstanding." There was no way

Theo's mom had suddenly come around to see my perspective. She hadn't changed her views. All she wanted now was harmony and the optics of resolution for the sake of keeping peace at this stupid camp.

I untied my apron. "Honestly, that four-year-old is right. It doesn't make sense for a Korean American girl to be here, pretending she knows what life is like on a prairie."

I took a deep breath and then threw the apron on the ground.

"I quit."

SIXTEEN

FOR A MOMENT, MY DECLARATION WAS GREETED WITH silence. Then, Kalani looked at Fauxhawk. "She wasn't a very good pilgrim anyway." He nodded in agreement and yanked her pigtail.

Theo's mom let out a tired sigh. "Theo, can you see she gets reassigned to the afternoon session to replace Henry? It's the only one with an open slot."

I asked, "What session is that?"

He clapped his hands and rubbed his hands together. "Oh, it's going to be interesting, but a very different crowd from this."

Side Braid laughed bitterly. "I switched out of that to come here. Enjoy your new activity! Domo arigato!"

Did she just speak Japanese to me?

"C'mon, let's go. She's trying to screw with you," Theo said, lifting his hand and placing it on my shoulder, leaving a spot of warmth. "And I promise, I'll talk to my mom."

A message blared on his walkie-talkie. "Theo, they're in front of the community center, and the bus just got here. It'll take a while for them to unload."

"They? Who's they?"

He kept his signature coy smile on his face but didn't answer my question. What was he hiding? And why? "These kids are about to go on a hayride, and it goes right by your cabin where you can change. Let's hitch a ride."

Kalani squealed, "Hayride?"

The other kids screeched and hooted and hollered. "Yaaaaay! Haaaaaaayride!"

A rusty pickup truck with a long flatbed attachment full of haystacks barreled up the path and parked right in front of us. The driver wore a straw hat, overalls, a bandanna, and a name tag that said *Farmer Raul*. He came around to the back, and Raul helped let the kids on, one by one.

"Good morning! Hola! Bienvenidos!"

After all the kids and teachers were loaded, there was no room on this flatbed for me and my wide-load, plumy dress. Theo held out his hand to lift me up. "We'll make room," he said, reading my mind.

"Can y'all kids move down a little?" Theo asked, and each kid shifted a little, making room for maybe half an adult ass, at best.

"I'll stand," I said.

"No, please sit. I insist."

Farmer Raul turned on the ignition and yelled out the window, "All aboard!"

All the children yelled, "Chooo! Chooooo!" adding even more historical inaccuracy to the day.

"I'll stand," I said defiantly. "My dress is too big for that spot, and besides, I'm a surfer, remember? I can handle a hayride."

Theo bit his bottom lip to unsuccessfully hide a smile. "Um, sure. Okay, LA modern woman, do your thing."

"The train is leaving the station!" Raul honked twice, and the truck lurched forward. Everyone squealed in delight.

Well, everyone except me. As soon as he hit the gas pedal, I lost my balance and screamed. Twenty pairs of eyes stared in horror as I stumbled backward toward the edge of the trailer. Theo grabbed my arm and pulled me toward him with a firm tug. Instead of plunging to my death off a hayride trailer, I fell into Theo's lap with a hard topple. So hard in fact, I wondered if I permanently injured his man parts.

My heart raced; I could have easily face-planted into the gravel path, but Theo caught me. His wavy hair blew into his eyes. He smiled at me and repositioned both of us so not all my weight was on one thigh. It was my first time in someone's lap other than Santa Claus, and here I was, like a hundred pounds heavier, wearing an unwieldy pilgrim costume and hideous bonnet. There wasn't anything unsexier than me in my current state.

Was unsexier even a word? Damn it, Theo was making my head swirl.

This was not how I ever dreamed an idyllic summer romance would go. Not that this was that. A summer romance.

I couldn't handle this Theo and Sunny role reversal in *Beauty and the Beast* any longer. While the truck continued bumping down the path, I scrambled off his legs and tried to steady myself on my feet.

"Hey, where're you going?" Theo asked.

A rush of heat rippled through my body as I tried to think of something to say. "I didn't want to crush your legs." *A slow clap for Sunny. Nice job.*

Fauxhawk said, "You need to look at the sign, ma'am."

Oh my God, why was this kid calling me "ma'am"? He pointed toward the driver. The sign pinned to the bale of hay at the very front: PLEASE STAY SEATED AT ALL TIMES.

Theo coughed. "Yeah, he's right, *ma'am*. You need to find a seat."

The truck hit a pothole, and for the second time, I lost my balance. And again, Theo pulled me in like a yo-yo, and I fell back into his lap. A softer landing this time. He whispered into my ear, "Is it okay if I keep you steady? I don't want you falling out."

I whispered back, "Or crashing into any of these kids. It would be a lawsuit waiting to happen."

His warm breath near my neck made my stomach flip and my

hands turn clammy. Amazing how I could go from uncomfortably hot to cold so quickly.

Scared I'd say something like "I hope I'm not crushing your legs" again, I simply nodded. Theo held his arms out like he was a comfy reading chair, and I placed my arms on his and leaned back into him.

"Shoot," he whispered.

"What?"

"We're basically here."

I was so fixated on Theo's skin touching mine and his deep, rhythmic breathing that I hadn't even noticed our surroundings. He was right: we were only about twenty yards from my cabin.

The hayride train climbed up the hill and slowed to a stop. I stood up cautiously, not wanting to leave my comfy position of course, and Theo rose to his feet too. Raul unlatched the back gate of the flatbed, and Theo jumped out first, landing on his feet like a cat. He held out his hand to assist, which I gladly accepted.

"Thanks, Farmer Raul," we both said in unison.

Raul tipped his straw hat and climbed back into his truck. He said to Theo out the window, "You look happy," and turned to me. "I've worked on this farm for over twenty years, since before this guy was born. He was a very unhappy baby."

Theo rolled his eyes and patted the side of the truck twice. "Thanks again for the drop-off."

The kids all waved and shouted, "Goodbye!" to us as their

hayride train rumbled away. They were still yelling and flapping their hands and arms at us as they disappeared over the horizon.

After sitting in someone's lap during a hayride, I thought it might lead to some sort of conversation about it. But it didn't. Silence fell between us as we marched to my cabin, not discussing what had happened. But maybe this wasn't a big deal for him. Was this something he'd done before?

Maybe nothing happened? The circumstances were so weird that maybe it was absolutely, completely meaningless and I was getting worked up over a little thing.

In conclusion: it was nothing.

Once we reached the door, he finally spoke. "Can you put on something not as hot really quickly, like super fast?"

I couldn't help myself. "You think this is hot?" Grabbing the skirt part of the dress with both hands, I swished the fabric back and forth like a can-can dancer.

Blushing hard, he said, "Oh, I—I didn't mean that. I meant temperature hot, not—"

"I'm kidding. Everyone knows this dress is pretty much the opposite of sexy. It's maybe, like, pilgrim-fetish hot, but not modern-day hot. So should I wear civilian clothes? Or do you have another ill-fitting, oxygen-depriving costume you need me to wear for this mysterious new activity?"

He barked out a laugh and shrugged at me but didn't answer the question.

"Not even a hint as to what I'll be doing? Can you at least tell me if I need outdoor clothes?"

"Civilian casual clothes are fine." He really wasn't giving me any info, was he? "Maybe you can wear something like I have on." My gaze traveled down his gray cotton shirt tight against his chest. Then over to his strapping arms. Back to his chest. Oh God.

Yeah, I didn't have clothes that fit me that well. Not like his did.

"Or if you have the camp shirt they gave you on the first day, you can wear that."

The first day seemed so long ago. It was hard to believe two weeks had passed. Two weeks of knowing Theo. I knew I was a Theo fan from the moment he'd entered registration with that armful of bottled water and expertly handled the argumentative landfill girl. Maybe there was something to this nonurban lifestyle, because it would hard to be #TeamTheo without also being at least partially #TeamCampSunshine. Was I warming up to all this...farm BS? Was I #TeamMotherClucker?

#CluckMe.

Oh no, Theo's weird farmer-ness had rubbed off on me.

Looking out the open window of the cabin, I could see him leaning against the post of a nearby wooden fence, his hands resting on top as he looked out at the empty field. He was staring out into open nothingness. No device to distract him but no singing or humming either. And he wasn't talking to himself or anything. Theo was one hundred percent okay with the quiet.

I turned my attention to why I was in my cabin in the first place. Peeling off the pioneer clothing was the greatest pleasure of my life. Liberation! Not only was I able to freely get oxygen in my lungs now, but my skin could breathe too. It was like kicking off a thick comforter on a warm night but better. At last! Freedom from corset captivity.

After throwing on a crumpled, clean camp shirt, camo utility shorts, and flip-flops, I met Theo, who was now dreamily staring up at the clouds by the fencepost.

"I'm ready! Let's go," I barked. It came out more authoritatively than I'd expected. I sounded just like my mom. Not exactly someone's shoes I wanted to fill.

"Yes, ma'am!" Theo jolted upright and gestured with his head to follow him. He didn't seem phased by my snappiness. I felt a little bad, interrupting his daydreaming so abruptly.

With a softened tone to lessen my bark, I asked, "So tell me, do you love it here? Living on a farm?"

He stopped walking. "I get that question a lot. People can't believe we live here and have been able to sustain this place for so long. I usually answer yes, because that's what people want to hear."

I shoved my hands into my shorts pockets and pulled out a piece of lint. "And when you're not usually telling people exactly what they want to hear?"

He chewed his bottom lip. "It's not an easy answer."

His response surprised me. I was in the "Theo loves the farm camp!" camp.

He looked down and kicked at an embedded rock, loosening it. "Most of the kids I know have families who are farmers, but they're the new kind of farmers. Around here, they're buying up land for commercial agriculture that is heavily mechanized and automated. Did you know the average size of a farm is four hundred and thirty-five acres? We're maybe an eighth of that. Nowadays, farming is more about robots and spreadsheets than getting your hands dirty. And they specialize, like they only have one or two field crops. Some only have pigs. Our farm, in terms of size, is hardly a farm at all compared to everyone else around us. We diversify by doing a little bit of everything in an old-timey, sowing-and-hoeing way, which I like because you don't see it anymore around here. We're not a farm that makes money from harvesting. At least not anymore. The bulk of our revenue is from group tours and summer camps."

Theo revealed an awful lot, but he didn't answer my question. "So do you like it here or wish you lived somewhere else?"

For a brief moment, I tried to visualize him living in LA, going to school with me at Westminster Prep. He was smart and attractive and made me laugh with his weird farm sayings, and no doubt he'd be one of the guys everyone liked. Sure, he spouted off obscure nerdy facts no one else could possibly know, but this was so cute. But the more I tried to envision him outside his life at Sunshine, I couldn't fully picture it. He didn't belong there. Just like I didn't belong here.

"I like it, but this is the only life I know. I've never been on a plane or seen the ocean. I think I'd like to someday." He sighed. "But there's so much to do here. I'd love to modernize some parts of the farm and change Sunshine's business model so it's more profitable by reaching out to more farm-to-table restaurants and going to more farmers' markets."

With a few swift kicks of his feet, stones rolled down the path ahead of us. "We're sort of barely squeaking by, to be honest. For so long, we had all our eggs in one basket. Sorry, another farm reference." He smiled briefly. "The camp business was down because not as many churches were coming here in the summer, as you probably heard, and tours and visits are much lower year over year." He resumed walking at a much more leisurely pace. Good for walking and talking without huffing and panting.

Never in a million years would I have thought I'd be talking about the state of the small farm industry. My question was meant to be a conversation starter. Something that could make things easy between us again to get back to the fun of maybe getting a third time on his lap. But this was spiraling into an unforeseen territory and not necessarily a bad one. It was eye-opening.

I ran ahead and kicked one of the rocks hard, knocking it off the dirt trail altogether. "I'll be honest, I thought until a nanosecond ago that you all have a pretty simple life here. With everything you said, I can see how running this place would be hard. You have crops and animals and groundskeeping and personnel on payroll. Plus daily programming and meal planning with annoying dietary restrictions. Us digital detoxers have got to be more of a pain than the Bible folks, right?"

He scoffed. "Honestly? You'd be surprised. Some of the kids who came to church camp in previous summers were pretty wild. Or they went hog wild once they came. There've been major issues with kids breaking curfew and sneaking off the premises and illicit drug use. There are stashes of it everywhere here, I'm sure of it. You detox campers are different in some ways but surprisingly the same in others. And each year, there's always a troublemaker."

I didn't want to break it to him that I had an illegal phone in my possession in the special zipper pocket in my shorts.

We'd been talking about depressing stuff for a while. I didn't mind a good non-jokey conversation, but we were far from the upbeat mood on the hayride. Time to lighten things a bit. "So what's the activity? Can you tell me now or at least give me some kind of clue?"

He slowed to a halt. His lips twisted into a smile, and he cocked his head playfully. "Well, you'll never guess, so I'll tell you. You remember when there was a nationwide toilet paper shortage?"

How could I forget? It was all my friends messaged about and was always on the news. Rolls of toilet paper were selling on eBay for up to seventy dollars a pack, and Amazon wasn't even shipping it because there was none in stock. Amazon greedily shipped anything and everything, even Japanese matcha Kit Kats and candy canes and neon-yellow marshmallow Peeps year-round, so it was hard to imagine an Amazon without TP.

He continued, "Well, we're taking the corn cobs we used for dinner last night to the fallow field to dry in the sun."

"Corn cobs? For what?"

"It's what they used long ago before toilet paper was invented," he said in a matter-of-fact tone.

My eyes widened. "Corn? Cobs? Really? Are you selling them as, like, a farm export? Or are you using them here at the camp?" Well...crap. Literally. I was off to make crap-wiping tools with Theo. Things had taken a dark turn since the hayride.

He looked straight into my eyes but quickly looked away. "I had you going, didn't I? You thought I was serious?" He coughed with laughter as I slapped him hard on his arm. And again a second time. I went for swat number three, but he jerked away and laughed as he ran ahead of me on the path.

There was no way to play this off like I was too cool or smart to fall for his corn cob charade. I believed we were making corn-cob butt wipers. Theo exuded niceness and thoughtfulness, and I never once pictured him as the kind of guy who would lie about making poop-wiping products with a straight face. He'd earned some major points.

I shouted at him, "Okay, I admit I fell for it. What are we *really* going to do?"

He slowed down and waited for me to catch up with him and held out his arm—elbow out—for me to grab. When I did, he looked at me and smiled. Tingles shot down my arm and throughout every part of my body. He had a hypnotic hold over me. Was it possible this camp experience could be the absolute worst *and* best thing to happen to me? I wanted to hold his arm forever.

Theo escorted me to an area with tall, white fencing. A crooked sign on the gate read, SUNSHINE FARMS FAMILY ZONE in what could best be described as brightly colored "kid font." The door creaked with Theo's light push. He put his hand on my back, sending a current of warmth down my spine. Theo and I were back in sync again, just as we arrived.

He nudged me through. "Your destiny awaits."

SEVENTEEN

A HUM OF LIVELY CHATTER EBBED AND FLOWED, BUT I couldn't make out what people were saying. Ahead, a group of ten elderly people yapped while standing around a pen of small farm animals. In unison, they all yelled, "Theo!" as we approached.

My handsome escort grinned and waved. "Good morning, Mrs. Davis. Mrs. Raymond, you're looking well. Glad to see you back, Mr. Fuller." Amazing. He knew everyone by name, and they were so utterly charmed by his presence. It was hard not to be.

I cleared my throat, and Theo's grin spread even wider across his face. "Well, class, you're in for a treat. Last week, we had a session on scrapbooking, but today we're gearing up to launch our first petting zoo. Eventually, this might turn into a mobile petting experience or something that's trending hot right now, like goat yoga. You're our guinea pigs, lucky you! Henry's out sick today, but the very capable, animal-loving Sunny Song will be joining us to assist!"

"I'll help with everything except goat yoga. Or with horses. I refuse," I joked.

The old man asked, "Goat yoga is a load of bull. Will there really be horses? I'm allergic to horses. And I hate them."

A man after my own heart.

Theo replied, "Mr. Fuller, if you follow me inside the pen, you can pet the miniature horses, mini pigs, llamas, and goats. No full-size horses."

Mr. Fuller crossed his arms. "Aren't mini pigs just piglets?"

Yeah, wasn't that what *Charlotte's Web* was all about?

Theo replied, "They're full-size Vietnamese potbellied pigs, but they're much smaller than the large Tamworth hogs we have here. Any other questions?" He unlatched the small wooden gate, and it creaked as he let us through the pen. It smelled like hay and horses. Yuck.

"My helper will pass out bags of diced apples and dietary-appropriate feed. Feel free to walk around and feed the animals. They're used to being around the staff." He motioned his head toward a cart a few feet away.

I brought the cart over and passed out the meals on wheels. There were baby bottles too, so I asked, "Oh! Can we feed them milk too?"

"Only the goats. The little ones." He smiled and turned to the larger group. "Petting zoos are good for your well-being. Animals can increase the stress-reducing hormone oxytocin. They can also decrease levels of the stress-inducing hormone cortisol. If you're feeling anxious or depressed, our animals can help with this."

From a distance, a goat bleated. One of the women muttered, "They're probably nicer and less stressful than my grandsons. They're all hooligans!"

Theo pointed behind him. "Feel free to feed and pet the animals. And most importantly, have fun!" Everyone scattered to search for their preferred animals, and I took off ahead of the pack, bottle in hand, desperate to find a baby goat.

When I couldn't find one, I assisted a woman by feeding an alpaca while she stroked his side.

A tap on my shoulder startled me. It was Theo, carrying a black baby goat under his arm like it was an oversize football. He placed the animal by my feet. "Be firm but gentle when you feed her a bottle. She likes head butting, so watch out for that."

She was adorable! "What's her name?"

He laughed. "We called her Kid as a joke, and it stuck. So that's her name."

In a baby voice, I asked, "Are you weady for a wittle bottle, Kid?"

The goat replied, "Meh."

"Well, you're getting one anyway!" I tipped the bottle, and the baby goat took to it right away.

The woman I helped with the alpaca said, "Oh, that's so sweet! I'm going to take a photo. Stay just like that. One. Twoooooo. Three! Cheese! Perfect." She looked at her phone screen and tapped a few times. "Huh. I can't send the photo to my grandniece."

I asked, "Is your grandniece into goats?"

Her brow furrowed as she tapped her screen. "No, she takes the photos I send her and uploads them to my Facebook account."

Theo and I exchanged looks. Before I could, he asked, "You don't post directly? You need your niece to do it?"

She nodded as Mr. Fuller walked over. "I ate the apple pieces in my bag. Do you have any more food for this pig? He keeps following me around." He gestured with this thumb over his shoulder. Sure enough, a waddling pig headed our way. "And I'm like Ms. Johnson. I need my teenage grand-people to help me with all technical stuff. We didn't have that garbage when we were young. We stayed outside all day and only came home when it got dark. We sent each other photos in the mail sometimes." He whistled. "They were expensive!"

I asked Ms. Johnson, "Do you have social media apps on your phone?"

She passed me the phone. While Theo refilled some milk bottles, I figured out an easy way for her to post herself. But the reason her photo didn't go through was a problem I knew all too well. No signal.

I showed her step-by-step how to pull her photo off her camera roll, add some filters, and post it on Instagram, which had an option to post to Facebook too. It didn't occur to me that this was something I shouldn't do until I'd already finished my tutorial.

"Thank you! Theo, this girl's a tech whiz. We should have her help us!"

My cheeks warmed. "Sorry, Theo, I forgot I wasn't supposed to use any technology. I was just trying to help."

Mr. Fuller looked at Theo. "Screw the animals. I want to learn about photo and video editing. Selfies. Hash browns too. My grandson is always talking about hash browns. I need some hands-on training so I don't look like an ass in front of my grandkids. I can have Maggie ask your mom, Theo. Mags is working on some talent show nonsense and couldn't come today."

Theo scratched his chin. "So you all want digital training or tutoring?"

All the elders nodded.

His face scrunched in deep thought. "I'll run this by my mom. At the farm, we try to promote other kinds of learning, hands-on activities, away from screens. But we also have a special relationship with you all at Sunshine Retirement and want to encourage well-being and happiness and foster community." He offered me a lopsided grin. "Coach will have to sanction this too. To make sure it's okay for you to be around tech after only being here for a couple of weeks. And I'd love to assist you if this gets approved."

I smiled back and nodded. While I helped baby goat Kid finish her bottle, I thought about how I'd always been so focused on how I could use technology to help me and my platform that I never thought about how I could use it to help other people. Maybe there was a purpose to this camp after all.

The baby goat looked at me with a satisfied half smirk. "Blehhhhh!"

I looked down and laughed. *Yeah, Kid, that's how I usually feel, but today feels a whole lot better.*

EIGHTEEN

ON MY WAY BACK FROM THE PETTING ZOO, I STOPPED BY the commissary to get a drink and on my way out bumped into Theo's brother, Henry.

"Hey, I've been paging you on the intercom. Didn't you hear it?"

I flashed him as charming a smile as I could muster. Charming wasn't exactly my thing though. "I didn't. I'm sorry. I was busy." *Busy working with the elderly since you backed out, being "sick" and all, thank you very much.*

His scowl stayed put on his chiseled, handsome face. "You have an emergency. We've been trying to find you!"

My stomach lurched. "Wait, what? What do you mean?"

He motioned for me to follow him to the office. We walked at a brisk pace at first then broke into a jog. I tried to gauge the severity of the situation by his speed. Surely, if this was a super-emergency, we'd be running to the point of puking.

Henry shouted over his shoulder, "I don't know much. The call just came through." He held open the rickety wooden door with two hands while I passed under his arms, London Bridge-style. Wow, he was tall. A lot taller than Theo. Broader shouldered than Theo too.

I tried to read his face. "Is it my sister? She sent me an SOS-type message in my last care package." Panic swept through me as I considered other possibilities. Mom? Dad? Who? It had to be Chloe.

Maybe my parents kicked her out of the house. But this didn't seem possible, because she was still Mom's favorite. If anything, they'd send her here, for me to keep an eye on her as added punishment for me.

I could see that.

Could this be Chloe with an exaggerated makeup or fashion emergency? I could see that too.

Maybe the note I got from her wasn't a note, it was some kind of cryptic ransom letter I'd completely misinterpreted because I was too distracted by the snacks. I could also see this happening too, sadly. And I'd thrown it away. Shoot.

Theo held the phone handset on his ear while he wrote on a pad of paper. His somber face brightened a little when I saw him and fell again immediately as he spoke, covering the speaker. "I'm on the phone with your grandma. Honestly, it's been hard to hear her. She wanted to speak with you directly."

My body stiffened with this news. "My halmoni?" She was in Seoul…how the hell did she get my number at Camp Sunshine? It made zero sense at all. My mom and dad would call on her behalf if there was any family news.

"Hold on one second. She's here now. I'll let you speak with her." His voice wavered as he handed me the phone. Worry filled his eyes as I held the phone to my ear.

"Halmoni?" My voice sounded small, like a five-year-old child's.

At first, there was silence, which I thought had something to do with the long distance. I repeated, louder this time, "Halmoni?"

More silence. "Hello? Yeoboseyo?" Here I was, self-consciously speaking broken Korean, and it was so bad, my own family couldn't even understand me and respond.

"Sunny?" A voice crackled. "I'm sorry. It's Maya. I used Google translate to speak Korean to whoever answered the phone. God, I feel like an idiot. But don't freak out. I'm sorry I scared you. But I have big news!"

Don't freak out? She was asking for something impossible, like "don't blink when I blow into your eyes." What. The. Hell.

"Is there anywhere you can go to talk alone?" She was whispering, but her excitement was palpable. Henry and Theo pretended to work on their computers, clicking things occasionally, but were obviously eavesdropping. And the cord on the phone was overstretched but couldn't make it to the hallway.

I said simply, "No."

"Okay. I'll be fast! And quiet. Starhouse was promoting a LOT of your content the last twenty-four hours. They just shared on social media today that they picked their final two contestants, and you're one of them! I think you have a real chance at this! Did you get my package? The signal booster?"

The entire time she spoke, a scream pushed to escape from deep inside my lungs, like I was on a roller coaster rising and plunging: the adrenaline, excitement, danger of this news had me on the brink of exploding with tension. HOOOOOOLY SHI—STARHOUSE. But to pull this off in front of Theo and his brother, I had to remain calm. "Thank you for asking. I haven't had a chance to use it—"

She cut me off. "You need to set it up ASAP, and you really need to find Wi-Fi, because the Starhouse team is going to give you a specific assignment for this last round. They're supposed to send it in a few days, and you need a good connection to upload videos. Otherwise, you'll be waiting forever on LTE for stuff to upload and download, and there's still no guarantee it'll go through. The other finalist has more followers than you, but you have a lot more engagement with comments and discussion. She's big into sports, and she's super intense, so she's an interesting choice. WowWendy—she's from the East Coast. Sunny Song is smart and scrappy. You can take her!"

Brain. Broken. "I understand, Halmoni. Thank you for letting me know."

"Okay, I'll let you go so you don't get in trouble. Congratulations, chica! Text me as soon as you get connected, okay?"

Click.

I kept the receiver to my ear long after she hung up on me, my hands shaking from the overwhelming update. Could I pull this off? What if I got caught and this whole thing came tumbling down like a house of cards?

Going along with this grandma emergency ruse, at least for now, was plausible, but I needed a good cover story. Especially since I didn't burst into tears. My cheeks strained to fight an eager smile, but I had to keep cool. I was on the phone way too long to feign confusion and say, "Wrong number, who dis?"

Putting the receiver down, I tried to keep a poker face. I'd never played poker, so I didn't even know if I was doing that right.

"Everything okay?" Theo asked softly. His green eyes were hypnotic and made me want to fess up on the spot.

"I—" That was all I could get out. The crease between his brows and his downturned mouth made me feel terrible. Whatever else came out of my mouth would send me in a liar trajectory.

"Looks like you need a Henry hug." Before I could react, Theo's brother enveloped me with his muscular arms, and boy, did he look and smell good. But I wished it were Theo.

It was hard to peer over Henry's biceps, but when I did, Theo rolled his eyes.

"Uh, thanks." I pulled myself from Henry's firm hold and took a small step back. It was wrong to accept his consolation hug, not when I had my secret. A FAKE granny had called from somewhere *not* in Korea to alert me of a FAKE emergency. And if that weren't shady enough, this whole thing involved hiding illegal imports and taking part in a high-profile social media competition while at a digital detox camp.

The scent of Henry's freshly laundered shirt hung around me. "If you need another hug, hit me up. Anytime." Henry flashed a smile at me. With a flirty wink, he sauntered out the door. He was the most insanely hot guy I'd ever seen in real life, and it was flattering for him to offer me his muscular cuddles, but he wasn't my type. He was too perfect.

With him gone, that left Theo and me alone.

"Henry, always the hero," Theo muttered. He asked, "Do you need to leave the camp? I—I hope not."

I let out a fake sad sigh. "Oh, she just wanted to keep me apprised on things." It was sort of true. "My grandpa's health isn't great." True. "There is a situation, but she thinks everything will work out just fine." Also kind of true. I didn't need to tell him the situation at hand was a contraband phone hidden in a glasses case lodged in my cargo pocket, to be used to record content for Starhouse.

Relief flashed on Theo's face. "Oh good. I'm glad you'll be staying!"

Well, as long as I don't get kicked out. "I bet you'd say that to all the campers here," I teased.

He stood up from his chair and walked over to me. He wasn't as tall as his brother, but he was the perfect height in my mind. Tall enough to put his hands on my shoulders in a non-awkward way. Short enough to stand on my tippy-toes and kiss. You know, if I had to for some reason.

His arms and chest looked like they'd be perfect for hugs.

We stood in silence. Each of us waiting for someone to make some kind of move. He smelled like fresh laundry too, like Henry. But not like bleachy detergent, more like a mix of spring rain and fresh-out-of-the-dryer clothes that were comfortable and broken in. A relaxed, cozy smell. A Theo smell.

The ringing phone cut through the tension but also scared me to the point of my heart nearly stopping. For a second, I thought it might be the phone in my pocket, the one I thought I'd turned off. He hopped on the desk and leaned on it to grab the receiver. "Sunshine Heritage Farms, how may I help you?"

My heart throbbed louder and harder. Was it fake Halmoni again? After a few seconds, his face went a little sour, like he smelled mildew somewhere but couldn't place the location. "Camper phone usage is restricted to emergencies only. If it's not urgent, we encourage correspondence by mail."

He paused and hung up. "Well, you're in demand today. That was someone named Rafael Kim. He said he's been hoping to hear from you. You might want to reiterate the camp rules in your next postcard."

Rafa.

I forgot all about him.

Lifting himself off the desk, Theo headed to the door and opened it for me. "Have a good night, Sunny," and waited for me to pass through. As soon as I did, he let the door slam behind me.

NINETEEN

THE NEXT EVENING, AS THE LAST SESSIONS AND ACTIVI-
ties ended for the day, campers streamed out in droves from all
the buildings like during dismissal time at Westminster Prep.
The chargrilled smell of hot dogs and hamburgers wafted toward
me, making me salivate, beckoning me to follow it.

But I went in the opposite direction from the mess hall,
toward the barn. The gravel path kicked up dust as I walked,
covering my toes and flip-flops in a light-gray grime.

Time to look for a signal again. I needed to set up the booster
so I could find out what the finalist video submission would be.

Once I was near the barn and hidden from view from the
camp's main area, I turned on the phone and held it at nose
height, slowly turning in a circle. It switched from one bar of
LTE to 3G and flipped back and forth between the two rapidly,
like it was possessed by poltergeist phone demons. I needed the

connection to stay steady, or I wouldn't be able to get the booster properly installed.

After a moment, I got one text. "This is Rupert from the Starhouse talent search. Please reply C to confirm receipt."

Before the bars completely disappeared, replaced by no-service dots, I smashed C and return.

"Thank you! We will be in touch shortly with your final assignment. From all of us at Starhouse, congratulations!"

I couldn't help but smile. Being in the Starhouse collective would be a dream come true. After all these years, after so many posts and videos and all the hard work to get new followers every day, if this could happen—it would be life-changing. All the collaboration prospects. The sponsorships. The fame. I'd finally be somebody bigger than Goggle Girl.

My stomach twisted with guilt though. Even having the phone was a slap in the face of everyone here. Especially Theo. There was no mistaking that electricity flowing between us on the hayride, the sense of connection we had as I sat on his lap, tuning everything out except for him. My heart thumped hard at the mere thought of him. Of us, together.

Was all this worth disappointing Theo? Or getting kicked out of camp and school? Expulsion. Dad wouldn't speak to me again. But that wouldn't last long, because Mom would kill me. On second thought, maybe this consequence wasn't worth all this. Maybe it was time to scrap the phone and head back to the cabin.

Excited chatter nearby made the hairs on my forearms stand at attention. I fell to a crouch behind a tractor-like machine, making my knees pop so loudly, they could pass for firecrackers or an accidental gunshot or two. By some wild luck, a lone cow in one of the barn stalls let out a short *moo?* at the same time, covering up my noise.

"You think you dropped it here? Are you sure?" Fifty feet away, two of the male camp counselors in their emerald-green polo shirts paced back and forth, examining the ground.

"Yes, I was here right before I noticed it was missing, when I reached into my back pocket for my bandanna. It must have fallen out. Ugh, that's like a week's salary."

In the distance, the sound of chimes echoed across the field. "Shoot, it's already dinner time? We can come back later to look. Maybe tomorrow if it gets too dark."

"Later?"

"It not like farm animals are going to find it."

The duo took off in a hurry, leaving me alone to continue hunting for a steady signal. But given what I'd witnessed, how could I not snoop around to see what one of them might have left by the barn?

I tried to do both: look for signal while searching for a mysterious treasure. On the shady side of the barn, there was a whole area covered with brown grass and cracked dirt, littered with all the signs of being populated recently. Hidden behind some gardening tools were cigarette butts, empty beer bottles, Slim Jim wrappers, and a bong. It was the epitome of anti-farm life, but none of it looked like it could be the counselors' scavenger hunt item.

After roaming zigzag over the wide field of weeds, I was able to get a fleeting bar of signal. Sometimes even two bars in small blips every few seconds. It made sense this area was a hangout spot of the staff at Sunshine—it really was the only place on the entire premises with any cell service. And a spotty one at that.

I combed the area for something not easy to spot with the naked eye. Like a watch. Or a class ring. Maybe a box of unused condoms? After milling around fifty square feet of gravel, dirt, and grass, I didn't see anything valuable—only an old vaping pen, a few bent bottle caps, and worn pennies.

A twig snapped behind me. I bristled, and all my muscles clenched tight. This wasn't a gang of chickens sneaking around—I would have heard them coming from a mile away, they were such noisy little jerks. The fact that it was still light outside gave me a false sense of security. I'd been careful about no one seeing me come here, but why hadn't I considered the danger of coming here alone, without anyone knowing where I was? Stopping in my tracks, a terrifying thought entered my mind. Here I was, a teenage girl behind a dilapidated barn in dire need of a remodel, with no security cameras anywhere. This had "Netflix murder mystery" written all over it.

God, I was an idiot.

"You looking for this?" The familiar female voice behind me sent my nerves screaming. I whipped my head around so fast, I almost gave myself whiplash. Side Braid dangled a ziplock bag of pills from her thumb and index fingers. "Well, well, well. Look what I found by the tractor."

Wasn't I just at that dumb tractor? So much for my twenty-twenty vision.

I groaned. "They're not mine."

"Riiiight. If they're not yours, whose are they? This is pretty good shit, by the way. You've got good connections."

I shrugged. "I've never seen those pills before." My hands grew clammy. Beads of sweat threatened to push to the surface of my forehead. Given that I was truly innocent, why was I such a sweaty, nervous mess?

Maybe it was because Side Braid wanted to end me.

And maybe it was because I had a phone in my hand that she hadn't noticed yet.

"Good try, LA. If you don't know whose it is, why the hell were you looking for them?"

Before I could say something, anything, she walked right up to me and pulled the phone right out of my hand.

OH NO.

"Drugs *and* a phone? This is my lucky day! I can't *wait* to get you kicked out of here!" Her eyes lit up with excitement as her lips curled into a smile, like she had just played an arcade bear claw game and it had accidentally dropped two prizes into the retrieval door.

Think fast, think fast.

Faster, please.

Dang it, Sunny.

I said the first thing to pop into my head. "Who's to say those are mine? It's not like my name is on any of it. They could have just as easily been yours. And you're the one holding *all* the illegal stuff right now. Drugs plus a phone can get you in much bigger trouble." I held my stare. Who would the administration believe? Maybe me, because she was such a horrendous human. Or maybe her, because I still didn't know who she was, only that she was Wendy from New Jersey. For all I knew, she was a VIP.

"Your fingerprints are on this stuff too," she snapped back.

"Not on the drugs."

Blood drained from her face. "If you turn me in...I'll say you sold this to me."

I channeled my ruthless lawyer mom who always seemed to settle out of court. "Look, let's take a step back here." I'd always heard her say it on her morning conference calls, and it sounded businesslike and perfect for this moment. Would she be pleased I used it in the correct context? "We can both come out of this unscathed. Give me the phone, and you can take the drugs or leave them, I don't care. But we can call a truce and both walk away from this and pretend none of it happened." Okay, so this wasn't exactly channeling my ruthless defender-of-justice mom—I was acting more like a shady, corrupt politician having a secret meeting in a creepy, deserted location.

A few seconds passed, and I was sure she would say, "Screw it!" and risk the consequences. She looked down at my phone, and her eyes bulged.

The congrats message from Starhouse was still up on my lock screen.

"Wait, you're the other finalist?" She shook her head. "But your Goggle Girl account is so embarrassing. How's this even possible? Is this a joke?"

My stomach fell to the ground. Side Braid was WowWendy?

She rolled her eyes. "Well, that's just perfect. Me versus Goggle Girl." Her eyes narrowed. "Now excuse me as I toss this phone into the lake."

I blocked her with my arm. "Give it back. Or I'll tell Theo's mom that you had a phone."

She laughed. "You idiot. I'll tell her the same about you."

"But you'll have a phone on you, and I won't. Plus, I'm sure you have your own phone on you or hidden in the cabin somewhere. Who would they believe? Plus, you have a bag of drugs, remember? With your prints on them? That pretty much means you'll get kicked out and get jail time. For me, all I'll be is a snitch."

She shoved the phone at my chest. Hard, right in the B cups. Could boobs bruise? "Fine. I'll keep the bag. You keep your phone. I can play fair because this isn't even a contest. I'm going to win because *Goggle Girl* is an embarrassment to the internet, and I have more followers than you'd even know what to do with. If you *try* to turn me in, by the way, you'll go down too. Whether it's here or online. So stay the hell away from me, and get out of my face."

There was one thing I knew for sure. There was no way I was going to put the booster and antennas up knowing she would benefit too. If Theo was right and there was a dude ranch on the other side of the lake, the guest Wi-Fi would be my holy grail.

Side Braid, a.k.a. Wendy, turned on her heel and walked back to the main campground, the bag of pills hanging by her side. Then she stuffed her collection of drugs into the top elastic of her pants. But not before I was able to snap a few photos.

Gotcha.

TWENTY

ON THE DAY I WAS HELPING THE SUNSHINE RETIREMENT folks with digital tutoring, Coach escorted me to the session and dropped me off at a rustic building with cedarwood walls. The brown wooden sign staked in the ground read COMMUNITY ROOM.

"You'll do great in there, friend. You've been here two and a half weeks, and you're making wonderful progress since our first meeting. It'll be good for you." Coach had approved this activity, and part of the agreement was that he basically acted like a prison warden, escorting me to the dangerous room filled with cell phones, tablets, and laptops. After the session, Theo would clear me for dismissal.

"I'm surprised you allowed this," I told him. "I thought the point of this camp was to distance ourselves from technology."

He cracked a smile. "For some people, yes, that's what they need. For you, though, I have a good feeling about this activity.

But if you feel uncomfortable, I'm just down the path, and you can come find me. Have fun."

Coach turned and waved as he walked away. Taking a deep breath, I opened the door. The whoosh of the air conditioner was a welcome comfort after spending most of the morning outdoors, with oppressive heat and humidity hanging all around me. Instantly, my mood lifted, and I gave in to the strong gravitational pull of the nearest AC wall units.

Theo stood in front of the class and nodded at me as I entered. "Perfect timing, I know you can hardly contain your excitement! Today, by popular demand, Sunny's back and is going to teach you all the basics on how to download social media apps on your phone, mainly Facebook and Instagram, how to upload selfies and short videos, and answer any questions you have about posting, commenting, or connecting with friends and family."

"Wait, you can get internet access in here?" My heart skipped. My connectivity problems were solved!

Theo smiled. "Yes, but it's limited use only. We turn on this guest Wi-Fi only for classes like this. This used to be our office building."

Damn. But...maybe I can sneak a peek at my phone on a break.

He said to the group, "This activity is two sessions only. Next time you come back to Sunshine will be the last day of the program, which coincides with one of the last days of Sunny's camp. Please come prepared with a specific digital project, and

Sunny will help you with it. Something like 'putting together an online album' or 'sharing pictures on Google Drive' or 'adding cat ears and whiskers to my profile pic.' Today is more of a meet and greet, plus a technology assessment, and basic social media training. We can do a quick Q&A and troubleshooting. In the final class, we'll jump into the real action."

Someone muttered, "Why do kids these days want to look like other mammals in photos?"

Old Man Fuller said, "My grandson keeps talking about Tic-Tac videos. He says he wants me to like his Tic-Tacs. I told him I only like the wintergreen flavor, and he laughed at me but wouldn't buy them for me. Is this something you can help me with?"

Was it okay to laugh? Everyone in this class was so adorably cute and clueless. And I desperately wanted this grandpa to post TikTok videos by the end of next session. It was a must.

A woman who didn't bother to raise her hand interjected, "I already have these apps set up. The problem I have is all my friends have disappeared."

"Disappeared? What do you mean?" Theo asked.

"Disappeared, as in I had friends, a lot of them in fact, and now they've all been deleted."

Theo furrowed his brow and jerkily nodded his head toward her, my signal to help. I held out my hand. "May I see your phone?"

She lifted her chin and sat up straighter in her chair, giving her an air of snootiness. "I'm sure you've heard the saying, 'You see with your eyes and not with your hands,' dear?" While she fished her device out of her Coach clutch, I shot a look at Theo—one that read, *Please fetch my sweaty pilgrim costume. I'd rather be the historically inaccurate Korean pioneer back at the welcome station than put up with this BS.*

His mouth twitched into a smirk. He walked around the room and jotted down the make and model of a resident's flip phone, which I honestly didn't even know they made anymore. Someone else handed him a Blackberry. It had a full keyboard, and some of the print on the keys had been worn off from excessive use. While Theo had his back to me, I walked to the water fountain and connected my phone to the Wi-Fi but didn't have a chance to look at the screen.

When I rejoined the group, the "see with your eyes" woman fished an iPhone from her purse. "I also have an iPad in here."

She had the latest and greatest everything, devices that had been released the week before I arrived at camp. And her phone case was custom engraved with a metallic monogram. She chattered while I swiped through her screens. "It's hard to believe, but I have no idea how to use my phone at all. My family keeps buying me the newest technology, but honestly, all I want is a phone I can use to call someone, text my daughters and grandchildren, and remind myself to take my diabetes medication. That's it."

Others nodded in agreement. I suppose they were right. Most apps these days were overly complicated for the average user.

I clicked on her Facebook app and saw she only had two friends. A deluge of excitement hit me hard from clicking around. How many days had it been since I'd used social media? Was this rapid reacclimating to social media after weaning off digital devices...safe? Coach had assured me it would be fine. I chewed my bottom lip, contemplating checking my accounts and looking up my stats and likes and follows and subscribes and comments and shares...but with all these people staring at me, Theo included, there was no way that was possible.

Tap. Tap. Tap on the phone.

I took her iPad.

Tap. Tap. Tap.

With minimal exploration, I discovered what her problem was. "So...it looks like you opened multiple accounts. And all of them have different profile photos."

She furrowed her brow and grabbed the phone from my hand. "Are you sure?"

"Yep, I'm sure." *No eye rolling, Sunny.* "And you have different accounts on each device. Four in total. Margaret Davenport. Margie Davenport. Maggie Davenport. And Call Me Mags."

One of the women in the group with silvery-blue hair cracked up laughing. "So she has three too many! Maybe she has these fake ones for catfishing people!" She took off her glasses to wipe tears from her eyes.

How did this woman even know what catfishing was? One of the profile photos was a little more sexified than the others, with her hair windblown, wearing sunglasses and making a pouty face at the camera. Maybe there was some truth to the catfishing theory.

I found the account with the highest number of people, sixty family and friends, and reset her password. And with her permission, I deactivated the others. Within seconds, she was reunited with her loved ones on one account.

She posted, "I'm back, baby!" and added a GIF of a partying toddler.

"If you want, I can permanently delete the duplicate ones. Don't forget I also changed your password for your protection. It's to help make sure you weren't hacked, which you could have been."

Her eyes widened. "Hacked? Do you think you can find out who did it if I was?"

Um, no? "I'm not tech savvy in that way." I glanced over at Theo, who still had a look of amusement on his face. "That's a level of complication I'm not equipped to handle, I'm sorry. It's way above my pay grade. But this other stuff is easy, like deleting things and changing passwords. It's not rocket surgery."

Theo coughed out a laugh. "It definitely not rocket surgery."

Margaret-Margie-Maggie-Call-Me-Mags Davenport sat quietly,

clicking and liking all the recent posts she had missed. She laughed and squealed. "This is a miracle. What's your name again? I'd love to give you a tip." She rummaged in her purse. "I might've left my wallet in my room."

The woman with silvery-blue hair said, "Kids don't use bills or coins. Or PayPal. That's for old people! They're all cashless these days." She was the wisest, coolest silvery-blue-haired lady I'd ever met.

"I'm not allowed to take tips of any kind. But maybe you can subscribe to my YouTube channel."

Ms. Davenport peered up from her reading glasses. "You have a YouTube channel? That's surprising."

She sounded genuinely surprised. Her mouth had even formed a perfect O. I mean, she could have at least tried to play it off like she wasn't *that* shocked.

"Surprising? What do you mean?"

Her face and shoulders relaxed into nonchalance. "Video creators are a bunch of dropouts. It's not even a professional setup usually. It's just people making videos from their bedroom or living room." She smoothed her hair with both hands. "What kind of talent is that, making videos on a web camera or a phone? What kind of career do you have after five years? Or ten? YouTubers are all young, like you—but it's the most ageist place to be, and from me, that says something. I used to work in news broadcasting before I had children," she huffed.

Was it a possibility that my mom and dad planted this judgy woman here to do all their Korean parent nagging on their behalf? They'd raised those exact same issues about YouTubers—arguing with me in Korean and me disagreeing in English—in a holler-until-hoarse means of getting our points across. They didn't understand, and neither did Ms. Davenport. A lot of the people in the video community were business savvy, and the most success-ful ones were hard workers. Plus, there was branding, monetiza-tion, and creativity involved. It's like when people say surfers are lazy bums. Who else gets geared up and out of the house at four in the morning to do something they love? Not people like Ms. Davenport.

I took a deep breath and spoke calmly. "Most of the YouTubers I know aren't dropouts. There are ones in high school like me who go to school all day and make videos in the evenings and weekends. Then there are ones who graduated, and some may never pursue degrees because they're making a good living in their teens or early twenties. Some do it just because they love it, some do it because it's their job and they have to, and nobody should knock that. These days, going to college seems like a scam, a waste of four years of time and money. It isn't a measure of professional success." She shook her head as I spoke, and searing heat flushed my face. Even with the AC on, it was, like, a million degrees in that room. "It's a racket. A degree factory that takes your savings, and for what? You get dozens of years in debt for a several-hundred-thousand-dollar piece of paper with an institution's name on it? They're not even handwritten—it's impersonal and printed on a laser printer."

Her jaw dropped. I looked over at Theo to back me up, but he was shaking his head at me too.

He was taking her side?

I pointed at him. "Okay, Agro Boy, say it. Go ahead and say what you're thinking."

He turned beet red. "I'd rather not."

"I'd rather you did." I crossed my arms and waited.

Silvery-blue hairdo lady stared at me, then glanced at him. Then looked back at me. "Oh, this is going to be good," she said, rubbing her hands.

"I—I—I'm just old-fashioned, I guess. I think everyone should go to college if they have the means. Society favors the more educated; you can't dispute this. So it's more prudent to get a college degree or even better, a master's or PhD. That's what I'm planning to do. Because I care about my future. To be practical, someone needs to bring home the bacon, as an agro boy might say. It's better than chasing likes for glitz and glamour and fame."

Did my parents plant him here too?

Ms. Davenport clapped. "My favorite young man, Mr. Theodore. Your parents brought you up well."

Fury rippled throughout my body, and I wanted to punch

something. "Okay, let's put things into perspective here." Both of their eyebrows flew up in surprise. The looks on their faces were priceless, but they were clearly shocked and scared by my outburst, so I backpedaled a little in tone. "With all due respect, ma'am, 'Call Me Mags,' you're here today to get on Facebook or Instagram so you can connect with others. But in addition to the multiple accounts you duplicated, all your old status updates were written in shouty all caps." I whirled around to Ms. Davenport's favorite young man. "And you, Theo, you're judging me for my vlogger lifestyle, a life which I only partially chose, but you live on a farm. And it's, like, ancient. You have a camp website that isn't even mobile friendly. Honestly, I could build a better website with Comic Sans font and clip art, completely blindfolded. And you don't even carry around a phone at all when, like, ninety-seven percent of the world has broadband access. There's your perspective."

The room was silent, and I couldn't help but fill it with even more commentary. "I'm not saying my life is better or my way of doing things is superior to yours, but you two are definitely *not* the ones who have authority to say what people should do with their lives or how they get ahead in this world. If anything, we're all in the exact same boat because we're stuck here together, at Camp Hellhole."

The silvery-hair lady clapped and gave me a standing ovation. "Did anyone record that? I want to see it again."

Theo raked his fingers through his hair. "Would it be okay to table this and just agree to disagree for now?"

For now? With Theo and me, we were so different, we'd need to agree to disagree for all of eternity.

Mr. Fuller cleared his throat and pointed at me. "I like her the best out of the three of you." Ms. Davenport scowled at him, which made me smile. He asked Theo, "I hate to change the subject since this is such a riveting conversation, but do you have any vending machines here, or are we stuck eating a bunch of farm-grown crud today? I want Fritos."

I couldn't help but laugh, and so did others in the room. What a way to cut the tension, with Fritos talk. I wanted nonfarm food so badly, too, and didn't realize it until he said something.

I looked over at Theo, but he refused to make eye contact. He scratched his brow and said, "Mr. Fuller, you know how this works. You ask the same thing every time you come here. Remember our candlemaking class? And the glassblowing workshop? Every time you're here, you ask about potato chips."

"*Corn* chips. And I figure if I ask every time I'm here, you might actually do something about it."

Theo cocked an eyebrow and scrunched his nose. "You all can eat and drink what you want at the assisted living home, but when you're dropped off here, you have to abide by our dining rules. We don't have vending machines, only free fresh fruit, and our gift shop that does carry some farm-themed snacks is only open an hour or two a day."

Mr. Fuller snorted. "The snacks you carry at the gift shop are garbage. You only had overpriced animal crackers last time I checked. Sometimes you carry turkey jerky, which is bull-crap healthy jerky. As bad as bull-crap turkey bacon. But that's it. At a minimum, you should carry good beef jerky for Christ's sake. You have cows here. I don't see any turkeys."

This was good information. Note to self: don't bother with gift shop snacks. Stick with the care package treats. I chimed in, "Campers are allowed care packages though. Mr. Fuller, if you send me a box of Fritos, I'll bring them to you in the next session."

He nodded and frowned at the same time. There was no pleasing this grump. "I might have to do that. Can't an old man have his Fritos? I'm eighty-one. I should be able to get any food I like. And how's a man my age supposed to remember to bring Fritos with me every week?"

Ms. Davenport scoffed. "Bill, I'm pretty sure you're using this as an excuse to complain and nothing more. I've offered to carry things in my purse many times, but you always refuse."

He harrumphed. "I'm too distracted by you rounding up everyone and getting us into the van earlier than necessary. I don't have time to get my things gathered. I'm lucky to even remember these, and I need them to see." He took off his reading glasses and polished them with his shirt. "And now that you're spearheading the talent show and making everyone participate, it's nonstop reminder after reminder." He snapped his hand open and closed like a crab claw, imitating Ms. Davenport talking.

His words alone seemed a little biting, but the way his eyes sparkled and the smirk on his face made it clear this was a playful kind of belligerence. Was Mr. Fuller...hitting on Ms. Davenport? It was hard to tell with these two. They both loved to antagonize each other, which could be hatred or compatibility. He picked on her, and she nagged him back. They were annoyingly, perfectly weird together.

She crossed her arms. "Well, fine. Next time the van is ready to go, we can leave you behind, Bill!" She pulled out her makeup compact to powder her nose. I could see her beaming in the circular reflection.

Theo glanced at me with a crooked grin plastered on his face. *Oh, NOW he's making eye contact.* But I wasn't in the mood to play any coy "look at how cute these elderly bickering people are" games with him. He had offended me and implied my life choices were beneath his. My parents were already second-guessing me all the time—I didn't need another person in my life trying to make me feel small. When he saw I wasn't playing along or succumbing to his charming ways, his smile flattened to a straight line. *Good. Let your feelings get hurt, like mine did.*

His shoulders drooped as he made an announcement to the

group. "We're almost out of time. While we finish up writing down the makes and models of your phones, does anyone have questions about anything other than Fritos?"

Mr. Fuller took off his watch and waved it in the air like a small lasso. "My watch doesn't count my steps. Can you let me know how I can make it work?" I walked over to him, and he handed it to me.

After a minimal examination, I explained, "Um, sir, this is a regular digital watch, not a smart watch. It doesn't have a step counter."

He grabbed it from my hand. "What's this showing?" He pushed a button and turned the display toward me.

"That's...a stopwatch. And it's on right now. Counting up." I tried to keep a straight face, but I almost lost it.

He shook his watch like it was an eight ball. "Well, I'll be damned. I thought it seemed too high." He scrunched his face and put the watch back on. "I swore I had a different watch on earlier this week. Maybe I wore the wrong one today."

Theo asked a final time. "No further questions? Okay then, meeting adjourned!" He stood up from his chair and walked to the door. Once he pushed on it lightly, it opened fully on its own, and he flipped the metal doorstop down with his toe to prop it open.

I walked to the exit to say goodbye to my class. The procession of elders filed out one at a time, saying thank-yous to Theo and me and letting us know they were looking forward to our next session. Ms. Davenport reached out and grabbed both of my hands. "I hope you're not mad at me. You're such a promising young woman, I don't want to see your talent go to waste. I'm from another era, so I'm a bit old-fashioned. Please come back again." She slipped a flyer in my hand for the Promise City First Annual Talent Show. "It's free, but donations are welcome, and it'll be in the auditorium at our assisted living center. You should come. Everyone at Sunshine Camp is invited, and we're putting flyers up soon. The more, the merrier!"

Pursing my lips, I pushed down the laughter bubbling inside me as I drew a mental image of a doorman collecting a cover charge for this hot event.

"I'll see you next time." My shoulders relaxed a little as I folded the flyer and put it in my shorts pocket. My fingers bumped against my phone as I lodged the paper deep inside. I was willing to cut her some slack because she was from a different generation. But Theo? He was from *my* generation. No, what he said pierced my heart a million times. We were two Venn diagram circles that would never overlap.

Theo said, to no one in particular, "They complain a lot, but these folks like it here because it gets them out of their day-to-day routines. They always make fun of our place. It's like a requirement for them."

Mr. Fuller was last to leave. He pulled himself up from his chair by leaning on the table and pushing with both palms. With a long groan, he said, "Hoooey, I think I pulled a butt muscle." He shook out his hips and made his way to the door. "Sunny, I'll have my son mail you some Fritos. Make sure you bring me the Chili Cheese kind. Ms. Margaret Davenport hates the smell of those, but I think she needs to be more open-minded about snack food. And make sure you have me sit right next to her." He came over to me and shook my hand. A surprisingly firm grip for an octogenarian.

I laughed. "I'm obliged to help, but I do require a reasonable fee since this is outside my duties here. A Fritos fee. One bag for me for every one of yours."

He grunted. "You drive a hard bargain, miss, but I expected no less. Since I have no leverage here, it's a deal. Under one condition—if I actually go to this horse pucky talent show that Mags won't stop going on about, you'll help me if I cave and participate. But just so you know, there's only an infinitesimal chance."

"Sure." There was no way he was doing the talent show.

He said to Theo, "You witnessed our handshake agreement. You're like a notary public who makes this official. Please make sure she fulfills her side of the bargain." Mr. Fuller grabbed Theo's shoulder and squeezed. "I like her." Then he whispered, not in a soft or quiet way, "If you don't ask her out, I'll tell my grandson about her. He's a freshman at Northwestern."

Theo's face turned ruddy, with splotches resembling red amoebas this time. Judging from the intense warmth creeping up to my cheeks, my entire face was likely blazing red too.

Mr. Fuller looked at me. "I want to hear all about your plans after you graduate. I never went to college either and owned a successful e-commerce business. Didn't need a college degree for that. Don't listen to Theo here. He's careful, deliberate, and not a risk-taker by any means. You really couldn't be more opposite."

It was true; he and I were so dissimilar every way you looked at it. An uneasiness in my stomach bubbled up. Theo had said all those judgmental things about my choices in life and hadn't apologized. At least Margaret Davenport had, sort of.

"I'll be here with your Fritos in hand, I promise."

We walked Mr. Fuller to the van. Theo's mouth quirked into a timid smile as he glanced over at me. I pretended to not see it.

Nope, still mad at you. Was it possible to be completely, positively, unquestionably irritated with someone you liked? I'd discovered the answer was yes.

Theo walked back inside the building, giving me a chance to glance at my phone. Finally, I was connected!

One new message:

Starhouse

> Finalist assignment: Create a short video to describe your summer experience. Don't forget to tag us! Post it in a week and we'll share it on the Starhouse platforms. Highest engagement and shares wins. Good luck!

A video about summertime? LA summers to me meant outdoor concerts. Festivals. Food trucks. The beach.

What could I talk about here? Temperamental chickens?

I looked up WowWendy's accounts. Wow. Wendy. Almost six hundred thousand followers. Like me, she had enlisted help, and someone was posting on her behalf. Every few hours, in fact, a new photo from Costa Rica magically appeared. Wendy zip-lining. Ocean diving. Beach monkeys. Fancy hotels. Her fake life was so much more interesting than mine. Were these photos from a past trip, or did she have a body double?

I clicked over to my accounts. Maya had posted an RBG quote that morning. Most of my prescheduled photo and video posts were pretty basic, especially compared to Wendy's. A couple thousand new followers since I started camp. Not bad, but not on WowWendy's level.

The door slammed shut, and Theo fiddled with the lock. My screen wouldn't refresh because he'd killed the Wi-Fi. I shoved my phone into my pocket as he walked in the other direction. He either didn't see me or didn't want to see me.

But I had other things on my mind too. How could I beat Side Braid? She had high production and quality content. Over a half million subscribers. And me? #BrowniePorn.

I thought about Maya's last words to me. *Sunny Song is smart and scrappy. You can take her!*

Yes. Yes, Maya. I can take her.

TWENTY-ONE

THE PLAID WOOL BLANKET MADE THE BACKS OF MY LEGS itch, but it wasn't nearly as bad as when I sat on the haystack directly during my first week here. If I left this camp knowing one thing, it would be this: never EVER sit on haystacks if you're wearing shorts.

I'd been sitting and sweating in the same spot for two hours, trying to think of a video idea. The bucolic view from where I sat encompassed farm life to the point of being cliché. Chickens and cows straight ahead. The iconic red barn far to the right. The lake, stables, and cornfields straight and to the left. Yet the notebook on my lap remained blank. I had five days until the final video was due. I was running out of time.

The only thing that popped into my head: how funny it would be to build this farm in *Minecraft*.

Not helpful, brain.

I stared hard at the smooth, white paper, willing myself to come up with ideas, even if they were terrible. Frustration mounted into anger as the *Minecraft* idea reentered my thoughts. I grabbed my pen and threw it as hard as I could at a nearby tree, almost whacking Delina as she came up the path.

She brought the pen to me. "If you want to try ax throwing, there's a new station for that by the wood-chopping area. I haven't seen you around, and I wanted to give you this." Delina handed me a small orange-and-green box. "My aunt sent me these from her local international grocery. She shops there because the fruit and meat are cheap. Rice paper candies. So good!"

"My mom used to buy these. Thanks!" I peeled the cellophane off the box and shoved the clear wrapper into my pocket. I opened a piece and popped it into my mouth. Immediately, the rice paper enveloping the candy melted on my tongue, leaving the gummy-like chewy center. Delicious.

I offered Delina a try, and she grabbed one from the box. She chewed and asked, "What are you doing over here? They want us to distance ourselves from technology, but this is ridiculous."

"I just need some time to think about things." Things like summertime video ideas. And finding an internet connection. And beating WowWendy.

Her deep-brown eyes filled with worry. "Are you okay?"

Delina hadn't told anyone about my contraband phone, and she'd known for over two weeks. Could I trust her with this? It was weighing on me so much, to the point I couldn't eat and sleep. Maybe she could help fill my brain with something other than a useless *Minecraft* farm idea.

I gulped a breath and told her everything. Starhouse. The signal booster. The video deadline. And that Wendy was the other finalist. At the end, I took a deep breath and relaxed my shoulders. Wow, that felt good to tell a friend.

What I didn't expect was her to jump to her feet and pace the grounds. "You need a hook. And a videographer. An editor too. Can you use copyrighted music? You have any ideas?"

My shoulders tensed. "That's the problem. I don't have any ideas. The biggest videos I've had both went viral by sheer luck, not talent. It's not like I can do a Goggle Girl brownie-porn mashup while I do a 'why I love summer' essay voiceover." I stood up and stretched. "Time to walk. My butt's asleep."

We walked toward the main buildings. Delina asked, "Well, you have to be good at *something*. Everyone I've met here has talent of some kind. Maybe we can figure out a video format that works best for you, like a fake newscaster, or a movie trailer, or a commercial. What kinds of videos have you done on your channel?"

"A little bit of everything. Other than my fluke viral ones, just rants about school. And exam snacks reviews. I did car lip-synching and karaoke, but those didn't get traction. Well, except..."

"Except?"

"My friend Maya and I did a *Pitch Perfect* car karaoke tribute, and those were the most popular ones and—OH MY GOD."

She stopped walking. "What?"

I hugged my notebook and pen to my chest. "One song we never got to do was 'Party in the USA.' I can make a parody of it, about me leaving LAX and arriving in Promise City. The opposite of a small-town girl moving to a big metropolis."

Delina grabbed my shoulders and shook gently. "I LOVE it! Can I be your camerawoman and editor and music mixer and special effects person? I miss doing all that."

"Yes! Wait, no! I don't want to risk you getting caught." Delina was my friend. The last thing I wanted was for her to get tangled in my messy web of deceit.

She put both hands on her hips. "We won't. I've got eyes and ears here." She squealed and grabbed me by the crook of my arm. "Making a music video will be fun. This is the best thing to happen to me all summer. Everything will be fine!"

With Delina's help and friendship, I was more than fine. I was on cloud nine.

TWENTY-TWO

"WE'RE NEARING THE END OF WEEK THREE. HOW ARE you all feeling?" Coach scanned the room. "I know, this early time slot isn't ideal, especially for the summer. But if you don't liven up here, we might have to do a morning dance party, and you're definitely not going to want that." He received a few groans and yawns in response. "Okay then, everyone stand up in your seats and shake your arms and hands. Get some blood pumping!"

Most of us stood up, half-heartedly flapping our arms and stomping in place. One of the seated guys in a too-tight Cavs shirt and too-baggy basketball shorts muttered, "I make almost five hundred dollars a day from advertising and sponsorships. This kinder-camp stuff you preach here is tiring."

Coach shrugged. "This is the last group session of camp, if you can believe it. It's a little longer than usual, because it's our final time together. You'll be on your own from here on out. So why don't you help me by pushing through, okay, friend?"

Friend rolled his eyes but stood up and stomped around. Left stomp, right stomp, left-right-left-right, three-year-old tantrum style.

I asked, "This is our last session? What do we do the rest of the week in the morning? And next week?" I'd grown accustom to our twice-weekly meetings with the larger group and then coming together for more casual sessions, where we journaled and read in a quieter setting.

Coach smiled. "I'll have office hours from nine to noon every day, even on the last day of camp, if you want to stop by to chat or say hello. The emphasis we place in our detox program is on being intentional with what we do with our time. We want you to cultivate good habits around finding rewarding leisure activities so you turn to those instead of mindless wastes of time." More groans. "Okay, I know *some* of you appreciate these group sessions we've been having, but I do acknowledge for others this isn't as rewarding as activities around the camp." He took a sip of coffee and held the "Coaching is awesome!" mug with both hands. "In short, we want to reduce distractions so you can use the remaining time at camp to explore, reflect, try things, relax. All these things will help you when you leave Sunshine Farms."

There were still a lot of activities I hadn't tried yet. Making soap. Canning jam. Grooming horses. No, scratch that one. I couldn't leave here without milking the cows, though, so maybe that would be my activity tomorrow. What good was being on a farm without udder-squeezing bragging rights?

Coach announced, "Now that everyone's on their feet, if you could find a seat at one of the tables in the back—quickly, because we're running a little late—we can get started on our final project."

Surveying the tables, I noted some had better art supplies than others. I went to one with the new box of markers (the scented kind) and better stack of glossy magazines. Side Braid rushed to the other side of the room, avoiding eye contact with me, holding up her side of the bargain to stay out of my way.

Coach clapped his hands together. "For your final assignment, we're making memes!"

Confusion flashed on everyone's faces. Memes? How?

He handed each of us a small, white poster board. "Here's how you'll do it analog instead of digitally. You have art supplies and magazines at your tables; plus, along the bookshelf wall, we have other supplies like newspapers, construction paper, stencils, and a few Pentax instant cameras. What I want you to make is the meme 'Online Me vs. Real Me.' Take your poster board and split it in half. Each side can have drawings, photos, whatever you want. But no handwritten words."

A redheaded girl wearing a leather jacket in the excessive Iowa heat and humidity said out loud, "This is the first time I'll be making a meme that won't go viral." She sighed and grabbed a year-old *People* magazine from the top of the pile in front of her.

I couldn't decide if her remark was funny, depressing, or obnoxious. Maybe all of the above?

My fantasy-sports-addicted basketball player friend asked, "Which 'online me' do ya mean? I have my public one, exclusively for my sports stuff—it's kind of like my work account—and I also have my personal one."

It took a few seconds for Coach to answer. "Let's go with the one with the most followers."

A girl with platinum blond hair with noticeably black roots asked, "What if you have, like, six accounts and you use all of them and they have roughly the same numbers of followers?"

I had a few accounts too, like everyone else I knew. My public one was for Goggle Girl, and then I had one for family and outside friends. The other one was private: it was one my family didn't know about, for me being moody, broody, and petty, an outlet for non-sunny Sunny. I used that account to bitch and moan about my parents or sister or teachers. The most recent post complained about the principal threatening to expel me and how the other parents had him wrapped around their little paraffined fingers. But I only had three accounts. Six? That was too many.

Coach seemed to think the same. "How on earth do you keep up with six accounts?"

The girl grinned. "It's easy when you have two iPads, two

phones, and two computers. I don't want to say too much, in case I get in trouble. You won't subpoenaed if I don't divulge anything else."

Well, thank goodness for that.

The same girl asked, "What if your real self is the same as your online self?"

Coach paused a moment. "Well, two things come to mind. One, do you think your online self is quote-unquote real if you have so many accounts? And second, I have a question for you and everyone here: have you ever deleted posts that don't get enough likes, even if they're cool or meaningful to you? Why do you think you do it? Are you self-conscious? Or is it something else?"

We all fell silent. Who hadn't deleted posts because they weren't popular enough? The worst ones were when they had a ton of views but not many likes or comments in comparison. If anyone denied this, they were straight-up lying.

I raised my hand. "Changing the subject. You said we can't write words. Can we cut out letters to spell words?"

Coach twisted his mouth. "Like word art?"

"Sort of. It would look like a ransom note." I clarified, "Not that I know much about it."

He scratched his nose. "I'm going to say yes. You have forty-five minutes total, because I don't want you to spend too much time on this. We're not trying to find the next MoMA exhibitor.

We're only sharing this here in the class to foster discussion, so perfection isn't what we're aiming for. I'll give you a five-minute warning. The clock starts now."

Making memes was hard for me online—I'd spent hours on them—and this poster board version seemed even harder. I'd spent hours on them. Parodying other famous people's memes was so much easier than coming up with my own. This was going to be tough, especially without an image or GIF search function.

Thumbing through the magazines was tedious. *Seventeen*, *People*, *TIME*, and *Architectural Digest* weren't exactly the best places to look for a girl wearing goggles—finding goggles in glossies was like looking for a hay-colored needle in a haystack.

Online Sunny vs. Real Sunny.

Flip the page.

Flip.

Flip.

Flip.

I couldn't find any relevant images, and after a while, my zoned-out, compulsive behavior closely resembled me swiping mindlessly on my phone. Finally, I landed on a two-page article in *Travel & Leisure* featuring an editor's weekend foodie trip to Los Angeles. A photo of him surrounded by stacks and stacks of doughnuts made me smile. A doughnut fortress. He'd eaten at two Michelin restaurants, attended a *Food & Wine* exclusive VIP event, and somehow had no wait in line for Sprinkles cupcakes in

Beverly Hills or at Hama Sushi in Downtown LA. This article was all about the food culture in LA—and I loved eating, especially doughnuts—so this all was very *me*. The scissors were being used by someone else, so I carefully tore out the pages from the binding and put the magazine in my reviewed stack. I had my LA food-loving me—now I needed to find my "online me."

The daily edition of *Promise City News* was on my media pile too. Curious about what they reported on in the town's paper, I opened the pages and found myself engrossed by a feature spread on Sunshine Heritage Farms' experimental detox camp, with the title, "As a Last Resort, Device-Addicted Teens Turn Back Time." There were picturesque photos of the red barn, the wayward chickens, and some of the activities they offered, like horseshoes, salting meat (they loved their salted meat at Sunshine, didn't they?), woodworking, and more. Theo's brother, Henry, was in a lot of the pictures, which made sense given how handsome and photogenic he was. But there was one photograph of Theo holding a bow and arrow that made my heart skip. That day he taught me archery was the first day I spent one-on-one time with Theo and noticed things about him. His sense of humor. His boyish face. Those big, square hands. The way he got splotchy when he blushed. This was how he looked in my memories. And in my dreams.

My mental images of Theo would go home with me, but I'd be leaving Sunshine Farms with no pictures of him or of this place, except for the few I'd surreptitiously taken on my phone on my daily mission to find signal. I looked around to see if anyone was watching me, but the others were laser-focused on their own meme projects. I ripped out the full-page photo of Theo, folded the paper, and stuffed it in my shorts pocket for safekeeping.

The rest of the article talked about the history of Sunshine and how times were tougher now since churches and corporations had scaled back on camps and retreats. This digital detox camp was a way of diversifying, but if it wasn't lucrative, the camp was in danger of foreclosure. In an interview, Theo stated, "I would love to live in a bigger city or get a degree in agriculture or hospitality at Cal Poly Pomona or Cornell, but this is a family business, and I need to help keep it afloat." The column went on to say he would likely apply to the University of Iowa part-time for college in the fall, a few hours away, to earn a business degree. His bio mentioned he was a rising senior at Promise County High who was inducted into the National Honor Society, played varsity baseball, and had led a statewide initiative to establish greener farming practices like organic soil treatments and natural insecticides. Worm composting at Sunshine was all his idea. An effort to modernize while still preserving what was special about the farm that had been in his family for generations.

This kid was Boy Wonder, and I had called him *Agro Boy*.

More memories of Theo flashed in my head, and I played them over and over in my mind. In regular speed. Then slow motion. Rewind and playback times a thousand. Registration day. The mail deliveries. The hayride. The hayride again. Him bringing me a baby goat to bottle feed. Our blowup about the value of being a content creator. We had our differences, and he dismissed me, but I had dismissed him, too, and chalked it up to incompatibility.

I shook my head hard, hoping to rattle these thoughts out of my brain. When that obviously didn't work, I pressed my fingers to my temples and squeezed my eyes shut.

"Sunny, are you almost finished?" Coach's words startled me. "You look like you're concentrating pretty hard."

My eyes flew open. "No." My stomach pulled into a tight knot. "I need more time."

"Try to wrap it up. I can give you five more minutes. That's it." Coach was a nice guy and fair but no pushover. Five minutes was it. To show real Sunny and online Sunny. Were they even the same people?

I pulled the stack of magazines closer and quickly skimmed old monthlies of *Vogue*, *InStyle*, and *Billboard* before coming back to the local paper, the one with Theo's photo in it. I thumbed through the pages and found the picture I wanted. While the other campers at my table were hanging up their memes on the corkboard in the front of the room, I hastily trimmed and glued images to my poster board.

Coach announced, "Scissors down, everyone."

I took two pushpins and added mine to the wall. An assortment of pictures glamorizing LA food and lifestyle on one side, and a lone image of Sunshine Heritage Farm's hayride on the other, plus the letters spelling my Korean name—Sun-Hee—pieced together in fragments from different fonts, colors, and sizes. That was me: individual pieces adding up to a Frankenstein whole.

The range of everyone's "Real Me vs. Online Me" collage cutouts ranged from slapstick comedic to heartrending. There were photos of crush-worthy celebrities, billionaires, fashion icons, and sports stars. There were also washed-up musicians, former child actors, and Britney Spears. Photos of darkness. Some images of violence. Abstract images of shattered and broken objects. Coach pulled out a tattered and thin washcloth from his pocket and patted his upper lip then dabbed the corners of his eyes.

For a while, no one spoke. But then one of the campers broke the silence, a teen comedian who was Yuksta in the outside world. No one at camp knew his real name. He was firmly anti-Sunshine when we got here, but now he said he was more at peace and relaxed because people didn't expect him to be "on" all the time. "I didn't like this project at all."

Coach sat on a stool near the collages. "Why not?"

"I got rubber cement all over my hands." He raised his hand, then peeled and stretched the adhesive with the other, like it was alien skin. Gross, but a few of us laughed. Much needed comic relief after all the silence.

"Anyone else?" Coach looked for volunteers, but no one raised their hand. "Let's break into smaller groups to get some discussion flowing. I'll come around and ask some questions." He split everyone into groups of three.

Me, the Comedian, and Side Braid.

Ugh.

Wendy crossed her arms and slumped her body in her chair, making zero effort to get up. Yuksta and I had to come over to her table. I made sure to place myself at the opposite end from her, as far away as possible. Our other group member looked at Wendy glaring at me on his left, then shifted his gaze over to me on his right. "Ohhhhsheeeeet, did I just place my ass inside a bitch sandwich? You two had better play nice for all our sakes. I don't want trouble."

Coach came over and sat down at one of the empty chairs next to me. "Which memes are yours? Show me and tell me a little bit about it."

Our comedian friend went first. "The one on the far left, top row. 'Online me' is on the left. Hasan Minhaj is one of my heroes. I put Jim Gaffigan there because he's a legend. There's also guys with nice suits."

"And the real you?"

Yuksta sighed. "The other side is more depressing. I found an old TV guide, so I cut out all the shows that have been canceled. That's the real me."

Coach knitted his brows and cocked his head. "I'd love for you to elaborate. Why do you feel like you're a canceled show?"

"It's like...I'm always trying to keep up with the next new thing, you know? I got on YouTube, Twitch, and TikTok early, and now there's all this new tech popping up. You can be successful on one thing, and then all of a sudden, a different thing comes along, and you gotta start all over again in case it blows up. A brand-new platform every few months. And it happens again. And again. I'm only seventeen and tired as fugginhell."

I nodded, and even Side Braid did too.

Coach asked, "Do you feel this way now? You know, tired as 'fugginhell,' as you say? Now that you're away from social media, is it helping or hurting?"

The Comedian pulled his baseball cap off and turned it backward. "Honestly? It's worse. Because while I'm here, cutting out pictures and playing 3D farmer life, the real world is rolling on without me. For all I know, another new media platform's picking up fast and I'm already too late. And worse, someone's already taken my username. I'm a future has-been." He fell back into his chair, arms flopping to his sides. "People always tell me to stop doing social media and do something else. But what? I can't do sports—even if I started now, I'm, like, at a beginner level. I used to do theater and liked it, but then theater somehow morphed into musical theater everywhere, and I can't sing. So yeah. A walking has-been."

Coach paused before speaking. "Thank you for being so honest. Looks like others can relate to what you said. This is good feedback for me, too, and also a great opportunity to loop in the camp counselor who will be available tomorrow for individual meetings. She specializes in adolescent anxiety, depression, trauma, and a number of other things as well. I want you to know you're not alone. I don't have any answers now, but we have someone on staff who can help you, and that's a start."

To my surprise, Side Braid shot up in her seat and announced, "I'll go next. I didn't hang mine up. It's here." She pushed her poster board at Coach. The left side was covered with black Sharpie scribbles. The right side was pretty much the same. More scribbly scratches.

This must be a visual depiction of what dark thoughts reside in her evil brain.

Coach pulled his reading glasses from his pocket and put them on. "Interesting. Tell me what's going on here."

She didn't say anything for a while. "This is me. Real me and online me. What you see is what you get."

Nailed it.

Coach scooted his chair back. "I see. Anything else you'd like to share?"

She cocked an eyebrow. "No thanks."

"Thank you for participating in this exercise." He turned to me. "It's your turn—"

Side Braid cut in, "Wait, don't you want to tell me some heart-squishy BS about why I'm here and how this camp is supposed to fix me? Aren't you supposed to lecture me to death?"

Coach's eyes widened. "Do you want me to tell you those things? Maybe you should tell me more."

Her nostrils flared as she spoke. "I didn't want to be here. It's punishment."

She had all our attention. Coach asked what we all wanted to ask. "What do you mean by 'it's punishment'?"

Wendy looked over at me, then picked at her fingernails. "My parents sent me here. Said I needed help, like they'd know. You know what? Never mind. All this is so stupid." She shoved the poster board in my direction. Up close, I could see it wasn't just black scratches and scribbles on there. She had glued some pictures of things in the background and written on top of them. With a lot of penmanship force, based on the indentions. One of them was a picture of a fancy hotel resort with a multilevel pool with water slides.

She really hated nice pools.

There were some photos of vacationing families and business-people there too, and they looked familiar. It was hard to make them out: everything was obscured behind a veil of permanent black ink. But then it clicked: they were the same photos from her

Instagram page. She said they were her family's properties, but these images she'd glued here came from celebrity magazines. Her online photos were...fake?

While I was processing all this, Wendy jumped to her feet, screeched her chair back, and shot out the door.

Coach turned to me. "I'm sorry we lost a member. I'll talk to her later. Would you like to go next?"

"Um. Sure." I'd need to think about what all this meant later. I pointed to my collage. "That's mine. I thought the foodie LA girl was me. But I don't know anymore; maybe it's not. I put the hayride in there too, because—"

Because on the hayride...I was Sunny. Not Goggle Girl.

Because on the hayride...I didn't feel the urge to check my phone.

Because on the hayride...something real happened with Theo.

Coach and the Yuksta stared at me. I cleared my throat. "Because I didn't hate the hayride that much."

Coach suppressed a smile. "Well, I'm glad you found an activity you didn't hate. That much."

I shrugged. "Thanks, Coach."

He put his hands on his thighs and stood up slowly. Addressing everyone in the room, he said, "I've saved a little time at the end to tell you some hard truths. I'm not a professor or therapist, as I've mentioned before on more than one occasion. But I've lived a long time and worked with kids my whole life. So here's what I know. Tech companies want to make money. The little guys want to be sold to the big guys; the big guys want to grow. They are not your friends or allies."

He paced the room. "Who benefits if you get dependent and addicted to their product? These companies, that's who. They're just as bad as big tobacco or the candy-flavored vaping companies, making it easy to binge-scroll for hours or because you're bored and they propose that the cure for boredom is their technology. It's a quick fix."

He looked up with a startle, like he'd forgotten we were all there. "Any armchair economists in the room? For those who took econ in school, what can you tell us about the law of diminishing returns?"

No one answered. I took econ, but I didn't have a grasp on the principles like Maya and Rafa did. There were some kids in class who understood everything, and it was intuitive to them, but not to me. I shrank down in my seat, hoping he wouldn't call on me.

"No takers? Okay, maybe I can explain it in a way so it's a refresher for some and enlightening for those who don't know, in an example that's relevant to where we are now. Let's say a farmer who owns Sunshine has ten acres of land with crops. He finds a certain number of farm laborers will yield the maximum output per worker. If he should hire more workers, the combination of land and labor would be less efficient because the proportional increase in the overall output would be less than the proportional expansion of the workforce with the finite use of land." He scanned our faces. "I lost you."

Yuksta chimed in, "Hey, Coach! I got a better example. Okay, let's say you buy a few orders of McDonald's fries, and you eat one handful. It's amazing—the crispiness, the saltiness. You eat another handful. It's crack on your taste buds—still delicious. By the sixth handful...well, it's not as good as that first bite, right? By the tenth, you're done. Ready to move on to a shake maybe. Or weed."

Coach laughed, and we all joined in. "We can all relate to the french fry example, can't we? I appreciate your thoughts here, but it's not exactly where I was going with this, although, everyone, he has a valid perspective. Maybe for many of you—or even all of you—technology is like that, eating fry after fry, where there is less satisfaction over time the more you eat." He shifted on his stool, causing it to creak under his weight. "What I want to share is what I've extrapolated from some lectures of a well-known professor of computer science at UC Berkeley. What if we do better at optimizing how we use technology? Would we then be able to increase the value of the returns? Here's an example: when you mindlessly scroll your feeds for current events or celebrity gossip or even check notifications nonstop, what if you had an app or an aggregator of some kind to curate what you want? Could some changes—restrictions even—allow you to enjoy the best of what social media has to offer, albeit in a more controlled or limited way?"

My basketball friend blurted, "Technology is supposed to be bad, right? Isn't this why we're here, living real-life Thoreau stuff? You cut us off cold...no devices, no internet at all, but now you're saying we can use it but differently?" His eyebrows expressively knit into an angry V formation. Like a flock of birds flying away in the winter.

"Yes and no. I'm sorry this is all so frustrating for you. Trust me, behind the scenes—the administration, educators, and counselors—we go back and forth every day about how to best proceed with our program here. It's not a perfect curriculum or plan." He sighed out through his nose, so hard, his mustache wiggled. "This is our last session, so I'll quickly lay out what I can. The goal here initially was to reduce distractions for you. To help you more easily identify when you're bored and lonely and to give you time to be intentional with your actions and choices. To provide opportunities for conversations, more personal ones, even if they were uncomfortable and unpleasant." I looked around the room to see if Side Braid had made it back here. She was still MIA.

"What tech companies do best is take advantage of you, to get you to use more and buy more. They get you addicted to their reward system. It's terrible. Especially when they don't help you differentiate between meaningful connections and loose contacts."

What he said was true, in a lot of ways. But what about

technology helping people like Ms. Davenport? And me helping people like Ms. Davenport? Was this what he was talking about? That maybe prioritizing my real friendships and connections would be more meaningful? See, this was problematic though: this theoretical live-your-best-life, blah-blah, rah-rah BS that sounded good when you read a book or article about it was one thing, but when you tried doing it on your own, it was ten-out-of-ten hard to execute. But maybe I could find ways to improve my life somehow, with some focus. Acknowledging there were high-value interactions and low-value distractions in my life was a big step for me. This would mean admitting my parents—after all the fighting, yelling, and arguing about my social media obsession and my life goals of being famous and doing social media as a career—maybe they were right to some degree. Or at the very least, they were right about rethinking things.

This was a lot to process. Coach may have fractured my brain.

Coach smiled. "I'm sorry for the info dump. I wasn't planning on that. But honestly, I've learned a lot from you, and I wanted to share what I've learned. It looks like we're out of time, if you can believe it."

Not only was the meeting over, but judging from my gurgling stomach, it was already nearing lunch time too. But while I was starving, I was dreading mealtime too: Delina was my breakfast, lunch, and dinner buddy, and she gave me the courtesy heads-up she wasn't going to make it today. Her breakout group was cooking hot dogs and s'mores at the campfire on their last day together. They'd all bonded, whereas my group continued to be a group of antisocial, incongruent misfits. Funny, since us being "social" was how we landed ourselves in this detox camp in the first place.

The end of group sessions was bittersweet: it meant we were closer to the end of camp, but the jumbled feelings uncovered in these groups filled me with a weird sense of satisfaction mixed with unease, like I'd seen a movie everyone loved but didn't understand the ending. I didn't connect with many other campers, but it was nice knowing all my feelings—the good and bad, the happy thoughts and the judgmental petty ones—weren't just something I experienced in isolation. Others felt the same way. I was not alone.

"Thanks for your help, Coach." I pushed my chair under the table. "From one fellow non-therapist and non-counselor to another, you were great and got me thinking. Though I wish you'd given us all the answers on how to live our decluttered lives once we leave here." My chronic overthinking resulted in me being hopeful yet worried about my life post-Sunshine.

He smiled as he organized some of the art supplies. "I'm happy to hear your wheels are turning. I wish I had answers for you, but as you know—"

"I know, I know, you're not a certified counselor or therapist. But maybe you should look into it."

After dumping a pile of paper scraps in the trash, he said, "Huh. Maybe. I'll think about it. Thank you, friend. Sunny. Have a good afternoon."

The door closed behind me, and I headed to the dining hall. My plan was to grab my lunch, wolf it down quickly, and leave. Or maybe sit with people from my cabin and hope they talked to me. Or maybe I could talk to them first?

I filled my plate with smoked brisket, baked beans, slaw, and a dinner roll from the communal table. Near the silverware, the basketball player and Yuksta were eating their meals. Ironically, the athlete had less on his plate than I did. The comedian had two plates full.

"Wanna sit with us?" asked my free-throwing friend.

Me? Really?

There was nothing I wanted more.

I put my tray down and sat next to him, across from the comedian.

"I'm Colin, don't know if you remember. He's Yuksta. But maybe he'll tell us his real name. Hopefully it's not as goofy as his face."

Yuksta looked at Colin and me and relaxed his shoulders. "Har har. Okay, fine. I'm Yehuda." He raised his burger with two hands and took a bite.

I smiled at him. "I'm Sunny."

Colin held out his hand. "Nice to hang with you, Sunny." I

didn't know if I should shake it, slap it, or go for a group hug. So I sort of did all three, and it was awkward—with mistimed hands, arms, and bodies moving at once, of various lengths and heights. But afterward, we all laughed at ourselves and chatted about nothing important over lunch.

TWENTY-THREE

WITHOUT OUR GROUP SESSIONS AND ACTIVITY rotations, Delina and I had a lot of free time on our hands our last week at camp. We brainstormed fun lyrics and cinematography ideas and would be ready to shoot the video soon.

Coach's words echoed in my head—to find high-quality leisure—so I also sought other ways to pass time that were enjoyable to me. Some alone time was nice, like going on short nature walks if I woke up early when it wasn't as hot, or burning marshmallows on sticks in the evenings with Delina, Colin, and Yehuda and eating the crispy, gooey goodness while it was warm. Crashing the kitchen and helping them bake cookies and brownies meant getting freebies during kitchen duty. Feeding the chickens, who had grown on me over the weeks, turned out to be one of my favorite farm chores. But most of the time, I hung out with Delina, and we played Uno, spades, and hearts in the rec room with the online gambler guys. They taught us Texas Hold 'em and blackjack and wanted to wager—of course—using dining food and care package treats as our currency, but we didn't give in. This was all for fun after all. The last thing I wanted was to fan the flames of their addiction by anteing up bets with my remaining Korean snacks.

Time ticked by, and before I knew it, I only had a couple of days to turn in the Starhouse video. And the last digital session with the assisted living folks was already here. Mr. Fuller's Fritos had arrived, and I brought them with me: an assortment of Chili Cheese, Original, and a kind I had never seen before—Honey BBQ Twists.

Frigid air blasted me when I opened the door to the community room. Theo stood on a tall, rickety ladder, trying to fiddle with the AC panel. The room was somewhere in the low sixties, freezing compared to the upper nineties outside. I caught glimpses of Theo's well-muscled body as his shirt pulled up and flapped from the high-powered wind.

I didn't know where we stood. Since the activity rotations ended, I'd seen him around camp, but he was mostly tied up in the main office or doing maintenance work with his brother.

He called out to me, "Can you spot me if I fall?"

I trotted over to him. "Sure." He smiled at me. We were okay. *I'd be happy for your strong, toned body to collide into mine, Theo.*

As if he could hear my inner thoughts, he glanced down, and

his mouth curved into a broader grin. With an amused look in his eyes, he asked, "Can you hold the ladder still while I come down? It's wobbly—I think it's missing a screw or something."

His firm, sturdy legs came down step-by-step. On the last one, he jumped and landed so close to me, I could instantly feel heat emanating from his body. My natural instinct was to take a step back, to give him space, but his presence was so compelling that I wanted nothing more than to go closer, removing all the space between us. My heart jolted as he took a small step toward me. He leaned in and whispered, "You're blocking me. I need to get by you to start the class." Before any disappointment set in, he brought his hands to my shoulders and gave a firm squeeze, sending a ripple of warmth through me. I let out a big breath as Theo walked past and started the session.

The group broke out into a few different teams: photos and filters, communication 101, and "freeloaders"—they were the biggest faction, the ones who wanted access to all things free, from library apps to photo stickers to sudoku puzzles and word games (all interrupted with annoying ads, of course). There was also a group working on independent projects. That was what I was assigned, and the only two people in there were Mr. Fuller and Ms. Davenport, who took no time before bickering about where they should sit.

Her: "If you sit next to Sunny, you'll block my view."

Him: "But if you sit there instead of me, you'll block me."

Her: "What if she sits in the middle?"

Him: "Then I can't hear if she turns her head to talk to you. You know I have a bad ear."

Her: "Yes, I know, you complain about it during all your waking hours."

I'd heard enough. "Let's arrange our chairs so you two can sit across from me. Then you can both hear me. And I can keep an eye on you two."

We arranged our seating in a bowling-ball-finger formation. Both of them had summer birthdays to celebrate, so they each wanted to create shareable albums of scanned family photos.

"Where'd you get a scanner?" I asked as they looked through their camera rolls to find the photos they wanted to include.

Ms. Davenport peered over her reading glasses. "The Promise City Assisted Living Center has a scanner they rent out, and it's currently in my room. Bill knocks on the door whatever time he wants, without calling first to ask if he can borrow it." She sputtered out an exasperated sigh.

My eyebrow quirked. "Oh, reeeeeally? Is that true, Mr. Fuller?"

He lifted his chin. "I can't control when my creativity sparks."

She bubbled out a laugh. "You just like to bother me when I'm trying to get some peace and quiet. It's like you can't stand me being happy."

"Can you two pick the photos you want? You can add them to your favorites folder. I need to talk to Theo for a second."

As I scooted my chair back, Ms. Davenport said, "One second isn't very long. To be more accurate, you should say 'a minute.' Maybe more."

Mr. Fuller's mouth quirked with amusement. "Jesus, Mags, let her be." He opened a bag of Fritos and held it up like he was toasting me.

"Well, obviously she doesn't have to take my feedback, Bill. And please, if you're going to eat those crunchy bits of heart attack fuel, can you do it with your mouth closed?"

I ran over to Theo. "I need your help."

He put down an iPad and furrowed his brow with concern. "Are you okay?"

"Me? Yes. Sorry, I didn't mean to scare you. We need to help Ms. Davenport and Mr. Fuller."

"Are *they* okay?"

"They are. But I can't tell if they hate each other or we need to get them together."

He snorted. "Those two? They're like two cans of soda that've been dropped and someone's trying to open prematurely. Are you kidding?"

"No, look!" I jerked my head in their direction. They were in each other's faces, verbally sparring as usual, but they were both relaxed, smiling, and making each other laugh.

His mouth twisted. "Huh."

"Isn't it obvious? They're totally into each other."

"I'm just surprised, they're both so..." He trailed off.

"Old?"

He coughed out a loud laugh. "I was going to say different. But maybe for Mr. Fuller and Ms. Davenport, opposites attract?"

I shrugged. "I guess so. How do we set them up on a date?"

Theo held up his palms. "Whoa there, Cupid. Let's not go overboard."

Tapping my fingers to my mouth, I said, "Oooh, I know. Let's call for a thirty-minute break. We can have them get some air by going to the canteen for a drink or ice cream. It's open right now, and it's got better snacks than the gift shop. I bet Mr. Fuller will like it; it's my treat." I offered him my most radiant smile. My family had sent me dining dollars, and this little experiment was totally worth the twenty dollars left in my account.

"You're like what my dad calls 'a dog with a bone.' I'll agree to the recess. But don't ask me why this little dating scheme of yours failed when it does." His barely there smirk turned into a wide grin. "Can you get back to work with those two so we can afford a recess break?"

In a mock salute, I chirped, "Yes, sir!" and trotted back to my duo, who were now not speaking to each other. All the banter, the quips flying between them—poof. As if I'd imagined the whole thing.

So much for my matchmaking plans.

"What happened?"

Ms. Davenport turned away from Mr. Fuller and unsurprisingly spoke first. "I'm waiting for an apology."

"She should apologize to me, not the other way around." He crossed his arms and fell back into his chair.

"Me? You're the one who said my precious grandchildren looked like the von Trapp family from *The Sound of Music*." She narrowed her eyes at him.

He held up her phone and showed me the photo. "Look." An army of children arranged in a semicircle, wearing identical Cape Cod prep attire, stiff as rods, all of them unsmiling.

I fought hard to keep a grin off my face. He was right. Gulping down a laugh, I said with warning in my voice, "Mr. Fuller, that hurt her feelings, and you know it."

"Fine. I'm sorry," he said with a wince, like it physically pained him to utter those words. "But I genuinely like that movie, so it wasn't meant to be an insult. More like an observation—"

"I think that will suffice, Mr. Fuller," I said. "Please stop talking."

Ms. Davenport relaxed her tightly pressed lips, so she no longer looked like she'd tasted a sour lemon. "All's forgiven." He returned her phone, and together they cropped, filtered, and uploaded their photo albums, then tagged their family members with minimal help from me. Success!

He looked at his Timex watch. "We're done. What can we work on next?"

"Well...let me think." I looked over at Theo to see if we were okay to leave the community room for our excursion. He gave me a thumbs-up. "Okay, I thought about it. We're going on a little walk. As a reward for finishing early."

Mr. Fuller leaned back in his chair. "You think a walk in this heat and humidity is a reward? Not with these hips."

Ms. Davenport's eyes brightened. She clasped her hands with delight. "I love walks! Come on, Bill. It'll be nice to get fresh air."

"There are mosquitoes out there. Did I mention the heat? I can't remember, I thought I did."

Theo came over. "Are we all set for our little field trip? We'll have you back in ten, maybe fifteen minutes." He winked at me, sending a pulse of electricity shooting through me and heat up to my cheeks. "We can't be gone too long. The other visitors will go buck wild without supervision. It'll be chaos!"

I asked, "Like chickens with their heads cut off?" Pleased with my use of farm lingo, I laughed at my own comment.

He broke into an arresting smile. "Exactly."

Mr. Fuller studied both of our faces before answering, "I see I'm outnumbered here." He rose to his feet and marched to the door. "C'mon then. Let's go."

Ms. Davenport looked at me, and her mouth twitched. "You heard the man."

Theo led the way, and I trailed right behind him. He turned his head and whispered to me, "Do you really think the two of them have a chance?"

I looked back at Ms. Davenport, who hung back to keep Mr. Fuller company as he shuffled down the path. She had a perfectly symmetrical blondish-gray bob and wore a floral dress that would be perfect for a Sunday brunch. Her slides were on the not-so-stylish side though, like Birkenstocks and Crocs got together and had an ugly shoe baby. But a very comfortable ugly baby. Mr. Fuller wore a short-sleeve button-down and khaki shorts, which revealed his blindingly white legs. He had a full head of gray hair, which I had to imagine sparked envy among his elderly peers.

Theo slowed down so he could walk next to me. "I bet you an ice cream *with toppings* this thing you're trying to make happen isn't going to happen."

"And why not?" I folded my arms across my chest.

"I've known them longer than you have. The two of them don't make sense. He's, like, a hundred and fifty—and she's, like, half his age. He's a finance and numbers guy; she likes to organize bake sales and go to art walk charity events. He complains all the time about everything. You saw him go off on the non-Fritos snacks we have here. Did you know his grandson goes to Northwestern? I know this because he tells me about him every time he comes here. He can be really annoying. Don't get me wrong. She can be aggravating too, as you know." He opened the screen door to the canteen and gestured for me to pass through.

"You mean how she always corrects my grammar?"

He laughed. "Maybe they're both compatible after all...in that they're both infuriating in their own ways."

The two of them finally caught up to us, whispering and stealing little glances as they passed through the doorway.

Theo looked at his watch. "That took longer than I thought. Let's grab some ice cream and walk back. No time for sitting today."

The canteen staff member said, "We only have chocolate, strawberry cheesecake, and vanilla. Whipped cream and sprinkles are extra. Napkins and spoons are on the table behind you."

"It's on me," I said. "You all pick whatever you want, as long as it doesn't go over five bucks."

"If I get, like, a triple scoop, is it an out-of-pocket cost?" Theo hunched over with his hands planted on his thighs, peering into the ice cream display. I couldn't help but peer at his bare, muscular arms and his powerful set of shoulders. My gaze traveled down his back to his—

"I'm ready!" Mr. Fuller tapped at the glass. "One scoop of chocolate on a cake cone." He looked at Ms. Davenport, who was still surveying her three options.

She glanced at her final choice. "I'll have strawberry cheesecake. In a regular cone."

Mr. Fuller made an exaggerated *blech* face.

Theo's amused green eyes met mine. He shrugged and sent me an "I told you they weren't compatible" look.

Ms. Davenport said, "For your information, I already had a small scoop of chocolate earlier today at the ice cream social. I wanted to try something else. Something less boring." Her wide-eyed, proper, and innocent act was a ruse—she was dishing it right back to Mr. Fuller!

He snorted. "Ice cream social? How did I not know about this?"

"Bill, you never go to anything. The talent show's in a few days, and you still haven't confirmed participation. It's like you make it your life's mission to be impossible."

Should I make a Tom Cruise M.I. joke? It was something corny that my dad would say. Nah, I didn't want to ruin this crackly spark between them. Plus, they probably wouldn't even know who I was talking about.

Ms. Davenport grabbed Mr. Fuller's arm and moved him toward the register. I looked at Theo, beaming.

The canteen worker scooped our ice cream orders. When it came time to pay, I handed her my dining card, and Theo pulled out his. "I'm paying for hers though. I think I lost a bet."

He shot me a *you-win* glance, filling me with joyous satisfaction as I said, "We said ice cream and toppings, right? The amount of ice cream was never confirmed." I grinned at him.

"I'll take two more scoops, chocolate and vanilla. Plus whipped cream and sprinkles." If I was going to bask in the glory of this win, I was going to do it with a large ice cream purchase, savoring every bite with smug delight.

When the girl behind the counter handed me my ice cream, Theo said coolly, "Enjoy."

"Oh, I will!" Theo, Ms. Davenport, and Mr. Fuller waited by the door as I took a wad of extra napkins. By the time I joined them, Theo had already eaten his vanilla scoop and was nibbling his cone.

I looked at him with disapproval as I held the door. "Why'd you eat yours so fast? You should try to enjoy it next time."

"I did enjoy it. I always eat fast. I like cold, firm ice cream better than the drippy, melting kind. Like that."

He pointed at Mr. Fuller trying to lick faster than the ice cream dripped. Right now, it was a perfect balance with drips and licks, but we'd only been out in the sun for maybe ten seconds. After thirty, it might be a different story.

Theo polished off his cone and gently elbowed my side, sending me into a fit of giggles.

"I'm ticklish. Don't do that unless you want me to puke this winning ice cream all over you."

Mischief glinted in his eyes, but he refrained while we walked. Just outside the community room, he poked me with his elbow again, causing me to jump back into Mr. Fuller, who fell into Ms.

Davenport, who somehow caught both of us human dominoes. I scrambled upright and somehow saved the ice cream from spilling from the cup.

"Wow, nice save, Ms. D!" Theo held out his right hand to high-five her. She couldn't reciprocate because she was still holding Mr. Fuller up with both of her arms.

I joked, "Maybe this can be the talent you showcase at the talent show, Ms. D. You've got superhuman upper body strength."

Ms. Davenport whispered a strained, "Pilates," as Theo and I pulled Mr. Fuller to a standing position.

He brushed off his pants, even though he hadn't fallen or spilled anything on himself. Mr. Fuller turned around and said to Ms. Davenport, "Looks like I owe you one. A fall like that would've meant emergency hip surgery."

"I think you owe me much more. A talent show confirmation for one. You can take me to ice cream again soon too." She blushed. "We can sit and enjoy it next time." Ms. Davenport looked at Theo and me. "Maybe we can all go. Another fun *double date?*"

I choked on chocolate ice cream.

Theo's walkie-talkie blasted, "Theo, you're needed in the front office. Have Sunny finish up the tech session and dismiss the visitors."

His face went insta-blotchy and red. "Gotta go! Camp emergency!" Theo jogged away, avoiding eye contact with all three of us.

I opened the door, and cold wind hit our faces. Ms. Davenport said, "Well, he didn't even say a proper goodbye. Or confirm his talent show attendance."

"Sunny will bring him." Mr. Fuller's eyes crinkled as he belly laughed. "Did you see how fast he ran?" He looked at me. "You're just like me, Sunny. He's just like her." The two of them went back to their table and worked quietly until Mr. Fuller called me over. More specifically, bellowed. He held his two hands together to his lips to form a circle and yelled, "Sunny! I need your help!"

Ms. Davenport had gone to the restroom. I walked over and said, "You know, you could have come over to me. I wasn't far from you."

His eyes twinkled. "You walk faster than me, and plus, I needed to ask you something while Mags isn't here." He glanced at the door. "I agreed to do the talent show."

"That's great, Mr. Fuller! I can't wait to go."

He waggled his eyebrows. "I convinced her to ballroom dance with me."

I squealed. "That's so exciting! And it's good exercise!"

He wiped his brow with a handkerchief. "We're doing the Viennese waltz because it's the easiest for me. I'm rusty and need a lot of practice. The last time I danced was at my first wedding. Would you mind practicing with me after this session? Not very long. Only enough so I can get the hang of it again."

"I—I don't know how to ballroom dance." I had one year of

mandatory dance in fifth grade: we learned the foxtrot, waltz, tango, cha-cha, and rumba. The waltz was the easiest for me to learn, but all five dances were a mess of clumsy feet, stiff arms, and mistimed moves. Reliving this gave me heart palpitations.

He grinned. "Well, this is your lucky day. I used to be a great dancer. And I'll teach you everything I know." He hummed a waltz tune and moved his arms to the beat, swaying in his chair. How could I say no to this man?

Ms. Davenport headed back toward us so I gave him a short answer. "Great."

He put his arms down. "Great!"

Great.

Everyone but Mr. Fuller loaded on to the van. When Ms. Davenport popped her head out the door, he explained he had some questions for Theo's mom and someone would drive him back. She didn't look convinced but closed the door anyway. He and I headed back into the community room and pushed the chairs and tables to the perimeter to clear out space for us.

Mr. Fuller was right: he was a great dancer. It was a shame he had me as a practice partner. My biggest fear, as I stepped on his feet over and over, was that dancing with me would make him worse.

Even though he was trying to be patient about my inability to do a simple box step, even after fifteen minutes of practice, his deep sighs were a dead giveaway. "Right forward ONE, left side TWO, close right THREE." *Sigh.* "Then left back ONE, right side TWO, close left THREE." *Sigh.* Over and over again.

My feet were supposed to be tracing the outline of a square, but mine was more like a lopsided trapezoid.

He paused the music on his phone. "I'm leading, and I go forward, and as the follower, you go backward."

I laughed. "Maybe I should lead. It's like my brain can't go backward or something."

His face turned contemplative. "You know, I have no problem with this. You lead then."

I was joking, but he turned on the music again, and I took lead. And holy cow, it was effortless.

After only a minute, we'd mastered the simple box. "You were born to lead, Sunny!" He went on to explain what happens next. "The step is then rotated, to the right in quarter and next half turns. Remember the dance direction is counterclockwise."

After we danced without mistakes, he tried out a few different waltz tunes to see which he liked the best. He turned off his phone, and a huge grin spread across his face. "Mags is going to be so surprised! I can't wait. Maybe I should offer to let her lead too?"

I grinned back. "Honestly, I don't think she'll care either way, whether she's leading or following, but I know that you asking which one she'd prefer would mean a lot to her."

We walked to the office together so Theo could drive him back home. Mr. Fuller chattered on and on about how many girls he'd danced with in his lifetime and how much energy he had when he was my age, but it was clear there was only one woman he was looking forward to dancing with now, and I couldn't wait to be in the audience to watch that happen.

He and I had such a funny little friendship. Mr. Fuller was a straight shooter, and I liked him a lot. Sure, he was a little rough around the edges, but he had a big, grumpy heart. Mr. Fuller was also a businessman, and I wondered if he could advise me on a decision I needed to make.

"Okay, I can tell you're thinking about something—you slowed down so much, I'm outpacing you. Spill it, missy."

Was it obvious? "It's nothing really. I need to decide on something soon. A hypothetical something, I mean." I bit my top lip. How much should I tell him, and what details could I disclose? Delina and I had woken up at 4:00 a.m. for three consecutive days to make the video. Funnily enough, the original "Party in the USA" video took place in a dusty field with beat-up pickup trucks and vintage cars, and Delina found an easy way to arrange the car props: there was a tractor and rusty car "graveyard" on the farm premises. As for the talent, a group of friends she'd made here offered to help. I had a decent enough singing voice to Miley Cyrus-ize the lyrics to be about hopping off the plane from LAX, arriving at a detox camp where "everybody seems so famous."

The parody worked perfectly. The final video was flawless. I was even able to send a shortened clip to Maya so she could preview it. All I needed to do now was send the final one to her.

Would Mr. Fuller understand any of this? Up until recently, he thought computer viruses were something you could catch. Successful business guy, though, even if he was blunt and a bit gruff. I decided it was best to hold back on disclosing details and discuss this philosophically instead.

"I can do something morally gray, well, more like light gray because it's not against the law or anything—and it could have a huge financial and career upside for me."

"But?"

I sighed. "But it might hurt people I care about. And I might get kicked out of this camp. It might also mean getting expelled from school, but I'm not sure about that."

He scratched his head. "You lost me. Why would you do something like that? Can you start from the beginning?"

I nodded. "Let's say you were given a once-in-a-lifetime opportunity, but if you went for it, you might succeed, but it could ruin a family's livelihood." I'd thought about this over and over again, and there was no way that a video filmed at a digital detox camp, clearly flouting its rules, would reflect well on this place. It would crater their reputation. "A place you've grown to appreciate. And people you care about might hate you forever, or at best, a very long time, because they'll feel deceived. But if everything works out, you'd get everything you'd wanted. What would you do?"

"Honestly, you lost me again," he said. "But this sounds like it could be a good Hollywood movie. You want to hear what I'd do?"

I nodded vigorously.

"I would do what felt right. Is this opportunity really everything you want? And all those people you hurt, are you better off without them, and are they better off without you? Or is your life better having them in it? I'm not saying don't do it. If you mess up, you can always try to apologize and fix it. But sometimes, as you get older, you need to make your own decisions and deal with the consequences, and an old man like me won't be able to help you with my outdated life advice. You need to learn how do to this on your own. Life's all about making choices, and sometimes they're good ones. Sometimes these decisions turn out to be the wrong ones, and that will, as you kids say, suck donkey balls."

"I don't think kids actually say *donkey balls*, but I get your point."

"Have you heard of a lady named Marie Kondo? She's always talking about purging things from your life that don't bring you joy. But maybe that's all a load of malarkey." Mr. Fuller pointed at the office a few yards away. "I can get Theo. Thanks for dancing with me."

"Sorry I sucked donkey balls."

We both cracked up. He said, "Well, when you take lead, it appears you don't. Your donkey balls shine."

A compliment from Mr. Fuller? Giddiness and relief passed through me as he shooed me away. It was time to make some choices.

TWENTY-FOUR

A SMALL CLUSTER OF DUCKS WADDLED TOWARD THE lake, entering the water near a patch of tall grass by the kayaks. I'd been sitting at a picnic table watching them for nearly an hour, like it was a live airing of a Discovery Channel show. I couldn't tear my eyes away from the adorable, carefree fowl family.

The smell of algae hung around me, a strange combination of mildew plus seaweed with sprigs of spring flowers, but I got used to it after a few minutes. This was the first time I'd spent time at the lake since I'd gotten to camp, partly because of the heat, partly because the dragonflies, horseflies, and mosquitoes limited my lake enjoyment considerably. There was also a yellow jacket nest somewhere nearby, which brought my overall satisfaction down a few hundred notches. We didn't have these aggressive kinds of bugs in LA, at least not where I lived.

But this time, I had a reason to be at the lake. I wanted to get across it. If there was Wi-Fi at the property there—and Delina heard from a reliable camp source that this was true—I could use the phone on the premises. But not to send or post the final video. It was to tell the Starhouse talent search team "thanks but no thanks" in the nicest way possible. I would send off a few important messages and emails, then dump the phone somewhere off the Sunshine Heritage Farms property lines.

If you had asked me even a day ago, I might have had a different plan. That last group session messed with my head, and after talking things through with Colin and Yehuda at lunch, discussing it with Delina in the wee hours of the night, and then chatting with Mr. Fuller, it made me question whether being a social media mogul was all I thought it would be. Maybe people like Theo were onto something. Taking a little time off to experience, explore, and enjoy other things in life was an option I hadn't considered before. And taking more time to think about my options when I got back home seemed like the right move.

My gaze drifted away from the mama duck posse to Theo, who was hard to miss, wearing a bright-orange life vest in a canoe, a stark contrast to his pale skin and brown hair. There was a girl in the canoe with him, wearing a pink sleeveless shirt that showed off her slender yet athletic arms. Her life jacket gave her a cute and outdoorsy look, not an awkward and bulky one. Performing for his canoe-mate, Theo imitated the rowing of a gondola, nearly tipping them both over in the process. Small waves thumped on the shoreline as the two of them drifted toward me. They drew close, and as Theo turned the boat to back into the bank, he nearly fell again. The gravel scraped the bottom of the metal canoe, making a sound as cringy as a locksmith making keys. His guest giggled and squealed like she'd never seen anything funnier in her life. I watched as she sat up straight and tossed her hair back. This girl's flirting game was set on expert mode.

Theo hopped out to drag in the canoe so his passenger could get out. Then he unclasped the two buckles on his vest, peeled off the buoyant neon layer, and put it in the boat. Reaching out his hand, he helped the girl stand and exit. My stomach dropped as she held his hand and carefully climbed out. She tottered but caught herself as both feet steadied on the shore of the lake. Then she fell into him.

Expert. Mode.

He propped her upright, and she removed her vest.

She asked, "Can you believe that in a few days, these detox kids will be gone? Was it you or Henry who called them 'toxers? It's so perfect. I hope next year the churches get funding again. I miss those guys. Not a 'toxer fan."

'Toxers?

The acid churning in the pit of my stomach made me want to vomit.

She walked closer to Theo and blocked my view. All I could

hear him say was, "It was Henry." I couldn't tell without seeing his face if he was conveying, "Ugh, Henry" or "Such a genius, that Henry." But what he *didn't* say was more telling. He could have just as easily added, "You know, this isn't cool. You and Henry shouldn't say that."

She took a few steps back, giving me a better view. "You want to go grab a bite at the canteen? Some ice cream maybe? It's hot out here." She flapped air into her shirt, conveniently revealing from many angles that she was not in fact wearing a bra.

Could I keep watching this courting ritual? This was torture. She was using her siren ways to lure Theo to the canteen for ice cream and who knew what else. Actually, I knew exactly what else.

Why couldn't I do that—be forward and confident like her? Maybe in my time of self-reflection and decluttering, this was another thing I could examine about my life. Why I was always in a perpetual state of singledom.

The ducks had concluded their tour de lake and were headed right to where I was standing. My picnic table offered partial shade plus a bonus of leftover sandwich crusts and cookie crumbs from some messy campers.

Theo noticed the ducks too. Then he immediately noticed me.

Even with our thirty feet of distance, I could see his face light up. New blotches on his neck and cheeks made him speckled from afar. "Hey! Sunny! Did you want a canoe ride?"

Was this his signature move? Wooing smitten women with a canoe ride, charming them, then breaking their hearts on shore as he refused their tokens of ice cream?

I needed to get across the lake, though, so I approached with hesitant steps.

He gave his gondola date an apologetic smile. "Thanks, Soph. You can have my ice cream—two frozen treats can definitely beat this heat!"

The girl tossed her hair back again with an angry, whiplike fury, making me thank the heavens she didn't have beads or anything in her hair. She could have easily weaponized her mane and taken all our eyes out with one flick.

"Last chance for ice cream? Or a milkshake maybe?"

When he didn't jump on the opportunity, she left with a scowl and made her way toward the main buildings.

Theo gestured to his canoe. "Your timing is perfect. This VIP yacht sets sail in one minute."

Cute, really cute. I needed to resist his charisma. I had a mission to get to the other side of the lake, and that 'toxer comment left me simmering, even a few minutes after it was made. I reached in the boat and lifted the life vest by the buckles. Why was it damp? It didn't make sense that a life vest would be so wet. Worse, it smelled like a mix of vanilla Glade PlugIns and strawberry body wash, the overly fragrant kind from Bath & Body Works that made me sneeze in the store.

"You need to put it on. No shoes, no vest, no service." Again, pretty cute. But no.

I shook my head. "I want a different one then. This one...isn't going to work."

"Okay, LA. You're so picky." He swapped it with the one he'd been wearing. When I clasped Theo's vest around my chest, his scent wrapped all around me, embracing me in a tight hug. It was hard for me to focus on what Theo was saying, which was apparently, "Can you help me push this in the water?"

With the boat a third of the way in, he motioned for me to get in and said, "Sit facing the back, please." Then he pushed a little more and stepped inside. He plopped down on the other seat facing me.

Using his paddle as a giant, wooden push-off device, he scooted the canoe into the water. After a few seconds passed, he broke my concentration by asking, "So, are you gonna help me paddle or what?" His strokes were moving us just fine, but I wasn't contributing at all because I'd been lost in my thoughts.

"Sorry. Where's my paddle?"

He pointed at my feet.

Oh God. It was right there.

"I was kidding," he said. "You don't have to do anything. In fact, watch this." He lifted his paddle, and we continued to drift toward the middle of the lake. "See? It's like at Walt Disney World, where the boat rides are on tracks. No effort needed!" Theo's eyes sparkled as he searched my face for a response.

I laughed. For a second, I forgot how quirky his sense of humor was. I wondered if the other girl appreciated his jokes. "So was that your friend in the canoe with you earlier? Or... girlfriend?" *Really smooth there, Sunny.*

He coughed. "Soph? No. Definitely no. Absolutely, definitely no, because she used to date my brother, and that's just...gross. Why? Did my brother say something to you?"

"She seemed like she was, I don't know, into you." He made a face like he might projectile vomit, so I added, "Into you two getting ice cream."

His face twisted into a scowl. "Our families go way back. She's a big flirt. Plus, she's not my type."

"You two look like you pair well together, like, I don't know, cheese and crackers."

He snorted. "Am I more cracker-like or cheesy to you?"

My face flushed. "I didn't mean—oh God. I meant, like, you two seem like you go together. You're compatible. It didn't come out right."

A hopeful glint appeared in his eyes. "So what about us? How compatible are we?"

"Y-y-you and me?" My pulse raced, and I could feel the blood pumping through my body, like something was trying to burst out of me. "We're opposites, right?"

He offered a slight smile. "I guess. It could be something else. Maybe we're complementary."

I swallowed hard. "Complementary? That's a surprisingly nice thing for you to say. There's a compliment for you."

He threw his head back and belly laughed. "You're such a goof sometimes."

"A complimentary goof." I unsuccessfully suppressed a giggle.

"I like complimentary goofs." His neck, face, and ears all speckled with red splotches. "Anyway, I'm not into her. I'm into you."

My body heat went up a few degrees, instantly activating Theo's vest scent.

There was no denying that sparks flew between us when we were near each other. I wanted to say, "I'm into you too," but wrong, awkward words lay thick on my tongue. I blurted out, "Even if I'm a 'toxer?"

Theo raised an eyebrow. "What? Where'd you hear that?"

Again, he could have said, "I hate that word!" or "You know, not cool. People shouldn't say that."

My heartbeat quickened, beating fast and hard against my chest. Could he hear it from his side of the boat, or did the life vest muffle the sound of the thumps with the thick, protective padding?

His shoulders slumped. "My brother used that term in a

camp staff meeting. He was trying to make a joke, but it offended a lot of people. It wasn't supposed to leave the room."

Was I reading too much into this by noticing all the things he didn't say? Like, "I'm sorry. I don't share his views." Or "He and I disagree all the time. Especially on this." Something.

Anything.

I spoke up. "But you see me as one, right? I'm just an LA surfer girl who is obsessed with social media and doesn't think college is worth the money?" I didn't know why I wanted to air this out between us, right then and there, in the middle of a lake while wearing uncomfortable life vests. But here we were. The last time we had a blowup, he wanted us to "agree to disagree." Well, not this time. I needed to know where we stood.

He put his paddle down on the floor of the canoe. "I'll be honest with you if you are with me. I did have my biases when you all came here for digital detox camp. A bunch of kids who were addicted to their devices were coming here, to my family's farm, to rehabilitate? This has the makings of a bizarre reality show, to be honest." Theo bit his bottom lip. "But then...there was you." He gulped and looked away before speaking again. "This girl from LA, who had her own YouTube channel but couldn't find the bathroom on the first day. I admit, I lumped you in this same category as everyone else. I looked at all of you like—like—"

"Influencer aliens?"

He laughed. "Your words, not mine."

"So you admit to being judgmental. About us 'toxers." My voice warbled, but I got the words out.

He fidgeted with his vest straps. "As a wise woman once pointed out, I live on a crusty old farm, so who the hell am I to be judgmental?"

"I never used the word *crusty*."

His gaze met mine. "True. My whole life, I've had a plan. To work on the farm, to go to school and college, then work on the farm when I graduated. But I started to get into the finance and operational side of the farm lately, and I'm enjoying it. Maybe even want to make a career of it for a nonprofit or for developing country governments someday. But not today. Not when the farm's in bad financial shape." He looked over at his family's property. "Developers are like vultures, circling this place, and my parents refuse to sell. Things are better this summer, now that we switched to a wellness camp when the church funds dried up. Anyway, what were we talking about?"

I shrugged, and he laughed.

"I think we were talking about how you judged me and how I judged you too," Theo said.

I dropped my gaze to my feet. "I'm sorry. You made me think twice about doubting people. I'm ashamed to say I realized how judgmental I was after you pointed out my bias." I pulled out the folded newspaper article from my pocket and handed it to him. "Your story here about the farm and all the amazing things you've done—I didn't know any of that because I didn't ask questions. I assumed things. I've been so me-focused, I couldn't even see how I was acting. Sorry I called you Agro Boy the other day, especially in front of all those people."

"Agro Boy was definitely a new one." He took his time reading the page in silence. After about ten seconds of awkward quietness, I kind of wanted him to either read faster or provide some commentary. *Say something, Theo.*

I couldn't handle it anymore. "I enjoyed reading about the camp's history. And about you. I feel so stupid that I assumed you were—" My words caught in the back of my throat. "That you were just a boy who lived on a farm."

He smirked, which I wasn't expecting at all. "This is like that old movie with the awkward British guy and Julia Roberts. *Notting Hill!* I'm just an agro boy, standing in front of an LA surfer girl—"

Asking her to love him?

I knew that line. My parents loved that movie. But like all cynics of my generation, I dismissed it as Hollywood storytelling and not anything like real life. Mocked it online with memes. But maybe this really was how my life was supposed to go. For me to fall for a boy wearing an orange flotation vest...in the middle of stagnant algae water. At a historic farm.

He held on to both sides of the canoe and kept his balance as he rose to a standing position.

"What are you doing?" I shriek-laughed. "You're not doing

that gondola crap with me. You already did that before with the other girl. I saw you."

He planted both hands on his hips, elbows out. "Oh, so you were watching me, eh?"

Don't be weird now, Sunny. Channel your inner Soph, who would ask him out on an ice cream date.

I flipped my hair. "I was."

He belly laughed. "I know. I was watching you too."

My cheeks grew hot underneath my slick sunscreen. This time, rather than overthink every little thing that could go wrong with me or him or us, I tried to make my mind go blank and go with what fate had in store for us.

Bzzz.

A yellow jacket flew by.

Bzzzzz.

Then another.

Bzzzzzzz!

When the third one came by and landed on the edge of the canoe to my left, I scooted all the way to the right, quick. So fast that Theo didn't stop me in time from upsetting the peaceful, blissful, harmonious balance of the canoe.

His arms flapped like he was doing the elementary backstroke, and he toppled backward into the lake before I could piece together what had happened. How could one quick scoot lead to so much mayhem? In the water, he lay on his back with his eyes shut. My instincts were to jump in after him to make sure he was breathing and hadn't hit his head on his way down. I knew my way around water, but I had no idea how to get out of a canoe other than tipping the boat and ungracefully falling in.

So that's exactly what I did, with emphasis on ungracefully.

The moment I hit water and tried to orient myself, sunscreen dripped into my eyes, causing momentary, burning blindness. Did I mention excruciating? That too. I wiped my sunscreen away with my palms while trying to keep my vest from pushing up past my neck and suffocating me. After a few swipes, using the lake water with who knows what kinds of microbes to flush my eyes, my vision returned. Theo was still floating on his back a few feet away from me, bobbing a little from the waves I'd made from all my commotion. I made my way to him, hoping he was okay.

His eyes were closed, but he had a grin plastered on his face. When he heard me approach, he said, "That took thirty seconds. I thought you'd be quicker with all your swim camp experience."

I used both arms to scoop waves of water onto his face. He lurched into a vertical position, and I hit him with another tidal wave of algae water. He wiped his face. "I'm just an agro boy, treading water in front of a slow-moving LA surfer girl, asking for a truce!"

Pure adrenaline pumped hard when Theo fell out of the boat and again when I tossed myself out of the boat to check on him. Now, I had all sorts of emotions flowing through me: attraction and annoyance were the dominant ones, followed by frustration, excitement, and an exponentially growing need-to-punch-his-face feeling.

He called out, "Race you back to the boat?"

The canoe had drifted many yards away, but at a glance, it appeared equidistant from us both. This would settle a lot, about how fast or slow I truly was and whether LA swim camp was, in fact, useless. But only if I could take off the stupid vest. I yelled out my terms for buoyancy removal, and he agreed. We both unhooked our vests and let them float away freely. We would come back to retrieve them when the race was over. It wouldn't take long.

I treaded water, waiting for him to count to three. Flashes of swimming memories popped into my head: being by the ocean, my body covered in sunscreen and sand. My middle school and junior high early-morning swim meets. My parents cheering in the bleachers. My hair, crunchy and lighter with blond tips from the chlorine. I never won any swim awards, but I loved being in the water. And I enjoyed the company of my teammates, some of whom were still my friends today. My parents and Chloe came to every meet, and afterward, we all went to brunch together. When I quit swimming, all that ended.

I'd given up much more than I thought.

"Three!"

DAMN IT. I'd missed Theo calling out the other numbers.

His laughter rang in my ears as he took off into a front crawl.

Judging by his speed, this wasn't a cute, coy, flirty game he was going to let me win. He was gunning for a victory.

I wasn't going to let him get the satisfaction.

I had two choices—a less embarrassing front crawl or my fastest move, the backstroke. The boat hadn't drifted and was a straight shot from where I was, so I eyeballed the distance and flipped over. The sun was at its highest point in the sky, so with my eyes closed, I swam like my life depended on it.

When I reached the distance of an Olympic pool, I flipped over to finish the rest of the way with the forward crawl. Who knew I'd roll into my last days of farm camp using a medley of rusty swim strokes?

Definitely not me.

Theo had a slight head start, and he was powerful, but his strokes were inefficient. I'd learned how to control the splashing in my millions of hours of training. We approached the boat at the same time, both tagging the canoe with both hands, hitting it hard with hollow, reverberating slaps.

We were both panting hard. His eyes gleamed with mischief as he huffed, "You almost beat me. I take back all my trash talk. Want to teach me some of your moves?"

It was impossible not to notice his paper-thin shirt clinging to his lean, well-built chest. Or his hair, mostly slicked back except for the one section in front that fell close to his eyes. Or the wry smile he was making with his full lips.

I thought back to Soph. Her hair flip. Her forwardness. How jealous I was of her. How much I wanted him to be mine.

I'd beat myself up later if I didn't make a move.

He's right there! Don't overthink this, Sunny.

KISS HIM.

And don't say something like, "Here's a move you won't forget!"

I made my way closer to him and put my trembling hands on his shoulders. With his left hand still on the boat supporting us both, Theo reached around to my back with his other one and slowly pulled me into him, our bodies not only touching but fitting together like interlocking fingers. Could he feel my heart hammering?

Sliding my fingers down his chest, I could feel the physical effects of his farm labor as my fingertips traced the ripple of his muscles down to his stomach. Through his white shirt, I could see everything. And I wanted everything I could see. I shivered.

Closing my eyes, I took a deep breath and inhaled his scent. With my head tilted upward, my lips brushed against his, gently exploring at first, like we were saying a shy hello. But our second kiss was the one to remember: he pressed his lips against mine, and the intense bolt of electricity flowing between our bodies was so intense, we needed a circuit breaker between us. I raked my fingers through his wet hair, curling and uncurling my fingers each time his mouth met mine.

My eyes opened as he loosened his grip on my waist. He

planted light kisses on my forehead, then down my neck, and pulled away from me slowly. His soft gaze made my heart and stomach turn little flips. With a wicked grin, he said, "Let's continue this ashore."

"And get these wet clothes off?" I asked coyly.

He laughed. "Yes, please. But first, let me stabilize the hull by holding it so you can climb in first." He scrunched his nose. "Actually, maybe I should go first so I can pull you in once I'm inside. Or maybe we can climb in on opposite sides and stabilize it with our weight. But you can't let go or give up, or the canoe will flip."

"I vote for the last option."

He nodded. "Okay, we can do it on the count of three," he said and went around to the other side. Steadying the boat by climbing in simultaneously could work. My upper body strength was nonexistent, seeing as how I hadn't done any physical activity in the last year other than backstroking and front crawling to the canoe, but this was the best option.

"Three!"

I missed it again!

The boat seesawed a little because he had a head start, but I used all my body strength to pull myself up. This was one of the hardest physical challenges in my entire seventeen years of existence. Once I got my shoulders up and over, I lifted my torso out of the water, turned lengthwise, threw my right leg around, and rolled into the boat, flopping in like a large, wet fish. Sitting up, I could see the boat had drifted to the other side of the lake, my original destination. Theo looked at me with bewilderment on his face.

"If you want to talk about how ungraceful that was, save it for another time."

"What's this?" In his hand, he held my phone.

Oh no. It must've fallen out of my pocket when I scrambled out of the boat.

His face clouded with confusion. "You have a message." He turned the screen toward me. There was a text from Maya on the lock screen.

Maya

> The camp parody clip you sent is HILARIOUS! Where's the rest of the video? It's due soon...

My voice wavered as I spoke. "It's not as bad as it looks." Tears threatened to fall as disappointment, sadness, and anger at myself swelled inside me. "Okay, some of it is as bad as it looks. I have an illegal phone. But I swear I wasn't going to send camp footage. I like this place, mostly. I'm sad to be leaving." He wouldn't look at me. "I'm sad to be leaving *you*. I wasn't going to send them anything, I swear—" Words caught in the back of my throat, and I gulped hard, hoping to find my voice again. But the more I talked, the worse it got.

"Who is *they*? Can you show me your camera roll?" He handed me the device. None of my photos were sorted, and I didn't know if the older photos or newer ones would appear first. When I hesitated, he lifted his paddle and stroked a few times to get us close to the edge of the lake.

No, I couldn't show him the photos. All this would show that I didn't adhere to the camp rules. The very fact that I had a phone was in direct conflict with the entire purpose of this camp. Plus, one of the first photos was of Side Braid holding a bag of pills. And there were outtakes from the music video too, but taken out of context, with us wearing cowboy boots and hats and overalls, it would look like flat-out mockery of the farm, but it was actually just like the original video.

The canoe bottom hit the gravel on the shoreline, and Theo jumped out as if the boat were on fire.

I whispered, "Can I please explain?"

Holding the boat still, he wore a blank expression on his face. "Honestly, I can't even talk to you right now. I can't look at you. I can't. Whatever you say won't make sense. And I'm still deciding if I turn you in or pretend none of this happened. *None* of it." He pointed to our left and our right. "It's safe to walk back on your own. It's a half-mile loop to your right, and a little longer if you go to your left." Theo closed his eyes, took a deep breath, then opened them again. "I need time to think. And I need to get the vests out there."

My shoes made a loud deflating squish sound when I hopped out. I looked at Theo for any sign of connection between us, but distrust darkened his eyes, and his face and body stiffened, signaling to me this wasn't the right time or place to talk about the phone or about us.

The creak of tall trees echoed far above me as leaves rustled in the wind. The breeze pushed his hair into his eyes, but he didn't take time to swipe it away.

He said one more thing to me. "I'm just...so disappointed in you." He stepped back in the canoe in a hurry and pushed off with his paddle, setting sail without me. As the distance between us grew, my body ached with fatigue and grief.

On the other side of the lake, I predicted he would woo me with a charming canoe ride and immediately break my heart on shore.

He wooed me all right, but I shattered his heart, not the other way around. Then I shattered my own.

Even worse, I didn't know how to fix any of this.

But I had to try.

TWENTY-FIVE

THE TALL GRASS TICKLED MY ANKLES AS I WALKED TOWARD my destination. All the leg-brushing made them itch like crazy. Only a short distance remained between me and the clearing ahead.

Beyond that point was the grounds for the newly built resort, where the guest Wi-Fi would be. Where I would be able to fire off all my messages, a few steps past the signs REST AND RELAXATION ZONE AHEAD! and WELCOME TO PROMISE RANCH. PLEASE STAY A WHILE!

The instant I picked up an LTE signal should have been a time of joy and celebration. But the moment was ruined because Side Braid was casually sipping a Coke on one of the wooden benches near the path. In her other hand, she held her phone. She staggered to her feet as soon as I approached, leaving the sweaty can of soda on the seat, knocking over a small, empty bottle of rum I hadn't noticed before by her feet. My brain couldn't process anything: Wendy had alcohol! How did she get a refreshing can of Coca-Cola? As she stumbled toward me, I punched a few keys on my phone and tucked it back into my pocket.

She laughed. "I posted my Starhouse summer video a few minutes ago, and it already has over a thousand likes. First mover advantage." She raised her Coke. "I took this from a room minibar while one of the housekeepers was in the bathroom. I'd share, but, you know, I don't like you."

"Thanks." I licked my lips, not realizing until now how thirsty I was.

She barked out more laughs. "You know what bugs me the most about you? All my content is so much better than yours. Your feed, it's the absolute worst." She stumbled back a step. "*You're* the worst." The *t* dropped off her last word, thanks to her rum-induced slurring.

In her current state, she was vicious but also melancholy, like a depressed cobra. If this were anyone else, I'd feel her out for a friendly hug, but she was no friend. She'd made this crystal-clear on the first day of camp.

"Is this trash-talking really necessary?" My cheeks flared with anger as she walked in a giant circle around me, sizing me up.

"Yes."

Well, I had to hand her that. Brutal honesty.

Wendy looked at her watch. "Ten minutes left for you to send your video." A sinister smile crept across her face. "But I'm not going to let that happen."

"Honestly, I'm not here for that."

She narrowed her eyes. "Well, Goggle Girl, I don't believe you." A fit of giggles erupted, followed by a hiccup.

My hand fished inside my pocket and pulled out the phone just enough to see it had two bars of LTE service. I had a lot of data to send still, and with her here, preventing me from getting closer to the main resort grounds, I wouldn't be able to connect to the Wi-Fi anyway. She brought the can to her mouth and took a long sip while her sociopathic eyes held my gaze.

She coughed. "Wow, that really burns when you drink it too fast."

While Wendy put the can on the ground, I pulled out my phone, firing off all my prewritten messages one by one, hoping the cell service still worked.

The first one to Maya.

Then to my parents.

Last one to Rafa.

"Hey!" Wendy barreled toward me, and I pulled up the photo with her holding the drugs and held it up so she could see. "Stop! One more move, and this gets posted."

Side Braid slowed to a full stop and peered at the phone from a few feet away.

"It's a pic of you holding the ziplock. Of you know, um, drugs." My phone hovered over the Send button.

"You can't tell it's me; it's taken from behind."

"True, but it won't be hard for people to figure out."

She snarled and lunged at me, clawing at my phone. Taken by surprise, I lost my footing and fell backward onto the lawn. We both came crashing down, her on top of me and me pinned underneath in submission, like a mixed martial arts match between two people of unequal skill.

After the day of swimming and canoeing, I had no energy left to grapple with Side Braid. My adrenaline had spiked earlier that day, a few times, and though my heart was beating hard and fast from the tussle, I couldn't push her off me.

Wendy pried the phone from my fingers and whooped with delight when she pulled it away. Still sitting on my chest, boobs squashed, she fiddled with the interface. "Wait, where's the video?"

While she was distracted, I pushed to my side and wriggled out a little, barely enough to breathe. "I deleted it," I croaked.

She clenched her thighs so I couldn't move anymore. "That doesn't make sense. Why?"

I motioned for her to move. She sighed and moved down my torso, more toward my stomach. I coughed and took deep breaths. "I have other priorities."

My phone bleeped with messages. Then pinged with urgent

emails. A voicemail. Then another. Her mouth dropped open when she saw the notifications stream in from the "I'm withdrawing from the competition" social media announcement Maya put up on my accounts. Coach had warned us that getting likes and notifications could be as addictive as smoking tobacco or vaping, and these "little ding-a-lings of false fulfillment" were short-term "hits." My post urged everyone to create positive, genuine relationships online and to use social media more intentionally.

Her face drained of all color, contorted with agony, then stirred with rage. I'd found a real reason technology could be embraced: it connected me with people who truly cared about me, and these notifications were proof that they pulled through for me.

Ding!

Ding!

Maya must have posted the online fundraiser to save the farm.

Or maybe it was the save the date: Delina and I would do a joint mukbang to raise money for Iowa's oldest historical farm in two weeks.

It could have been Rafael posting his photojournalism article about Sunshine Heritage Farms for his internship assignment. The first entry was "Going Hard-Core Cottagecore at Camp Sunshine."

I'd learned the hard way that you can't silence social media.

It had always had a life of its own—an untamable beast, for good or bad. But the other lesson I took away from #BrowniePorn was that if there's an opportunity to get ahead of a story, to control the narrative, you should take it. In this case, I would use my short-term social media buzz to help Theo's farm stay afloat with online fundraising.

"What is happening here?" Theo's voice echoed above my head, but because I was still pinned under Wendy, I couldn't make eye contact.

He surprised both of us by taking a photo. "I'm sure whatever it is, you don't want me sharing this picture of you bullying Sunny."

Wendy scrambled off and pushed down on my chest to help herself stand. "I—was just—s-she was trying to use an illegal cell phone, and I was trying to stop her."

I rolled to my side, sat up on my knees, and wheezed.

Wendy slurred, "This isn't my phone." She jabbed a finger in my face. "It's hers."

Theo held out his hand, and Wendy gave him the cell. He looked through the camera roll. "All that's here are a bunch of nature photos and a picture of you holding a bag of something that doesn't look like vitamins." He pulled out his walkie-talkie. "Theo here. I need a camper escort to meet me at Promise Ranch. We have an intoxicated, disruptive detox participant on neighboring grounds."

Crackle—"a counselor on the way"—*crackle*.

Theo said to me, "I got back to camp, and there'd been no sighting of you for a while. I got worried, so I came looking. I thought you'd gotten hurt or lost."

My eyes brimmed with tears, relieved he at least knew things weren't what they seemed here. He offered me a half smile. We still had some things to work out between us, and his almost smile meant the world to me. It meant there was hope for Theo and me.

Theo's walkie crackled at full blast. "Theo, is Sunny with you? We need you both back here immediately. We have a major media problem on our hands."

He pulled me up to my feet. I winced from the achiness in my arms and rubbed my chest and shoulders. Getting in that altercation with Side Braid was not at all what I was expecting. Especially so soon after I'd been kissing Theo in the water.

The escort came quickly, and Theo briefly explained what had happened, then he and I walked to the shore.

"You okay?" Theo glanced at me. His hair was dry now, but errant brown wisps clung to his forehead. I wanted to push them away, but I didn't dare.

He held the canoe so I could get in. I said, "There's a lot to explain, and a lot of it didn't make sense until I came here. But I understand if you're tired of me and don't want to talk about it."

He launched us into the water. Seated now, with his full

attention on me, he said, "It'll take some time to get across the lake. I'm listening."

Tears tumbled down my cheeks, and I told him everything.

TWENTY-SIX

THEO'S MOM AND COACH WERE WAITING FOR US IN THE main camp office. When we opened the door, they both gestured to the two empty chairs facing them. On the desk was a Camp President wooden plaque that someone had painted and shellacked. The faint smell of pine mixed with instant coffee was a welcome combination given the other rancid animal scents pervading the camp.

Once we were seated, I nearly fell backward when a video image of my parents appeared on the large monitor.

"Mr. and Mrs. Song, I appreciate you were able to video chat on such short notice. I'm sorry for the technical difficulties, but it looks like this link worked." Flashbacks from my scolding in the principal's office flickered in my head. My heart raced, and I swallowed down the panic in my throat.

Everyone looked so serious. This situation warranted

seriousness, of course, so it was understandable. But it was uncomfortable, especially since Theo was here, and my parents would witness whatever punishment the camp deemed appropriate. The muscles in my shoulders clenched, and I was unsuccessful at willing them to stay down.

Theo's mom cleared her throat. "I presume you know why you're here, Sunny."

I nodded slowly and glanced at the screen. My parents offered no comforting looks.

Theo's mom pulled a spiral notebook from a nearby stack and thumbed through some pages. "Today's daily log says you went on a canoe ride with my son, and Theo came back alone. While he was searching for you, we received several calls and emails in a row from prominent individuals and various organizations in our area, inquiring about the camp availability for next summer. And one of our board members shared a recent social media post from your account, in which you promoted a fundraiser to save Sunshine and something called a...Muck. Bang. And it appears this unauthorized fundraiser has passed five thousand dollars in donations." She took her reading glasses off her face. "What were you planning to do with these funds? My husband, who will be here shortly, is our finance person, and he's unaware of any of these so-called plans. Were you planning to embezzle this money?"

I let out a loud laugh. Me? Embezzle thousands of dollars?

I didn't even have a bank account that wasn't cosigned by my parents. Um, no.

I looked at my parents as I spoke. "My plans were to raise money and send the funds electronically. I've done successful fundraisers before, for my school. My parents can attest." I looked over at Theo's mom and then back at the screen. My mom and dad nodded, their faces calmer. I loosened my shoulders and took a deep breath in and out.

For someone who had five thousand dollars dropped into her lap, Theo's mom still hadn't shown any emotion other than stoicism. Coach's worry lines weren't as deep anymore, which was good. Maybe things weren't as bad as I thought?

"We received something called a Google Alert. Someone had posted an article with photos of our camp online, and the time stamp also happens to be today. Were you by chance involved with this too? My guess is yes."

I glanced at Theo. He made eye contact and nodded slowly.

"Yes," I croaked. "It's only photos, and they're all good ones. Like, you could make postcards out of them."

For the big finale, she would disclose that I was getting expelled from camp. Waiting for that other shoe to drop was brutal.

"Well, as you can imagine, we have questions, such as how you were able to post those photos in the first place. When did you plan all this? Do you have anything to add?"

I did have something to add. "I brought an illegal phone into camp. Honestly, I thought I needed it as, like, a safety blanket, and when it didn't get confiscated, I didn't know what to do with it. At first, I checked for signal all the time, then a lot less, and after a while, like only once a day." Should I mention the Starhouse competition? Nah. Bad idea. "I found out you were in financial trouble, so I went searching for Wi-Fi to put into motion all the things you mentioned today. Even though I hated most of my stay here, no offense, I've found that this place—Coach and Delina and Theo especially—helped me not lose sight of what matters most to me."

Theo's mom quirked an eyebrow. "And what is that?"

"Relationships. Ones that matter because they're real and true." I looked at Theo, whose upturned face buoyed my confidence. A warmth expanded in my chest as I shot him a look of gratitude.

Theo added, "Wendy was involved with some illegal activity too. But her infractions were so much worse." He showed her the drug photo on my phone and the video of Wendy sitting on my chest.

Her lips curled. "I see." She jotted something down in her notebook. "When we're done here, I'll call her parents and notify her school that she didn't complete the program."

"What Wendy did is far different from Sunny's actions," Coach said.

Theo's mom closed her notebook. "Agreed. This brings us to the decision we need to make. Sunny violated the rules by bringing a cell phone onto the property, which, as you know, warrants immediate removal from the program. Mr. and Mrs. Song, that's why we asked you be present."

Theo's mom's phone rang, and she sent it to voicemail. It rang again, but she tried to talk over it.

"We have a 'one strike and you're out' policy here." A video call request popped up on her phone screen. "Oh, this is a call from Promise City Assisted Living. We take all their calls in case there's an emergency."

Mr. Fuller's face appeared when she answered. We could only see his nose and mustache. "Hello? Can you hear me?"

She sighed. "Yes, loud and clear. Is there an emergency, Bill?"

"Of course there is! You can't kick out Sunny."

"How did you hear about this?"

Mr. Fuller explained, "I have a lot of friends who keep their ear to the ground." He raised the phone so we could only see his eyes now. "She's the one who taught me how to make video calls. And now look!"

My parents murmured in Korean, "Who is that strange old man? Why is he so loud?"

"I appreciate your call, and we will take note of your praise and your concerns."

He squinted. "That's BS corporate speak, and you know it.

I'm telling you, she needs to stay. She's helped a bunch of us figure out how to work technology in a useful way. We're talking to our kids and grandkids now, more frequently and easily. Oh! And I need her tomorrow afternoon—she's my dance coach for the talent show."

I threw a look over to my parents, who gave me the most priceless WTF look in the world. I shrugged back. *I know, Mom and Dad. Me, a dance coach?*

"I don't know if any of this helps her case, but I want her to stay. Mags does too. We all do. It's only for a few more days. Have a heart."

Theo's mom's lips pressed into a hard line while she took a deep breath in and out of her nose. "Coach, any thoughts here?"

He shoved his hands in his pockets. "I'm Team Sunny. I have been from day one."

My eyes teared over. If he said anything else, it would turn into a full-blown ugly cry.

But then my parents broke me. "We're Team Sunny too." It was my mom. Speaking for the first time.

"I'm sorry." My voice cracked. Small, uncontrollable heaves shook my body.

I *was* sorry for bringing the phone. For #BrownieGate and #BbrowniePorn. For disappointing my parents. For not telling Theo about so many things. Sorry for ruining our moment.

Sorry for everything.

Theo scooted his chair right next to mine and put his hand on my back. It wasn't a hug, but it was just as nice. He leaned over and whispered, "You know what team I'm on."

My dad spoke. "Don't be sorry, Sunny. We sent you to camp without having time to think everything through." He glanced at my mom. "Your mom and I have talked a lot about this, and it was a knee-jerk reaction."

My mom jumped in. "*My* knee-jerk reaction. I'm the one who should be sorry for not listening. To you, to your appa. It was my dream to be a mommy blogger, not yours. I'm ashamed to say this, but I—" Her sentence cut short as her words caught in her throat. She looked at my dad and said in a soft tone, "I pushed you into this life. And then, I not only lived vicariously through you but got a little jealous too. I had to go back to the law after I had you and Chloe, all while you had exciting opportunities laid out in front of you at such an early age. But as you got older, you struggled with the burden of it all, and I wasn't there to support you. You're a strong-willed, thoughtful, and headstrong person. I've known this your whole life, and I need to step aside to let you grow to be the person you were meant to be."

"Really?" I wiped my eyes with my palms.

Mom smiled. "You do what you were meant to do. Make your own path."

Dad added, "We've gotten a family counselor. We're also trying some new things when you get home. We noticed that you enlisted Maya's help for your social media accounts. We're impressed with your resourcefulness." He nodded and smiled. "When you get home, you'll see some changes. Mom's taking a three-month paid sabbatical to work on self-care. She might even start blogging again. I'm going part time at work while I ramp up my real-estate consulting business. When you're back home, we can see what changes you want to make, if any. We're Team Sunny all the way. Chloe is too."

Something inside me shifted. My whole body became less tense, and a sense of relief washed over me. Whatever happened here, whether I'd be kicked out or not, I was in a better place now. I was Team Sunny all the way too.

Theo's mom cleared her throat. "Well, I've never been outnumbered by so many people before. Sunny, with less than a week left at this camp, I'm leaning toward you staying. Mr. Song, if you're starting a consulting business in real estate, we might need to figure out the best way to upgrade our facilities with the new funding Sunny's secured for us. I would love some advice— for a friends and family discount, of course." Her mouth cracked into something that resembled a smile. She made a joke!

I glanced at Dad in the video screen. His face brightened as he leaned in to the camera. "Sure. Give me a call tomorrow!"

Theo's mom looked at her phone. "I forgot you were still on, Mr. Fuller. Thank you for your input."

He bellowed, "You're welcome!" while dropping his cell on

the ground. After a loud scramble and a lot of cursing, he hung up abruptly without saying goodbye.

"Sunny, I also wanted to say sorry for my insensitive comments when we were at the welcome station. They were uncalled for, and Theo's helping us implement diversity and inclusion training soon, and I will be an active and eager participant. I'm going to strive to do better." She offered an apologetic smile. "But back to the situation at hand. While we appreciate your help with keeping our farm afloat, we still need to issue appropriate punishment for your actions. So effective immediately, please head to the sheep shearing station. It seems a lot of campers have skipped out on sheep duty, and our ewes have taken on a Bob Ross look."

I leaned over to Theo. "Who's that?"

"I'll tell you later," he whispered.

"Afterward, you'll need to clean the kitchen tonight, and then, bright and early, please clean the bathrooms in the mess hall. And you can clean up again before the talent show."

"I can stay?"

"Yes, as long as you take your duties seriously. Thank you again, Mr. and Mrs. Song for joining the call. We'll let you go now."

"Bye, Mom! Bye, Dad!" With both of my parents smiling and midwave, Theo's mom clicked out of the video call window.

Theo stayed behind to chat with his mom as I shuffled out of the office. Exhausted from the day's events, sheep shearing was the last thing I wanted to do, but it was better than being sent home. How nice would it be to sleep right now? And I knew what Agro Boy would say if he were here: *Can't wait to hit the hay?*

I snorted and walked to the barn.

TWENTY-SEVEN

"THERE'S BEEN A CHANGE OF PLANS," MR. FULLER BARKED as he let me in through the back entrance of the Promise City Assisted Living Center's auditorium. "It's a long story, and we don't have time to go into it because the show starts soon, but I need you to dance with me onstage."

My mouth fell open. "Wait, what happened to Ms. Davenport?"

He shrugged. "She's mad at me and said she'll dance with Theo. I made fun of the talent show this morning, and now she's not talking to me. She's too busy flitting around with supervising this event and won't listen to my apology."

"What did you say exactly?" I braced myself.

His face paled. "I said she needed to ease up with her stress. It's not like this event was something important, like finding a cure for STDs." He picked at his fingernails. "I guess I could've been more sensitive."

"Mr. Fuller, I'm the worst when it comes to advice, but when someone's stressed out, it's maybe best to offer to do something useful, like help them with groceries or bring them food if they're strapped to their desk. Something like that. A gesture."

"A gesture," he echoed. "Okay, next time."

He offered me a seat in the front row, beside him. "She's over there, with Theo." He pointed across the aisle to the seats opposite ours.

I waved at the two of them, but only Theo saw. He nodded toward the front of the auditorium and mouthed, "See you onstage."

The room was mostly full, with a quarter of the audience from camp. The lights dimmed before I had time to skim through the talent show program. Whistles and clapping erupted when the emcee of the event took the microphone. He had slicked-back gray hair and wore a navy-blue sequined jacket and pants, like something you might see at an upscale show in Vegas. He was rail thin, but the outfit gave him some bulk.

"Ladies and gentlemen! Welcome to the first annual talent show, which we've named Promise City's Got Talent! I'm your host, Ricky Suggs. Tonight, we have magicians and jugglers and musicians—the list goes on. There's juice and cookies in the back. And if you're prone to falling asleep and snoring—I'm looking at you, Jimmy—be sure to sit near the back so we can get you out quickly. If you don't, we might mike you and turn it into a comedy act." The audience roared. "So without further ado, let's bring Marion Smith to the stage to perform an interpretive dance to 'The Star-Spangled Banner.'"

According to the program, we were on next, and the national anthem was only two minutes long. I stood and pulled Mr. Fuller to his feet. My hands were clammy. Some of it was performance anxiety, but I knew deep down, my stomach was clenched tight from Theo being here. I took deep, steady breaths as Marion the interpretive dancer left the stage.

"Coming to the stage next...we have Bill Fuller and Mags Davenport, dancing to—" He squinted and asked, "Which songs, Mags and Bill? It's crossed out."

Ms. Davenport said, "'Come Away with Me' by Norah Jones." Theo was standing next to her on the opposite side of the stage.

Simultaneously, Mr. Fuller shouted, "'*Game of Thrones* Theme'!" I looked over at Theo, who laughed and shrugged.

These two hadn't even agreed on the music! The *GoT* theme was a much faster one-two-three step, and I tried to picture how fast the song would be in my head. My God, we hadn't practiced that one.

Mr. Fuller whispered into my ear, "I think she's also mad at me for switching the song."

Oh, dear God.

The emcee laughed. "Well, we're here to have fun, so let's

do that. DJ, could you please play both? Let's do *Game of Thrones* first, to get the energy up."

The audience applauded as we took the stage. My breathing came out unevenly as panic wriggled through my body. *It's only a dance. One, two, three, one, two, three.*

The haunting theme song to *Game of Thrones* blasted over the speakers, and we began our dance.

One, two, three, one, two, three. Basic steps, like we practiced.

I was so focused on the counting that Mr. Fuller leaned in and said, "Kid, it'll be fine. It's music. Follow the beat."

I relaxed my shoulders, and he and I waltzed around the stage. *One, two, three.*

This wasn't so bad. *One, two, three.*

It was actually kind of fun. *One, two, three.*

We had stepped toward Ms. Davenport and Theo, who were also having a good time. I smiled at them, and they returned one too.

When the music switched to Norah Jones, a much slower tempo, Mr. Fuller loosened his grip on my hand and waist and pulled back. He turned and took Ms. Davenport as his dancing mate before I could even react, leaving me partner-less.

Theo, standing a few feet away looking as confused as ever, was alone too.

I walked over to him. "May I have this dance?" I bowed deeply. He pursed his lips to hold back a laugh and gave me a little cross-ankle curtsy.

He offered his right hand, and I laced my fingers in his. With his left hand on the small of my back, he said, "After you."

"I have to take lead," I murmured.

"I noticed."

And so I did. His eyes sparkled as he gazed into mine. We waltzed, and my stare dropped to his soft lips for a quick second. I shivered from the memory of the intensity of our kisses that day in the water. From his breath against my neck. From our bodies pressed together.

YOU, two, three.

WANT, two, three.

HIM, two, three.

The entire auditorium washed away. In a dreamlike state, my feet moved in sync while our bodies swayed to the count. He pulled me in closer, our hips nearly touching as we danced.

"I really want to kiss you right now," he whispered into my ear.

"So do it," I murmured.

We stopped waltzing, and he pressed his lips firmly against mine. One slow, intense kiss that made my legs quiver. He buried his face in my neck and wrapped both hands around my waist. My body ached for another deep, shivery kiss.

Mr. Fuller and Ms. Davenport waltzed over to us. "Trying to steal the show?" Mr. Fuller joked. "How's that for a gesture, Sunny? Here's another gesture—guest room forty-two is used for overnight stays of the family of residents, and I consider you like family. I hear they have nice sheets. No one will bother you there. I'm friends with the facilities manager. The talent show should take a couple of hours at least."

They giggled and danced away to the other side of the stage. I asked, "Do you think they orchestrated this whole thing? For us?"

Theo eased his hands farther down my back, sending my head spinning. I tugged on his shirt collar and ran my fingers lightly down his chest, then said, "Let's check out room forty-two. I hear it has nice sheets."

I took his hand and guided him off the stage. On the way out, Theo shouted curt hellos to the people who greeted him. Lucky for us, room forty-two was on the same floor, just around the corner. Electricity rippled through me as I turned the knob. Unlocked. Theo pressed into me as I pushed on the door. When it clicked shut behind us, my body flooded with uncontrollable joy. Theo turned the lock, and with my blood pounding through my body, I fell back on the bed and pulled him down next to me.

It was one of the last nights at summer camp together. We were going to make it count.

TWENTY-EIGHT

THE NIGHT BEFORE WE WERE SCHEDULED TO DEPART, THE staff gave us our devices and turned on the camp's Wi-Fi in the community room. Everyone had hundreds to thousands of notifications, and it was a real chore to get through a big chunk of them. Some were so old, it wasn't even worth responding to or acknowledging them. A lot of us added one another as friends, and we now could see who our fellow campmates were. Esports world champions and famous beauty bloggers were in our midst, and I didn't even know it.

Delina and I were more midrange types, and now that we were good friends and got along so well, we were going to collaborate on lots of projects when we got home. On our last morning, we hugged goodbye in the cabin.

She handed me a brown paper bag that she'd decorated at an art workshop. I peered inside. Fritos and brownies.

"Those are my grandma's special brownies. And I figured the Fritos would remind you of this place."

"Thank you. I'm going to miss you!"

"Don't get all sappy. We still have mukbangs and who knows what else we come up with—maybe some music videos?" We both burst into laughter and hugged again, one last time. "Need help carrying anything?"

"Nah, I'll be fine. Plus, you have some goodbyes of your own." Behind her, a line of girls were waiting their turn. I waved and made my way to the screen door that was propped open.

Before Delina tended to her fan club, she said, "Oh, before you go, I wanted to tell you that Wendy was disqualified from the Starhouse competition. Someone here leaked information anonymously that there was foul play involving Wendy at this camp, and now there are questions of whether the images in the video montage she submitted were hers or actually stock photos. Can you imagine? Even if it isn't true, how embarrassing is that? Anyway, who knows what'll happen. Maybe this whole thing was a publicity stunt for Starhouse and they weren't going to actually pick anyone. There's a rumor that the whole thing is going to blow up anyway because the members of Starhouse all hate each other now."

This was the best news I'd heard since coming here. Well, other than Theo admitting he liked me and his mom saying I'd get to stay at camp. Oh, and my mom saying she was supportive of me. So it was the fourth best thing.

I took my bags and headed toward the airport shuttle stop. While I walked, I studied my suitcase. It was weird to have gone on a trip and go back with basically the same amount of luggage, minus one burner phone, and with no souvenirs except for a Sunshine shirt for Chloe.

Coach saw me in the distance and caught up with me. He asked, "You think you'll miss this place?"

I smiled at him. "The fact that I'm not looking at my phone right now...probably."

"This was a challenging experience. I'm proud of you. When you get back, it's not going to be easy. You're going to be faced with a lot of choices. But if you've learned anything from me, you might be able to prioritize your time better."

"Thanks, Coach. I'm sure this wasn't easy for you either."

We arrived at the shuttle departure area and sat on the bench together. He knuckled a drip of sweat off his nose. "What do you think you'll do first, priority-wise, if you don't mind me asking?"

Theo came jogging over. "Hey, sorry I'm a little late. We had a call with our lawyer that ran way over time. What'd I miss?" He stroked my upper arm and gave me a light kiss on the lips.

"I was just about to tell Coach here my plans. Our plans." I took my reusable water bottle from my backpack pocket and took a sip. "Well, first I'm writing an essay my friend Rafael will help me get published. Then, I'm going to ask for swim lessons. And talk to my parents about getting a Korean tutor, a private one. Someone who won't laugh at how embarrassingly bad my accent is. I figured I should face my insecurity head-on and do something about it, not think about how I wished I'd learned Korean when I was younger."

Coach smiled. "That's a great idea."

"The rest of the summer, I'm still figuring out. I was pretty down on college before, but I'm not actually opposed to it. Maybe I could do it part time. Or defer. Or try a general studies program. Or maybe still not go. I need time to think through my options. Luckily, I'll have it."

Coach stood up. "I'll let you two be. Try to stay in touch if you can. You can find me on social media—I'm @TheGreatestCoachman1. It's a play off that musical. Anyway, good luck, Sunny." He shook my hand and walked back to the office.

Theo clasped his hands and squeezed them tight. "I forgot to tell you what the call was about with the lawyer and my dad. Thanks to your fundraiser and our advanced bookings, we're financially in the black this year. And it looks like we can roll out some of my new initiatives too!"

I placed my hand on his. "That's so great! Does this mean you can leave Iowa if you want?"

"I think so. When I visit UC Berkeley and UC Davis and the other Cali schools with agricultural business degrees, I promise I'll come to LA. You can teach me how to surf, and I promise

I won't make fun of it. And you can visit me when you look at schools in the Midwest."

Theo and I said in unison, "And we both look at Cornell." He and I planned to visit Ithaca in the late fall. Delina too.

The shuttle bus bumped down the dirt path. I looked into Theo's eyes with earnest. "So we video chat every day. Even if it's finals. Even if you have a football game to watch." Theo had bought a new state-of-the-art phone just to be able to video chat with me.

He nodded. "And even if you are doing a live mukbang with Delina, we talk. Every day."

The van braked short of where we stood, sending a cloud of brown, powdery dirt into the air around us. The driver got out and put my bags into the back. "Sorry I'm a little late. But unfortunately, this means we have to go now."

I stared into Theo's eyes one last time. "I'll miss you."

He put his hands on my shoulders and whispered into my hair, "Me too."

We kissed again. Soft and sweet.

Having to close the door on Theo was one of the hardest things I'd ever done. He waved and blew a kiss as the van barreled down the road. His silhouette grew smaller and smaller, and I thought about how much my world had widened. When I got back home, I wanted to work on minimizing my compulsive need to constantly communicate and connect. It wasn't a magic process that could all be figured out in a day. I was a work in progress—and probably always would be.

I didn't know what would become of my platform or of Goggle Girl, but I no longer had the same anxiety about it, and I'd make it my mission to no longer define myself singularly based on social approval or how strangers might perceive me.

My future—filled with more purpose, real friendships, and a new budding relationship with Theo—was brighter than it had ever been.

I didn't want to count my chickens before they hatched, as Agro Boy would say, but my summer had turned out far better than I'd ever imagined it would.

ACKNOWLEDGMENTS

I wrote most of *Sunny Song Will Never Be Famous* in the early part of quarantine when the country was sheltering in place. When you hear the phrase "It takes a village," well, for me, it took several villages from all over the country to get me back on track. Spontaneous Zoom meetups, group chats, and commiserating DM sessions helped me make it through those tough deadline months. To my high school, college, business school, and Saturday evening Zoomers, and to my writer friends who reached out and answered my calls, messages, and texts, thank you for making those early quarantined months far less lonely. Thank you for telling me it was okay to not be okay. Thank you for inspiring me to write again.

I wrote *Sunny Song* holed up in my apartment, looking all haggard while eating Doritos and wearing mismatched pajama sets—and I have a bunch of people to give shout-outs to because this book DID get written and delivered reasonably on time, all 73,000 words of it. A god-dang miracle if you ask me.

Thank you to Eliza Swift, my brilliant and wonderful editor, who helped shape this story into something much more relevant, coherent, and fun. It's scary how much you know about influencer houses, but there's no judgment here.

Brent Taylor, my agent and cheerleader, thank you for all of the emotional support pre-debut and post-debut; it's been a roller-coaster few years!

Thanks so much to my BFF Helen Hoang, my Pringles-loving twin, who is always there for me. Roselle Lim, as always, thank you for your friendship, sound advice, and fried chicken photos. Whitney Schneider, you're the best CP and writing buddy, thank you for sticking with me through the years.

Huge thank-you to my writer friends listed in a secret order only known to me: Liz Lawson, Dante Medema, Alison Hammer, Annette Christie, Judy Lin, Jenny Howe, Chelsea Resnick, Kristin Rockaway, Kathleen Barber, Chelsea Ichaso, Jeff Bishop, Danielle Paige, Sarah Henning, Kellye Garrett, Sarah Partipilo, Falon Ballard, Julie Abe, and Ann Kim. Early ARC readers Janet Rundquist, Amanda Sellet, Adrianna Cuevas, Alex Richards, Mike Lasagna and Cathy Janovitz, a humongous thanks!

Thank you so much to Sandhya Menon and Sabina Khan for the kindness you showed me during my debut week and going out of your way to host *The Perfect Escape* Instagram launch events.

In the bleakest time for me as a sheltered-in-place debut author, you brought me light and hope.

My MAPID writers group has been my local support system for several years, and I appreciate them so much. Ken, Michael, and Katrina, your early feedback on my projects has been invaluable.

The editorial, production, marketing, and sales folks at Sourcebooks Fire: thank you so much for your hard work and support. I love everything about this book, and it turned out wonderfully because of you! Thanks so much Ashlyn Keil, Katie Stutz, Lizzie Lewandowski, Cassie Gutman, Carolina Melis, Stephanie Rocha, Ashley Holstrom, and Manu Velasco!

Thank you to Kathleen Carter, who has been so steadfast and incredibly helpful during this release year. I appreciate everything you do!

Thank you to the generous librarians, booksellers, and established authors who talked up new authors till they were hoarse. And to the bookstagrammer community, I have so much appreciation for everything you do. Your enthusiasm for debut books gave me strength and purpose. In the months everyone needed comfort and escapism the most, you did your thing. And the energy you brought to *Sunny Song*'s release, wow—thank you from the bottom of my heart. Humongous hugs to nurse_bookie, inkstains.and.dust, booksaremagictoo, utopia.state.of.mind, and booksnraedunn for your friendships and support this year.

My family has been cheerleading hard since my debut release—thank you to my parents, siblings, in-laws, Ebrahimis, and Balmages (my extended family) for all of your encouragement. Trevor, thank you for being my foundation and calming better half, especially when it came to ordering takeout and delivery when I was on double deadline. CJ, your *Minecraft* crash course was super helpful. I also appreciated all of your impromptu keyboard and trombone concerts. You're the best kiddo in the world, and I love you to death.

And finally, thank YOU for picking up this book and helping make my writerly dreams come true. I hope it provided some laughter, escapism, and enjoyment. If it did, I would love if you left a review online (it helps new readers find riveting books about teens who go to digital detox farm camp). If you're on Twitter or Instagram, I'd love to hear from you—please reach out and say hello! I'm @suzannepark on both platforms, though I'm not on as much these days, because after researching and writing about digital detoxing, I've learned a lot!

Don't miss Suzanne Park's other hilarious rom-com, *The Perfect Escape*

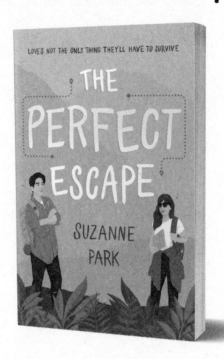

One guy. One girl.
One weekend-long survivalist competition.
What could go wrong?

ABOUT THE AUTHOR

© Joanna DeGeneres

Suzanne Park is a Korean American author who was born and raised in Tennessee. In her former life as a stand-up comedian, she appeared on BET's *Coming to the Stage*, was the winner of the Sierra Mist Comedy Competition in Seattle, and was a semifinalist in NBC's Stand Up for Diversity showcase in San Francisco. Suzanne graduated from Columbia University and received an MBA from UCLA. She currently resides in Los Angeles with her husband, offspring, and a sneaky rat that creeps around on her back patio. In her spare time, she procrastinates. She is also the author of the young adult novel *The Perfect Escape*.

FIREreads

#getbooklit

Your hub for the hottest young adult books!

Visit us online and sign up for our
newsletter at FIREreads.com

 @sourcebooksfire

 sourcebooksfire

 firereads.tumblr.com